TAKE
OUT

PRAISE FOR THE STEVIE HOOPER SERIES

An Easeful Death is a delightful pot pourri of police corruption, injustice, tangled emotions, treachery and misunderstanding—*Mary Martin website*

An Easeful Death is bound to keep you up at night—*Scoop Magazine*

[An Easeful Death] is tight and well-written—*Adelaide Advertiser*

An Easeful Death is an exciting whodunnit page-turner from a talented West Australian writer, and a welcome addition to Australian crime fiction—*Western Suburbs Weekly*

Felicity Young is an intriguing new addition to the upper echelons of Australian thriller writing ... *Harum Scarum* is a well-crafted page turner that explores themes that concern every parent—*Sun-Herald*

Harum Scarum is an enjoyable read with considerable credibility—*Aussiereviews.com*

Harum Scarum is a gripping, chilling thriller. A page turner—*www.eurocrime.co.uk*

FELICITY YOUNG

TAKE
OUT

 FREMANTLE PRESS

ABOUT THE AUTHOR

Felicity Young was born in Germany and educated in the United Kingdom, while her parents were posted around the world with the British Army, before settling in Perth. Felicity trained as a nurse, married young and, having always been a passionate lover of history and English literature, completed an arts degree at the University of Western Australia while her three children were growing up. In 1990 the family moved from the city and established a Suffolk sheep farm in Gidgegannup, WA. Here she studied music, reared orphan kangaroos, joined the volunteer bushfire brigade and started writing. Felicity's fiction includes:

A Certain Malice / Flashpoint
An Easeful Death
Harum Scarum
Take Out
A Dissection of Murder / The Anatomy of Death
Antidote to Murder
The Scent of Murder
The Insanity of Murder
A Donation of Murder (2016)

Visit the author at **www.felicityyoung.com**

To Ben, Tom and Pip
And to Mick, as always, with love

LIST OF SHORTENED FORMS USED IN THIS NOVEL

AFP	Australian Federal Police
APB	all points bulletin
CCC	Corruption and Crime Commission
COD	cause of death
DCP	Department for Child Protection
EEG	electroencephalogram
ET tube	endotracheal tube
GBH	grievous bodily harm
ICU	intensive care unit
ID card	identity card
MCIS	Major Crash Investigation Squad
OIC	officer in charge
PDQ	paint data query
RAN	Royal Australian Navy
SCS	Serious Crime Squad
SOCO	scene of crimes officer
UNIFEM	United Nations Development Fund for Women
UWA	The University of Western Australia
WACA	Western Australian Cricket Association
WAPOL	Western Australian Police

PROLOGUE

Mai and the other planters follow the farmer and his 'mechanical buffalo' as it chug chugs along, ploughing the ground into soupy mud. They separate the tied bundles of rice seedlings and then plant them individually into the furrows. It is back-breaking work, but neighbour helps neighbour. Soon a carpet of dazzling green will cover the paddies. The rice shoots will grow, the weather will dry the seeds and after the harvest there will be much celebrating in the village.

Mai thinks of the fun times to come and they are the only things that keep her going. She works alongside her mother and sisters. Her father leaves before the short lunch break. He tells them his back is sore. Mai's mother says nothing, but Mai knows she will be blushing with shame under the scarf that covers most of her face. With the help of these neighbours their own family paddy was planted several days before.

They break for lunch, flick the mud from their feet like cats and find a patch of ground a little less soggy than the rest to sit on. Mai's three younger sisters eat sticky rice and play jacks with the other children on a scrap of timber. Mai rolls her shorts further up her legs and steps into the tepid water of the drainage ditch to hunt for frogs and small fish to add to their evening meal of steamed rice. The liquid movement of a snake glides across the skin of her calf. She stands rigid, like a water bird on one leg, and concentrates on the buffalo on the bank. The buffalo's ears flick ineffectually at the surrounding halo of flies. Grass shoots are stretched and snapped by his lips and tongue, teeth crush and grind upon the pulp. The scent of his breath sweetens the metallic tang of mud from the surrounding fields. Damp air presses against Mai's skin. In the dishwater sky, heavy clouds roil. Only when she is sure the snake has gone, does Mai move again and continue with her lunchtime hunting.

When the day's planting is finished, Mai and her mother and sisters get a lift in the farmer's pick-up to their house in the village on the banks of the river Pai. The house is built on stilts to protect it from floods. A colourful assortment of open umbrellas hangs underneath the floor and sways in the weak breeze. Bicycles lie on top of one another under the shelter, chickens perch on rusty handlebars. All around the village, buffalos bellow at the approaching storm.

A satellite dish on the tin roof makes the roof tilt to one side. Mai's father says they are a privileged family. No one else in the village has a satellite dish and because of this he is a very big man.

But there is no noise from the TV tonight. Mai climbs the steps to find her father with the usual can of Singha beer in his hand, sitting on a fruit crate watching an Elvis Presley movie with the sound turned down. A stranger in an embroidered silk dress sits on a crate next to him. She wears dainty red shoes and carries a bag that sparkles like diamonds under the single light globe. The woman must be very rich: the TV doesn't get turned down for anyone.

Her mother places her hands together and gives the woman a little bow. Her father hauls himself up from the crate. 'See this woman, Mai?' he says. 'She used to live in a village like ours and came from a poor family too. She went to Bangkok and made lots of money.'

Mai bows to the woman as her mother has done.

'Would you like to come to Bangkok with me, Mai? Would you like to be rich like me?' the woman asks in a high fluting voice.

There is a long silence. Mai's mother starts to cry. Mai doesn't understand why. This is the most exciting thing she has ever heard and she finds herself gulping air like a frog. She is twelve years old and cannot take her eyes off the woman's diamond purse. She wants so badly to have a purse like that.

'You go with this woman, Mai,' her father says, 'and you will never be hungry again. You will have all the jewels and fine clothes a young girl could ever want.'

Mai glances across the room towards her three younger sisters. The food she has caught in the field today will never fill those hungry bellies. Her own belly begins to growl; perhaps it is the spirits giving her a sign. She lowers her eyes and nods her head to her father.

He pulls her into his arms. His skin is slick and he smells of smoke and beer. 'You are a good girl, Mai. You go with this woman. Help yourself and then you can help all of us.'

Mai knows of girls in other villages who have been visited by beautiful strangers. Their families boast about it, saying how rich the girls have become. Mai realises she must have been very special in her previous life to be chosen as one of the lucky few in this one.

Her mother hugs her. 'You will come back to visit?'

Mai looks to the beautiful stranger for an answer. The stranger nods her head and says 'yes' with a solemn promise.

As Mai is led to the door by the stranger's small manicured hand, she hears her father say, 'DVD players are going cheap in the market. I can buy one now.'

MONDAY

CHAPTER ONE

The dead cycad might look like a rusty buzz-saw in a pot, Stevie thought, but it was hardly a portent for disaster.

'Have you been inside?' she asked Skye, who had joined her on the front porch. Stevie's fingers grazed one of the plant's leaves. 'Ouch!' She pulled away, beads of blood welling along the small cut.

'Tetanus up to date?' Skye asked.

Stevie pulled her stinging finger from her mouth. 'Yes, *Nurse* Williams.'

'If I'd had the guts to go inside,' Skye went on, 'I wouldn't have bothered calling you, would I?' She gave a characteristic eye roll that made Stevie smile despite her irritation. 'Mrs Hardegan's positive no one's been home for days. I mean come off it, look at all this.' She waved her hand at the overflowing letterbox and the rolled newspapers cast about the lawn.

'And the grass needs a mow,' said Stevie, 'I can see all that, but why didn't you just wait for the local cops?'

'I told you,' said Skye. 'They never showed. 'C'mon, you owe me. Let's get this over with. I've still got another three home visits to make and she's watching.' Skye tilted her head towards the squat pre-war bungalow next door. Stevie caught a shadow of movement from a window, the snap of venetian blinds. With a resigned sigh she gave the lion-head doorbell three sharp jabs.

Skye fumbled in the pocket of her uniform for the key Mrs Hardegan had given her and reached for the doorknob. 'I rang before and got no answer, had a look around the garden, the back shed, looked through the windows—there isn't anyone about.'

To their surprise the door opened under her touch.

They found themselves in a cool front entrance with a high ceiling. A stained-glass skylight shone down on them and a black and white tiled floor chequered its way down the passageway to the left and right. There were plenty of larger mansions in the area, but this Federation-style reproduction was the biggest in the block. Stevie regarded the spacious lounge room ahead. Two modular sofas gripped the walls, the type found in airport lounges or hotel lobbies, not really designed for lounging. Not even a coffee table filled the void between them. The room was bare: there were no paintings, no TV, books or magazines. Stevie had seen display homes that looked more homey.

'Police! Is anyone here?' she called out, her voice echoing down the passageways.

No response.

'Nice place,' Skye mumbled.

'What exactly did the old lady say?' Stevie asked as they headed down the right hand passage, footsteps scuffing on the gritty tiles.

'Mrs Hardegan said she hasn't seen the couple for several days, and they always tell her if they're going away. She likes to keep an eye on things. It gives her something to do.'

'Good neighbour,' said Stevie, glancing into an open-plan dining room that contained a dusty antique table and no chairs. A picture window, designed to capture rolling farmland or sweeping cityscape, revealed a cramped backyard.

'She said she'd got her son to call the local cops—several times—and they promised they'd look into it, but they haven't. I tried them too, also with no luck. I reckon the old dear might've cried wolf one too many times.'

'So you called me instead.'

'Mrs Hardegan's recovering from a serious stroke and I don't want her having another. She's been getting more and more anxious over this and I can't see the harm in putting her mind to rest. Besides,' Skye added with an ironic smile, 'we were planning on catching up anyway.'

'This isn't exactly what I had in mind.' Stevie pulled at her paint-spattered overalls. 'I was doing the eaves of my house.'

Skye shrugged. 'Give a girl a spanner.'

Stevie thumped on the closed door of what she assumed to be the master bedroom, expecting and receiving no reply. 'Has Mrs Hardegan told you anything about the couple?'

'Delia and Jon Pavel, early thirties, filthy rich.'

Stevie opened the door and saw an unmade bed, scattered shoes, dirty carpet. The windows were shut and the room smelt sour.

'Filthy seems to be the operative word,' she said as she approached the bed. She poked for a moment among the tangle of forget-me-not blue sheets and floral pillows, noting the absence of doona or blankets.

Skye tugged at an earlobe peppered with empty holes. 'Stevie, maybe we shouldn't be doing this ...'

Stevie barely heard her. She was in full cop mode now and it was too late for second thoughts. She indicated an open satin box on the dressing table containing a magpie's nest of jewellery: gold chains, silver, diamonds and pearls, 'Look at all this—they obviously haven't been robbed.' Nodding to a plasma TV on the wall opposite the bed she said, 'And that would've been easy enough to take.' A knot formed in the pit of her stomach. Robbery was now the least of her concerns. 'Wait outside if you like, Skye.'

'No, no, you might need me, I'd better stay.' A tremolo underscored Skye's earlier confident tone. A uniformed constable would be a lot more useful than this skinny girl with the dark rings under her eyes, Stevie thought as she flicked her friend an unenthusiastic smile.

They picked their way around piles of unwashed clothes in the doorway of the ensuite bathroom. Scattered beauty products oozed over the vanity, blobs of dried toothpaste dotted the green marble top. The taps of the claw-foot bath were edged with slime, the tub ringed greasy grey.

Skye shuddered. 'Looks like my sister's bathroom,' she said as she toed a towel with a white Doc Marten, releasing an invisible cloud of mould into the air.

'What you might expect from a teenager, but not a wealthy couple in their thirties,' Stevie said.

A tap dripped a steady pulse into one of the double basins. The basin would have flooded over if the plug had been more securely rammed in the drain. Stevie reached for the faucet and stopped the flow. 'Their toothbrushes are still there, his shaving stuff, her make-up. Maybe they had toilet bags packed and ready to go?'

'Maybe. I only saw one car in the triple garage.'

'What kind of car?'

'A new Range Rover, very dirty, filled with burger wrappers and junk. Why bother going to the tip when you can carry it around with you?'

They continued to look around the east wing of the house, taking in the few pieces of expensive but carelessly arranged furniture, the layers of dust and the rippled oriental runners in the passageway. It seemed to Stevie as if the trappings of wealth were of little consequence to these people; things in this household were taken for granted, neglected. They passed a sweeping wooden staircase. 'We'll search downstairs first,' she said.

The family room and kitchen were cavernous. Stevie folded her arms and slowly pivoted on her heel. There wasn't enough furniture to fill the room or muffle their footsteps. There were no curtains on the windows or ornaments on the jarrah fire surround other than a mute carriage clock, hands stopped at 10.15. Possessions tended to give off echoes to Stevie but the few objects in this room told her nothing. All was silent except for the faint humming of the fridge and the popping of blowflies against the windows.

She ran a finger across a windowsill. The paintwork looked fresh under the dust. 'Have the Pavels lived here long?'

'Long enough for Mrs Hardegan to get to know them. The house is obviously fairly new, not bad for a reproduction.' Skye pointed out a row of brass light switches and the tracked ceiling lights. 'Expensive, too.'

Stevie's eyes were drawn to the adjacent kitchen area some metres away. The rancid smell of old food became sharper as she zeroed in on the kitchen table. Laid for two, it held the remains of an unfinished meal — TV dinners by the looks of the empty food packets on the granite bench top. Both plates contained thin slices of drying beef, crusty cauliflower and half nibbled cobs of corn. Flies skated on ponds of solidified gravy splashed across the tray of a baby's highchair.

The knot in Stevie's stomach tightened. '*Mary Celeste*,' she whispered.

'What?'

Stevie waved her hand. 'Forget it.' As she walked she kicked a scattering of shrivelled peas across the floor. A glass of pale liquid teetered on the table's edge, too close for comfort. She lifted the glass to her nose and sniffed.

'Stale wine,' she said, sliding the glass into a less precarious position. 'Looks like this food has been here for several days.' She pointed to the table. 'The meal's only half finished, the chairs are skewiff, as if someone left in a hurry.'

Heat still radiated from the electric oven. In it she found a baking dish containing several charred spheres.

'They never got their pies,' Skye said, voice hushed as she pointed out the carton of ready-made apple pies next to the other empty food containers.

Stevie replaced the oven tray and chewed on her bottom lip, trying to make sense of it all. At once she became aware of a strange sensation at the back of her neck, a warm breeze, the feathering of a breath.

Her sudden turn towards its source caused Skye to clap herself on the chest. 'Holy shit! Don't do that!'

Stevie spotted the open gap in the sliding window behind the sink and let out her own pent-up breath. 'Sorry, I thought for a minute someone else was in the room.'

'Look, I don't feel right about this—this place gives me the creeps,' Skye said, drawing a breath and exhaling with an unmistakable wheeze. 'I think we should leave and call the proper police. I reckon they'll listen to you rather than me.'

The 'proper' police, *jeez*.

'I'm not pulling out now,' Stevie snapped back. 'Wait outside if you like while I check out the rest of downstairs.'

Skye reached into her pocket for a Ventolin inhaler, took a couple of puffs and sidled a step closer to Stevie.

Two of the bedrooms in the west wing were empty and dusty with spider webs parachuting from the cornices. Another room served as a study. A computer on a fake antique desk stood next to a single bed with nothing on it but a bare mattress. A scraggly bottlebrush from the garden bed outside scratched against the window. Stevie cringed at the sound. Blood-red flowers pressed against the glass—as if anyone or anything would want to get into this desolate, inhospitable house.

There was still one room left to check at the end of the passageway, next to a bathroom. She sniffed at the odour leaking through the gaps of the closed door and felt nausea rise. Skye dug her bitten fingernails into Stevie's arm. The door creaked as Stevie eased it open. She drew a sharp breath.

'Oh my God,' Skye said.

CHAPTER TWO

The room was as bare as a prison cell. The only item in it was an old safe cot of the style now deemed politically incorrect. Like an old-fashioned meat safe its walls were made of tough flyscreen topped by a heavy wooden lid.

The cot reeked, the bedding a jumble of urine-soaked sheets, flyscreen walls clogged with lumps of faeces. A soiled disposable nappy had been flung to the far end of the saturated mattress.

The naked baby inside lay still.

With trembling fingers, Stevie fumbled with the latch and flung back the door, making the wooden frame rattle.

Skye pushed her aside before Stevie could reach for the child. 'Wait a minute,' she said. Leaning over the wall of the cot she gently inserted her finger into the baby's mouth. 'Airway's clear but the inside of his mouth is dry—he's very dehydrated.' Her finger pressed the side of his neck. 'Pulse rapid, but not too bad. We're not too late.'

The baby stirred, whimpered and sucked his thumb with increasing vigour. Skye ran her fingers over his dark, matted hair and looked desperately around the room.

'Here.' Stevie grabbed a cot blanket from the floor and

handed it to Skye who wrapped it around the baby and clasped him to her chest. 'Let's get out of here,' Stevie gasped, as the movement of the bedclothes disturbed the foul air.

In the kitchen they made the necessary phone calls. Stevie reported the incident to the local police, stressing the emergency and then took the baby from Skye so Skye could call for an ambulance. After consulting with the on-call medico Skye decided the baby could be given a small amount of water. She filled a cup from the kitchen tap and put it to his lips. He drank greedily, snatching at the cup with stained fingers, mewling like a kitten when she wouldn't let him hold it himself. 'Poor little bugger's still thirsty,' she said as she pulled the cup away and placed it on the kitchen table. 'We'd better not let him have any more, he might vomit it up—this should get him by until he reaches hospital. They'll need to know how much fluid we gave him, put an IV in.'

The baby didn't have the strength to yell; his eyes were sunken, his skin hot and dry. He soon gave up his fight to reach the water and flopped his head against Stevie's shoulder. 'How could anyone leave a baby like this?' Skye asked, rubbing soothing circles on his back, eyes glistening with unshed tears.

Don't go sentimental on me now, Stevie thought. 'Here take him.' She passed the baby back to Skye. 'Wait in the fresh air for the ambulance, I want to make sure no one's upstairs.'

She had a quick look around the upstairs of the house, relieved to find just three deserted, almost empty rooms.

Back in the family room rays of light shone through the French doors, highlighting the dusty coating of the tiles, sticky patches and faint footprints. Stevie slowly examined the tracks on the floor from different angles, all the while conscious of the smell of the baby on her clothes. It was during one of these shifts of position that she noticed a clean area of tiles in front of a leather chesterfield, as if the tiles had recently been washed. She pushed the couch back, the sudden draft making the dust-bunnies underneath tumble. Earwigs hiding from the light scampered away across ominous brown splats. She dropped to her knees to examine the stains. Could be spilled Milo or tomato sauce; could be dried paint. Or blood.

It was tempting to search the floor for further evidence, but fear of contaminating a possible crime scene held her back. French doors led from the family room to the small back garden; she'd cause less damage out there, she decided, as she opened the doors up.

The walled garden seemed as badly kept as the inside of the house, although the surrounding flowerbeds, crowded with roses as tall as Stevie herself, suggested a time when it had been well maintained. Somewhere in the distance she heard the wail of an ambulance.

At the swimming pool's fence she stopped. An ominous bulge pressed up from under the pool's cover.

Shit.

The gate creaked as Stevie opened it, hurrying across the weed-choked paving to the cover's reel. The pool surface gradually appeared as she wrestled with the stiff mechanism, and she found herself breaking into a sweat despite the mild temperature. Leaves and dirt swished from the bubbly blue surface, leaving black scum upon the green water. The reason for the bulge, a pink lilo, sprang from the confines of the cover. Globs of algae bobbed on the water's surface next to the body of a disintegrating blue-tongued lizard. It was impossible to see through the murk to find out what else might be down there and she decided she didn't want to know either; the rest of the job could be left to the police search team. Finding an abandoned baby was enough for one day.

She heard the ambulance pulling up outside the gate and walked a brick-paved path to meet it at the front of the house. The baby had fallen asleep against Skye's shoulder. She continued to rub his back, cooing something tuneless under her breath. Stevie explained the situation to the ambulance attendant and asked where the baby would be taken.

'Straight to PMH. Lucky you found him when you did.'

Skye pushed past him into the back of the ambulance before he'd finished swinging open the doors and settled on the seat with the baby tight in her arms. She cut the man off before he could voice his protest. 'I'm a nurse, I'm going with him.' She swung defensively to Stevie as if expecting to be challenged by her too.

Stevie shrugged. 'Good idea, you can tell me what the doctors say.'

Skye held up a hand as the doors were closing. 'Look in on Mrs H for me, Stevie, make sure she's okay, yeah? And call me: I want to know what's going on here—none of your secret police business.'

Easier said than done, Stevie thought. This was out of her jurisdiction; she'd be lucky if the local police confided in her at all. She pulled her blonde ponytail through her fingers as she watched the ambulance speed away, and tried to remember which police division covered the Peppermint Grove area, pondering the likelihood of knowing anyone in it. No names sprang to mind.

As she stepped out of the front garden gate, a small

Felicity Young

colourful object caught her eye. She squatted down to take a closer look and found a silk-covered button. Making a mental note of its location she reminded herself to point it out to the police when they arrived.

It had been about fifteen minutes since her call and there was no sign of them yet. A dark slit appeared in the venetians of the house next door. Perhaps Mrs Hardegan was anxiously waiting for the police too? Skye had asked her to check up on the old lady—surely a quick word wouldn't do any harm?

Rows of peppermint trees bordered the wide street, filling the air with a minty odour cut through by the tang of the sea to the west. Mrs Hardegan's was one of the few untouched houses left in the area, most having been extensively renovated or knocked down and replaced by modern concrete monoliths and elegant reproductions such as the Pavels'. Her Californian bungalow was characteristically squat with tapered columns supporting a heavy front veranda, and a gabled roof with winking leadlight windows. Stevie detected the smell of camphor before the front door was even opened.

'Where have you been, boy?' the old woman demanded. She wore a simple linen dress enlivened with screen-printed green fish and secured with a tight leather belt. She stood ramrod straight, her bright, level eyes fixed unwaveringly upon Stevie. Stevie may have been wearing workman's overalls, but she didn't think her gender was that ambiguous. She began to explain. 'Mrs Hardegan? I –'

'We've been waiting here for days. What's wrong with the smudgin' fullets these days, why so long?'

It took a moment for Stevie to realise the woman's

peculiar speech must be the result of the stroke Skye had mentioned. It might also explain why she'd been unable to call the police herself, getting her son and Skye to do it for her.

'I'm a friend of Skye's, Mrs Hardegan.' Stevie consciously slowed down her usual rapid-fire speech. 'She asked me to look into the Pavels' house for you. She said you hadn't seen them for a while and were worried about them. I am with the police, but not from Peppermint Grove. The Peppy Grove police are on their way.'

'A lovely boy, but the others are useless, quite useless. You'd better come in, have a cup of tea and tell us what's going on.' Despite the oddness of her speech, she had the cultured pronunciation of another era, almost English but not quite. Newsreel ABC.

Mrs Hardegan turned and clasped one of the bookcases in the dark hallway. As she eased herself down the passage-way, Stevie noticed one leg lagging slightly behind the other. Seeing no sign of a Zimmer frame or stick Stevie instinctively reached for the woman's elbow, but the well-intentioned gesture was shrugged away with an impatient scowl. On the wall above a bookcase, a black and white photo of a young Mrs Hardegan caught Stevie's eye; the hooked nose was unmistakable. She was dressed in the uniform of a wartime RAN nurse—it figured.

Mrs Hardegan led Stevie past several closed doors to a lighter, self-contained room with kitchenette at the back of the house, where it appeared she did most of her living. Recycling was sorted and stacked in tidy piles on one of the benches. The surfaces of the kitchenette were clean; soapsuds popped on the drying plastic dishes spread across the draining board. The single bed in the corner of the room was made after a fashion, the lumps disguised by an intricately embroidered cotton counterpane. Stevie found herself wondering how long it had taken the old lady to make the bed, how frustrating the disability must be to someone who probably required everything around her to be shipshape. Every free surface of the room was crowded with various arts, crafts and sewing paraphernalia: crushed tubes of fabric paint, bottles of varnish, glue, jars of bristling paintbrushes. A wooden contraption, like an old printing press, stood near one of the windows. It would be used for screen-printing, Stevie guessed. Several bright cushions of the same fish design as the old lady's dress were arranged in a precise line down one side of the bed.

An open door led into a bathroom. Stevie glimpsed a toilet and railed bath before Mrs Hardegan moved with surprising speed to close it.

'*Bloody Japs!*' The mechanical voice made Stevie whirl towards the source, a parrot, hanging in a dome-shaped cage from a ceiling beam toward the back of the room.

'Hello, who's this?' Stevie said as she approached, resisting the urge to poke a finger through the bars. The parrot stared back. It had bright black eyes and a beak similar to its owner's—it could probably shear a finger with a single snip. Bald in places, its patchy arrangement of feathers looked as washed-out as a favourite summer shirt.

'Captain Flint, our feathered friend,' Mrs Hardegan said.

The tea was made with only a few minor mishaps—Stevie given three lumps of sugar when she asked for none—and settled by Mrs Hardegan on a tapestried footstool in front of a high-backed easy chair next to the window. One side of the

Pavel residence was visible from this vantage point and the binoculars resting on a shelf nearby were no doubt used for further surveillance.

Difficulties of expression do not necessarily mean difficulties with understanding; Stevie knew that. But to be safe, she explained what she'd found at the Pavel house as slowly and as simply as she could. She cringed at the patronising sound of her own voice, so like the manner in which some people talked to her seven-year-old daughter, Izzy, but could think of no other approach. She would tread softly until she could work out the extent of the woman's brain damage.

But the hooked nose wrinkled when Stevie described the unkempt Pavel house and the blue eyes dampened when she mentioned the abandoned baby. Some of her doubts about the old lady's comprehension were put to rest.

'When did you last see the Pavels, Mrs Hardegan?' Stevie asked, speaking more naturally.

Mrs Hardegan leaned back in her easy chair, tented her fingers and looked sincerely back at Stevie. 'About twenty years ago.'

Stevie's raised hopes took a dive. 'Did you know them well?'

Suddenly the elderly woman's face twisted and she stamped her feet on the linoleum floor, the force of her anger surprising Stevie. 'We can't tell you—it's all our fault!' Tears spilled down the old lady's cheeks.

Stevie got up from the footstool and placed a calming hand on her shoulder only to have it dashed away with a string of unintelligible words. She looked helplessly around the room, wondering what to do next. This meeting was going nowhere fast — she shouldn't have even tried, should have trusted her instincts and not become involved at all. *Damn you, Skye.* What if she caused the old lady to have another stroke? She spied a box of tissues on a work table crammed with sewing paraphernalia. Stevie offered the box and Mrs Hardegan swiped at her eyes. 'Can't help it ... can't get out. Trapped ...' she said, tapping fiercely on her temple.

Stevie hadn't noticed the arrival of the police car earlier, and spotted it now parked outside the Pavels' house, one door carelessly left open.

With relief she said, 'I'd better go now ...' about to add a consoling 'love', she stopped herself in time. 'The *proper* police are here and they'll probably need to talk to you. If talking is hard, perhaps you could write down what you remember about the Pavels for them?'

Mrs Hardegan shook her head.

'Never mind,' Stevie said, injecting her tone with false brightness. 'I'm sure the other neighbours will be able to help out.'

Mrs Hardegan closed her eyes for a moment and took a deep calming breath. 'We're sorry, better leave now. Needed to do that.'

'Are you going to be okay?'

Mrs Hardegan nodded and reached into her sewing basket. Stuck into the padding was a row of pre-threaded needles of various shades of wool. Inspecting them in the window's light she selected a strand of lemony green. 'Too long,' she muttered to herself, cutting it to size with a decisive snip of the scissors, before picking up a swathe of cross-stitch tapestry. Stevie was dismissed.

She made her way unescorted to the front door. Mrs

Hardegan would be written off as a witness, even though it was obvious she knew more than she could tell. They'd have to dig into the Pavels' history from other sources.

Wait a minute; Stevie stopped halfway down the darkened, book-lined passageway. What was she thinking? This wasn't her problem; her problem was a can of paint she'd forgotten to put the lid on and some half-finished eaves she'd have to live with until her next day off. She looked to the west and noticed the brewing bank of grey clouds, hoping what she'd painted that morning had had a chance to dry; it looked like the weather bureau had got it right for a change.

All she could do now was have a quick word with the local cops, put the incident behind her and return to her family.

My dear, I trust this

My dear I hope this finds you
in a better state than when we last met.

CHAPTER THREE

A plainclothes cop in a snappy suit and crisp white shirt leaned on the car's bonnet, writing notes. He barely looked up when Stevie approached. 'Hi, I'm Stephanie Hooper; I called you. The Silver Chain nurse and I found the baby.'

The cop lifted his left hand in brief acknowledgement and continued to write. 'Detective Sergeant Luke Fowler, Peppermint Grove.' He put a full stop at the end of his sentence, straightened and inspected her through mirrored sunglasses. 'You're a painter?'

'No, I was painting my own house. Nurse Williams called and asked me to go with her to the Pavels'. The old lady next door told her there was something amiss over there.'

'Well she's got that right in one, no sign of the Pavels at all—but why did the nurse call you?'

'The old lady was getting agitated. She has speech problems and had already asked her son and the nurse to call in her suspicions to the police, but apparently the matter wasn't followed through.' Stevie made sure to keep her tone neutral; she didn't want to get off on the wrong foot. 'Nurse Williams decided to call me because we've worked together before. I'm with Central ...'

Fowler cut her off. 'That wouldn't be *Skye* Williams, would it?'

'That's right.'

Fowler ran his hand over his buzz cut as if to say, Jesus, that's all I need.

Stevie let the matter slide. 'Skye went to the hospital with the baby. Do you want me to ring her for you?'

'No, I'll get to her later,' he said abruptly. 'You'll do for now.'

'I might call her anyway.' Stevie delved into her overall pocket for her phone. 'I'd like to know how the baby is. He was badly dehydrated when we found him.'

He pushed her hand away before she could reach the phone. 'Leave it to the police please, ma'am; we'll handle this.'

Stevie felt a sudden pulse of anger. 'The baby's condition should be top priority, Sergeant—you might find you have a homicide on your hands. '

Before Fowler could retort, the uniformed officer who'd accompanied him appeared from the back of the house. 'Looks like the pool cover's been removed recently, Luke.'

'That was me,' Stevie said. 'I thought someone might've been stuck under it.'

Stevie might have been able to exercise a certain amount of control, but the same couldn't be said for Sergeant Fowler. He hissed out a breath through clamped teeth. 'Oh, is that so? And what else have you tampered with, Ms, er—'

'Hooper, Detective *Senior* Sergeant Hooper, Central Police.'

The detective paused. Stevie delighted in seeing the skin around his collar redden. He hitched his trousers and took off his sunglasses to get a better look at her. The blond buzz cut, the hard blue eyes and the razor-sharp scar on the cheek reminded her of someone or something she couldn't place.

'Did you spot the stains under the chesterfield?' she asked holding his blazing gaze with her own.

Unaware of the mounting tension, the tall uniformed officer did a double take, gaping at her through thick-lensed glasses. 'Stevie Hooper, what a sight for sore eyes! I've been following your exploits in *Newsbeat*. Congratulations, sounds like you've really wiped the floor with those cyber predator arseholes. I hear you've shacked up with Inspector McGuire—how is old Monty going these days—coping okay with your new-found fame?'

William Trotman had been a divisional colleague of Monty's some years ago, and obviously had climbed no further up the career ladder since. Staffed by the likes of him, the tardy response of the Peppermint Grove station now came as no surprise.

At last it seemed that Stevie and Fowler were on the same wavelength and neither in the mood for idle gossip. 'Save the chitchat, Bill,' Fowler told him. 'Notify the station and have a team dispatched over here asap. Then call the office and get them to phone the local hospitals, see if anyone's been admitted matching the parents' descriptions. The couple might have just ducked out to the shops while the baby was asleep and met with some kind of accident.'

Fowler turned back to Stevie while Trotman carried out his instructions on the car radio. The Pavel house would soon be a hotbed of police activity—though perhaps 'soon' was optimistic.

Fowler drew himself up, on full alert since he'd discovered

he wasn't dealing with an easily bullied member of the public. 'You were at the house next door when we arrived. What were you doing there?'

She could have lied, could have told him she'd been admiring the last of the bulbs in Mrs Hardegan's front garden, but to hell with self-preservation. Telling the truth and risking an official reprimand was worth every gram of pleasure she'd get from stirring up this self-important prat. 'I was talking to Mrs Hardegan, the woman who raised the alarm.'

Fowler rubbed his square chin. 'If you're involved with the cyber predator team, you must be with Sex Crimes. This is way out of your jurisdiction, Hooper. You've already breached police procedure; you should have waited here for me as instructed. How am I to know how you handled the witness, what false memories you might have sown in her mind?'

Stevie sighed — so much for amiable cooperation. 'I had to do something while I waited; you took long enough. Anyway, you won't get much sense from her. She's had a stroke and has trouble talking. I suggest you start with the other people in the street. Get a decent description of the couple and find out if there are any family members who can tell you anything before you start phoning the hospitals and stirring up a media frenzy. And now, if you excuse me, I have a call to make.'

She glared back at Fowler, challenging him to stop her as she punched Skye's number into her phone. A vanload of cops pulled up alongside the Pavels' driveway and he was called away.

Stevie listened gravely to Skye's report on the doctor's findings and told her a detective was on the way to interview her at the hospital. While they spoke Stevie watched Fowler brief the newly arrived cops and another plainclothes officer.

Toward the end of her conversation, Stevie was hit by a thought that made her laugh out loud.

'I don't see what's so funny. The baby's condition is serious.' Skye sounded miffed.

'Sorry, Skye, I'm not laughing at anything you said, I was just watching the sergeant marshal his troops. I thought I'd seen him before, and now I remember where.' She pulled herself together. 'Have you ever seen an Action Man doll?'

Despite Stevie's intentions of returning home, she felt uneasy about the way the investigation was being handled and couldn't bring herself to leave. For a while she loitered with the other rubberneckers in the street, trying to glean more information, hoping Fowler would feel her eyes burning into his back.

A TV news van arrived and Fowler gave a stony-faced interview loaded with cop-speak. He made a public plea for news of the whereabouts of Jon and Delia Pavel and briefly mentioned the abandoned 'male infant.' The journalist lost interest when Fowler said that, at this stage in the investigation, the parents' disappearance was not being regarded as suspicious, probably just an unfortunate misdemeanour or accident. Was he understating his suspicions deliberately? Stevie wondered. Was this all part of his procedural tactics, or did he really believe what he was saying? With Action Man wearing his sunglasses again, it was impossible to tell.

Hunger and boredom finally drove her to the corner deli. The family-run corner store was a rarity these days in the more gentrified Perth suburbs. Few owners could compete with the big chains or hack the long hours. Like Mrs Hardegan's house, this place was a bastion against change. A patchwork of colourful brand names covered the windowless sidewalls; private notices about lost pets, babysitting and piano lessons curled down one pane of the front display window. Toward the back, the battlements of an old brick dunny jutted over the top of a rickety wooden fence, and next to this, a sun-bleached weatherboard garage.

Stevie waited to be served behind a group of chattering landscape gardeners and found her gaze drawn to a rack of classic DVDs near the large front window.

'How much are the DVDs?' she asked at the counter when her turn came.

'Ten dollars,' the girl said, lisping through her tongue stud.

Stevie jingled through her purse, counting up the change. 'Damn, I can't make it.' She ordered a salad sandwich and an iced coffee, moved to the DVD rack and selected a copy of *Gone With The Wind*. 'Mind putting this aside for me?' she asked. 'It's the same collectors' edition I've had my eye on at Amazon.' Stevie's passion for old movies had developed with her time in The Job: the more she saw of real life, the less she wanted to see of it on the screen. Modern romantic comedies, especially those starring George Clooney, were the only exception to her nothing-under-fifty-years-old rule.

The girl made no comment and took down Stevie's particulars with one eye on the clock, no doubt counting down the hours till the end of her shift.

'I noticed a bunch of cop cars down the street—any idea what's going on?' Stevie said. Ancient movies might be of no interest to the girl, but surely this kind of action would.

'Oh yeah, it's soooo sad,' the girl said, brightening immediately. 'The poor little baby was left alone for days and the police can't find his parents anywhere—they think they might have been killed in a car crash.'

'Days?'

The girl shrugged. 'That's what everyone's saying.'

'That's terrible. Did you know them?'

'Kind of, they came in here sometimes. The baby was so cute, but the mum and dad were like really weird.'

High heels clacked across the tiles and a well-dressed woman with tight porcelain skin and a prominent gap between her front teeth appeared from the storage area at the back of the shop.

'What's going on out here, Leila?' the woman said. She might have looked like Madonna, but her accent was all *Kath and Kim*. To Stevie she added, 'I hope she isn't holding you up.'

'It's fine,' said Stevie, 'I was just asking about the missing people down the road.'

'Oh them, yes—a strange pair.'

Leila rolled her eyes. 'How would you know, Eva? You're hardly ever here.'

Eva did not appear bothered by the girl's insolent tone. She asked Stevie if the couple had been found yet.

'Haven't a clue,' Stevie said, conscious of the woman looking her up and down, glad that today she didn't look like a cop: maybe she could get something useful out of them.

Eva pointed to the DVD on the counter. 'I've given up on that one, makes me cry too much, 'specially when the little girl dies. When it comes to the oldies, give me something funny over serious any day—the Ealing comedies or the original *St Trinian's* movies—remember them? What a great escape they are.'

Stevie agreed. She had a feeling this woman had experienced more reality than she cared to admit to. She paid for her lunch with a clatter of loose change upon the counter.

But Eva wasn't ready to let Stevie go just yet. It seemed Stevie wasn't the deli's first visitor from the Pavel house that afternoon and it soon became obvious that the woman knew far more about what was going on up the street than she ought to. Stevie would have put money on the identity of at least one of the deli's recent customers—William Trotman, without a doubt.

Stevie adopted the role of gossiping tradesperson, leaning on the deli counter among the boxes of lollies, and took a bite of her sandwich.

'Apparently the poor little boy's in a dreadful state,' Eva said. 'They're not even sure if he'll make it. Just as well the Meals on Wheels lady from next door decided to look in when she did.'

Stevie smiled to herself—Skye would not appreciate the demotion. Eva turned to Leila who stood agog, listening to her boss gossiping. Evidently even she hadn't heard the whole story.

'Come on,' Eva said to Leila. 'We haven't got all day. You can listen and clean the grill at the same time.' The air was greasy with cooked onions even though the lunchtime rush had ended long ago.

Leila shot her employer a *whatever* look, took up a scourer and began to dab half-heartedly at the filthy grill.

'So what are they like then, this family?' Stevie asked. 'Rich by the look of the house—I'm glad it wasn't me painting all those eaves. Leila said they sometimes called by the shop.'

'They got their papers here sometimes. A quiet couple, not particularly friendly—I don't think I ever so much as heard her speak.'

Leila opened her mouth to interrupt, glanced at Eva and closed it again.

'Rich bitch, eh?' Stevie asked.

'Not many of the people round here like them much,' Eva said. 'You can't run a business like ours and not hear talk. Nothing major or bad enough to make anyone want to harm them, I'm sure. Just very inconsiderate neighbours from what I've heard.'

'What, loud music, parties?'

'No, not their scene. More like backwashing the pool into the vegie patch of the people behind them, burning rubbish on a windy day and covering everyone's washing in ash—that kind of thing.' The woman shrugged. 'They're eastern European; they're not like us.'

'Oh? Where in Europe are they from, do you know?'

'Couldn't say, they all sound Russian to me.'

'What do the police think has happened to them?'

'No idea. If you find out anything, come back and tell me, okay? I'll shout you a free lunch.'

Stevie said she would, wondering if a similar deal had been struck with William Trotman.

On Stevie's return she spotted a solitary crime scene tech pacing the perimeter of the cordoned area. A general duties constable stood guard in the doorway of the Pavel house. Stevie watched for movement through the windows and detected none, meaning that the remaining officers, including Fowler, must still be door-knocking the neighbours. She spotted a couple of cop cars parked further down the street. The lack of action had driven even the most curious of onlookers home and there wasn't a reporter in sight.

Chattering swallows darted in and out of the eaves of the Pavel house as they prepared for the approaching bad weather. The light was fading fast, dark clouds closing in. When the storm finally did come through, any outside evidence would be obliterated.

With this in mind, Stevie stepped towards the tape. She caught the attention of the crime scene tech treading the path outside, head bowed, covered with the hood of his blue forensic overalls like a meditating monk. He stopped his pacing when she told him who she was and regarded her suspiciously. She had no form of ID and no William Trotman close at hand to greet her by name. When she asked if he'd found anything in the garden bed by the kitchen window, he told her it wasn't in his brief. Nor would he tell her if he'd taken scrapings from the brown stains under the chesterfield—how did he know she wasn't a reporter? he said. But he did agree to check out the button near the front gate. He sounded bored, but polite enough, covering his options in case she really was who she said she was.

There was only one thing for it.

Stevie had more success convincing the hovering uniform in the street that she was part of the investigating team. No questions were asked when she strode toward the white van and pulled on a pair of overalls and booties from the storage box in the back and snapped on a pair of gloves. Stepping over the crime scene tape, she made her way across the overgrown grass towards the side of the house and the kitchen window.

Crushed weeds choked the garden bed below. She squatted on her haunches and combed through them with her gloved hands. What she was expecting to find, she had no idea. No footprints were evident on the dry surface, though it was obvious something or someone had recently trampled down the weeds. The flyscreen had also been removed and propped up against the wall.

She straightened and peered through the open window, seeing no sign of police in the house. She wondered if the substance from the floor really had been scraped up and dispatched to the lab. The thoroughness of the investigation at this stage would largely depend on how seriously Fowler was taking the disappearance of the couple; not very, if the interview with the press was anything to go on. With budget restrictions as they were he couldn't afford unnecessary procedures. This could, after all, merely be a case of crossed wires, such as a babysitter failing to turn up, or, as Fowler had mused earlier, a horrible accident. For all they knew the couple could at this very moment be lying on a beach in Bali, unconscious in hospital, or worse still, on a slab in the morgue.

If foul play was the last thing on Fowler's mind, why then was it at the front of hers? Perhaps it was the feeling she'd had earlier when exploring the house. Maybe it was the odour of the baby still rising up from her clothes. Whatever it was, she had been with the police long enough to know that these kinds of feelings should not be ignored. Bugger Fowler.

She approached the front porch and looked around. No one seemed to be paying her the least bit of attention. A couple of cops had returned to stand by their patrol car, lounging with their backs to the house, drinking from plastic cups. The

door of the house was open enough for her to slip through
without a sound.

The false dusk of the oncoming storm had made the
interior gloomy and the searchers had left all the lights downstairs ablaze, which was just as well because it meant she
didn't have to draw attention to herself by turning them on.
There didn't appear to be much evidence of the crime scene
tech's activities in here, no coating of fingerprint dust across
the surfaces of the kitchen and no apparent interference
with the food on the table. One of the chesterfields had been
moved, though, and Stevie did detect fresh scrapings in the
brown coating on the tiles. At least something had been taken
seriously.

When the unpleasant smell became too much, she decided
to have another look upstairs, an area she hadn't had the
chance to thoroughly explore earlier.

As with downstairs, a similar state of neglect was evident
here, but with less sign of human habitation. Things were
dusty and spidery, but not unhygienic. The stairs led to an
unfurnished room with a new looking grey-flecked carpet,
power points and an aerial connection. A TV- or playroom,
she'd hazard a guess. A bathroom and two bedrooms led
from this central room. One of the bedrooms was tiny, not
much more than a storeroom, and stacked with removalist's
boxes. She prised some of the lids and found an assortment
of cooking utensils, a collection of baby's toys, folded clothes,
a pile of old shoes. Stevie and Monty still hadn't unpacked
boxes in their house from their recent move, so there was
nothing strange about these. But Skye had told her the couple
had lived here for a while—were they preparing to move

house perhaps? If they were, the dusty lids must mean they'd packed a while ago. She must remember to ask Skye if she could discover more from Mrs Hardegan; find out just how reliable a source of information the old lady might be.

The other bedroom was much more spacious. It held four single beds with bare mattresses, giving Stevie the impression of a school dormitory on the last day of term. Unlike the smaller room, this one had an ensuite bathroom and a large in-built robe.

From a locked window Stevie had a good view of Mrs Hardegan's neat back garden. A car pulled up outside her house. Lights flicked off and a man climbed out. It might be Fowler returning to ask Mrs Hardegan more questions, she thought, until she saw the man take a key from his pocket and let himself in through the front door.

The wind picked up in an instant and whipped at the trees in the surrounding gardens. In the street below, the patrol car's door blew shut. The crime scene tech wrestled with his overall hood, but soon gave up, dashing to the white incident van as the first heavy drops of rain fell. Lights went on in the parked police cars as officers returned to exchange information gleaned from canvassing the neighbours.

Stevie felt as detached from the goings on below as if she were viewing it all from a CCTV monitor. The grey road gradually turned black, yet she could hear no sound of the storm, no hammering of the rain on the roof, rattling window frames or whooshes of wind in the eaves. In this room everything remained silent and still.

A sudden draft blew the heavy bedroom door shut. She drew a breath, whirled around and moved quickly. It was time to leave—the last thing she needed was for someone to come up and investigate the noise.

But when she reached for the doorhandle, there was nothing there. The handle was missing. She was trapped.

I very much regret
everything that has happened
and the part I played

the part I have played in your
misery

CHAPTER FOUR

Lilly Hardegan turned off her TV and leaned back in the chair with the lacy armrests, pausing for a moment to listen to the drumming of the rain on the orange tiles of her roof. Through her open window the metallic smell of fresh rain on bitumen gusted in. Forcing herself to try to relax and enjoy the scent, she attempted to block out today's disturbing events, closed her eyes and began to compose the letter she would never write to a person who would never be able to read it.

When she was writing in her head, she saw the words as clearly as if they were printed on a blackboard. But when she tried to say them aloud, it was as if the board had become coated with butter, and the words slid from it and flew around the room and all she had to catch them with was a large-holed net.

She began to compose, leaning back in her chair, fingers of each hand touching, *here's the church here's the steeple*, like the childhood game.

My Dear ... she began, setting the letter out in her head as if it were on a page. *I trust this finds you* ...

A noise from the front of the house disturbed the flow of words. Surely the police wouldn't be calling on her again when they knew she had so little to tell? She dimmed the table lamp and prised open the venetians. The Pavels' house was lit like the Gloucester Park trots. The police were still there: she could see silhouettes in the cars, sheltering from the rain, and an officer standing on the front porch, but it had been a while since she'd seen anyone in the street.

Her body tensed. She continued to strain for alien sounds, one hand creeping down the gap between the side of her chair and the wall under the window. The carved texture of the samurai sword's handle was a comfort, despite the weakness of her grip upon it.

When no more strange sounds seemed forthcoming, she let go of the sword and sank back into her chair. Sometimes she relished the idea of a fight, a chance to get even, with whom or what she still did not rightly know.

There had to be someone, there always was.

My Dear, I hope this finds you in a better state than when we last met

There it was again, a distinct thump, the sound of the front door closing. The passageway light clicked and shone under the door of her room—her sight and hearing were as acute as they'd ever been. The floorboards creaked more softly than usual, as if the person was treading on the tips of his toes, a sneaking teenager home well after curfew. Only two people had keys to the front door, and Skye said she was going home after her last visit. It could only be him.

Oh God, him.

Perhaps if she pretended to be asleep he would go away.

*I very much regret everything that has happened and
the part I have played in your misery*

No, too syrupy, too sentimental. Not like you at all, Lilly,
you can't write that nonsense. Too much too soon; get back to
that part later.

The door of the room announced his entrance with a slow
moan. She ceased her composing as if, like an EEG, he might
sense the activity in her brain. She kept very still in her chair,
her eyes closed, keeping her breathing firm and even. His
footsteps were softer than usual, as if he were trying to keep
silent. A silent little mouse creeping across the lino, *scritch
scritchity scritch.*

A shadow flickered through the red of her closed eyes.
She willed her lids to remain steady and not betray her with
vibrations. Her ears strained for the sound of his movement.
The shadow stilled; he was very close now.

A feeling of dark warmth descended upon her from
above.

'*Bloody Japs Bloody Japs!*' the parrot squawked.

Her heart gave an extra thud, her eyes shot open and she
sat bolt upright in her chair. 'You, boy — shock!'

He leapt back as if he'd been stung, clutching a green
velvet cushion to his chest. 'Christ, Moth, I thought you were
asleep. I was just fixing your cushion, wanted to make you
more comfortable.'

'Doesn't need fixing. Fine.' In hospital she'd overheard the
nurses joke about giving a troublesome patient the 'Tontine
treatment'. It didn't seem funny now.

'Well you shouldn't leave it on the floor, it'll get dirty,' he
said, frisbeeing the cushion onto the bed. He turned to the

parrot. 'And as for you, it's about bloody time you fell off the perch.' He tossed a blanket over the cage and made it rock. The parrot let out a final curse and fell silent.

Too vain for glasses, Ralph peered closely at her face. 'God, Moth, you're as white as a sheet, are you alright?'

'Of course we're alright, just a shock, you shouldn't call at this time of night, tired, worried, must go to bed ...'

'It's not late; it's not even six o'clock. I'm here because the police called me. They said you were upset, said the Pavels have gone missing—does that mean the cops finally got round to checking up on them? I rang them several times you know, like you asked, but I think they thought I was some kind of crank. So what's happened—no sign of the Pavels at all?'

She shook her head; it was so much easier.

'I'll make you a cup of tea.'

She didn't want a cup of tea; she wanted to go to bed.

'So ... what exactly did you tell the police?' he asked as he bustled about the kitchenette. People often remarked upon her son's resemblance to Sir Richard Branson—tousled grey hair and neatly trimmed goatee beard—and it was an image he seemed determined to cultivate, even adopting a similar dress style to the multi-billionaire. There weren't many engagements grand enough to get him out of those bright figure-hugging shirts and designer jeans and into a suit. He probably wouldn't even wear a suit to his mother's funeral, she thought without sentiment. His ersatz Branson image had won and lost him three wives quicker than the real Branson could polish one of his jets.

He told everyone he was a businessman, but to Lilly Hardegan, her son Ralph would never be anything more than a trumped-up greengrocer.

He put her tea on the table next to her sewing and settled himself on the footstool at her feet. He often complained about the stool, said she should have another chair for visitors, said he hated sitting at her feet like a child. It kept him in his place, Lilly liked to think.

'Listen, Moth,' he said as he took one of her hands.

She used to have such pretty hands, she reflected without self-pity. These days they looked more like something found under the lino—too much sun maybe?

'It's really important that you tell me exactly what you said to the police,' Ralph went on. 'It would be awful if they were given the wrong impression of the Pavels, or of me for that matter, wouldn't it?'

'Your friends.'

'Well, not exactly, Jon Pavel is a business associate really. It's not necessary to mention my connection with him at all. You see, if you mention me ...' He paused, his eyes becoming sharp slits, nothing like Branson's at all. 'You'll be dropping yourself in it too.'

I was stupid. A stupid, naïve, ignorant old woman. Lilly's head began to pound. She felt as if she might be having another stroke. Maybe it would be easier for everyone if she did.

His clammy hand gripped hers once more. He was worried now, really worried, but only for himself. No, erase that. He wasn't merely worried; he was bloody terrified; she could smell the fear in his sweat.

'I might have to go away for a while, Moth, just to be safe, just until this business with the Pavels calms down. I won't tell you where I'm going; I think it's best you don't know in case they come here looking for me.'

Who did he mean 'they'—the police? Or was he talking about those awful people he'd got himself mixed up with?

'Don't worry, they won't want you, they know you can't tell anyone about anything. In the meantime, I'm getting things in motion to get power of attorney. It's a pain I didn't organise it before your stroke. Things are tricky now, but I should be able to get it sorted—it's the only way, you can see that, can't you?'

No, Lilly couldn't see it at all. Skye had said she was making a splendid recovery. Her right leg had improved to the extent that she didn't need a stick any more, and her hand was now good enough to let her tackle a basic cross-stitch. Skye said her speech was sure to follow, and when that happened, she would be taught to read and write again. No, he didn't need power of attorney. She drummed her feet ineffectually upon the lino. *He didn't, he didn't, he didn't!*

I try to find words

the words to express my sorrow but words
as you know
are no longer friends to me
that is why I write to you

in my head

we have more in common than you

might think

CHAPTER FIVE

Stevie tried the other window in the room, but like the one overlooking Mrs Hardegan's place, it was locked and she couldn't find the key. 'What a bloody idiot,' she cursed aloud, kicking at the heavy door. Lucky she didn't get claustrophobia; lucky, too, the smells from downstairs couldn't reach her in this hermetically sealed room. On the other hand, could any air get in at all? She panicked for a moment, not daring to breathe. Then she spotted the two air-conditioning vents in the ceiling. The aircon was switched off, but at least it meant that a certain amount of air could get through from the roof space. She let out her pent up breath, *whew*.

Stay calm, she muttered to herself, pacing the room. You've got your mobile with you and you must use it. You don't get claustrophobia. Someone will get you out, and when that happens you'll just have to come clean and face the consequences.

But maybe, just maybe, she could find a way around this.

She reached into her overalls for her mobile, relieved to see she had plenty of battery power left. Her first call was to Monty.

'I'm going to be late home,' she told him. 'Skye called

with a problem. I need to stick around a bit longer and sort something out for her.'

'Fine, no worries — where are you?'

'I'll explain later. There's something I need to know, though.'

'Shoot.'

'Do you remember a guy called William Trotman? A general duties officer when you were with Joondalup Detectives.'

'Blinky Bill? What's he got to do with Skye?'

'For now I just need his mobile number.'

'Hang on I'll check my phone.'

He seemed to be gone an age. When he finally returned he told her he no longer had Trotman's number in his phone. She started to swear.

'But I did find it on the old Cardex in the study.' She tried to ignore the infuriating smile in his voice, remaining calm as he read out the number, returned his 'love you' and hung up.

A police car pulled away from the curb. Stevie prayed Trotman was in the remaining one, that he still had the same mobile number.

He answered on the second ring. 'William Trotman.'

'It's Stevie Hooper, Bill. Don't say a word. Just get out of the car and get away from the others. I need a private chat.'

The car door opened and she saw Trotman's gangly form unfold into the street. 'It's fucking raining, Stevie.'

'I'm trapped in the upstairs room. Come and get me out without telling anyone.'

Trotman let out a whooping laugh.

'Just do it, you bastard!'

The door opened easily from the outside. To stop Trotman from asking what she was doing in the upstairs bedroom, she quickly pointed out the missing doorhandle, asking if it had been noted.

'No idea,' he said as they thumped down the stairs. 'That's the first I heard about it.' They paused on the front porch, waiting for a break in the rain. A van pulled up alongside the police car. Stevie recognised the high-heeled form of the woman from the deli, hauling herself out with a box of snacks for the troops. Stevie's stomach gave a hungry moan. It seemed hours since she'd eaten that salad sandwich.

'But the room was like a prison,' Stevie said. 'I still think you should point it out to Fowler, just in case. Get yourself some brownie points.' God knows he must need them. Fifty-five if he was a day and still a constable first class.

'It's probably just something to do with the redecorating that's been going on,' Trotman said, as if she should know what he was talking about.

'Redecorating? What do you mean?'

Trotman took off his glasses and wiped them thoughtfully on his uniform jacket, making them streakier than they already were. 'The neighbours told one of the lads about a fire here last year. Apparently an electrical fault damaged quite a bit of the inside of the house and they've been slowly getting the place reorganised. I guess they were just waiting on some more doorhandles.'

That would account for the fresh paint and lack of personal effects around the house; possibly, too, the boxed items in the storeroom. But what of the dirt, Stevie thought, the neglect of a beautiful house by a family who could easily afford to pay someone to clean it? And more importantly, how could the state of the baby be explained? A figure ran through the rain towards the porch before she could continue with the thought.

Her heart sank. Luke Fowler.

It seemed that during her absence her kitchen had been transformed into a Chinese laundry. Stevie blinked as she looked around the place, at the sheets of pasta draped over every available surface, from the oven doorhandle to the chair backs, the kitchen shelving to the wooden clotheshorse. Limp doughy strips even hung from Monty's tropical fish tank. 'See, curtains for the fish!' Izzy proclaimed.

Stevie finally found the words. 'I don't believe this ...'

Monty, with flour on the end of his nose and a generous dusting through his rust-coloured hair, put out two placating hands. 'Don't say anything, not one more thing. When you said you'd be home late we decided to cook dinner ourselves. It'll be the best lasagne you've ever tasted — low fat everything, so don't freak out — and you'll enjoy it more if you don't see any of the cooking process. Grab a drink, have a shower or check your email or whatever you want to do and leave dinner to us.'

'But how can you say that? Just look at all the mess!'

'Get out of the kitchen, Mum,' Izzy commanded with a swish of strawberry-blonde curls. She was becoming more like her father in hair colour as well as temperament as the years passed, quick to anger but just as quick to defuse. A lot healthier than Stevie's own anger, which tended to curl inside her like a spring. 'We don't need you!' Izzy stated the obvious, giving the pasta machine a couple of decisive cranks and sending several more sheets flopping to the floor.

Jesus Christ.

Monty pressed a tin of Emu into Stevie's hand. 'Go and relax.' Relax? That was easier said than done. After what she'd just been through with Fowler she felt about as relaxed as a car chase. But she was too tired for further argument. The beer was good, icy and cold. She took it with her into their living room, the stripped floorboards rough and splintery under her bare feet. With an uncommon flash of despair, she took in the room, a microcosm of the rest of their recently purchased, run-down house near the beach.

Unlike the Pavels', theirs was single storey and authentic Federation, with many more years of neglect under its belt. That was the challenge, Stevie liked to think, of putting it to rights, making up for the sins of the past. The beauty of art was in its imperfection. With this in mind she'd opted to keep the original character of the house as much as practically possible. Crooked doors, sloped floors, the outside dunny, would remain. Obvious dangers like the sagging veranda roof and floor would have to be fixed up; the electrical wiring replaced, the plumbing modernised. It would be a long, painstaking job. In some ways the process was much like the circuitous road she and Monty had taken to arrive at this point in their lives. The house they would do together; it was their future.

The renovation plans were with the council now, waiting for the official stamp of approval before the structural changes could commence. Stevie had been doing what she could to make the place more comfortable, though none of it was necessary in this time of limbo. But pulling up mouldy carpets, stripping wallpaper and painting selected parts of the outside at least gave her restless energy some direction.

Monty had said it was a useless exercise, a waste of time, seeing the builders would probably destroy most of her hard work. But she'd bulled ahead regardless and had so far enjoyed every minute of the process.

Her workstation was tucked into a corner of the lounge room. The study was only big enough for one desk and Monty dominated that. His need was greater as he worked mostly from home at the moment, writing reports for the Corruption and Crime Commission, a desk job to lead him gently up to his heart bypass surgery—if he went through with the operation, that is. He'd pulled out a couple of months ago using the state of their new house as an excuse. And he'd given Stevie no guarantees that he'd go through with the rescheduled operation either, leaving her in another form of limbo.

This one she filled with police work.

Her squad had recently arrested three Perth men involved in an international paedophile ring. The highly publicised court case demonstrated that it was not as easy as it used to be for predatory scum like these to hide on the Internet. She had spent the previous week in court, using the weekend for catching up on paperwork and team meetings at Central. The end was in sight, the prosecution going well, with most thinking they'd have a verdict by the end of next week. When her part was finished, further legalities would be handed over to the Australian Federal Police and the appropriate international authorities, and then she would commence three weeks of well-deserved leave.

Her desk was even more of a mess than usual. It looked like Izzy had been playing here again despite its out-of-bounds zoning. While she waited for her computer to boot up she attempted to create some order in the chaos, sliding

Lego pieces into their box, picking up scattered crayons and textas. At least Izzy had had the foresight to protect the desk with a newspaper, Stevie thought, until she saw the page it was open at—the personal columns. Various lurid pleas and advertisements had been singled out and decorated with rainbow borders, love hearts and stars. Shit. She could only hope Izzy hadn't been able to read any of it. Imagine if she'd planned on taking this artwork to school for show and tell?

2 hot chicks wet and waiting

Buxom blonde eager for your call ...

Asian babes for all tastes

She snatched the paper from her desk and crushed it into a tight ball. Christ, she thought, I'm officer in charge of the cyber predator team and I can't even keep this junk out of my own home, away from my own daughter. Although this wasn't quite what she dealt with at work, the core elements were still the same, it was all a question of exploitation. Sometimes she wondered what chance in hell they had in stemming this flood.

She looked at the picture of Izzy on the mantelpiece. It was her first day at school, her school dress stiff and new. The wide, gap-toothed smile seemed to say, look at me, I'm about to take over the world. Like her dad before his health scare, she thought she was ten feet tall and bullet-proof. Stevie saw a row of little faces in the photo album of her mind, exploited little boys and girls she'd come across during the course of her career, many who would have once been like Izzy. Her mind went to the abandoned Pavel baby — God, how could she protect them all?

She took a swig of beer and tried to calm down. The day had left her overwrought. Things weren't all doom and gloom, she tried to console herself; her team in the cyber predator unit had proved that the system could work.

She scrolled through her mail and found the memo telling her what time she was expected in court tomorrow. It looked like it was to be an all day session, which meant nearly ten hours of skirt-suit and heels. *Shit*.

Luke Fowler's face filled the TV screen in their bedroom, pleading to the public for information regarding the whereabouts of Delia and Jon Pavel. The woman at the deli thought they sounded Russian: close — the newsreader said they were Romanian. Photos of the couple were broadcast along with their car rego and a picture of a green Jaguar similar to the one missing from their garage.

Earlier, between bites of lasagne — Monty had been right, it was one of the best she'd ever tasted — Stevie had recounted the details of her afternoon, including her brief imprisonment in the upstairs bedroom.

'Good old Blinky Bill, coming to the rescue,' Monty said again, killing the TV with the remote and plunging them into darkness.

She wriggled further into the covers; the nights were still chilly despite the warmer days. 'Yeah, well he may have got me out of there, but he didn't do anything to help when I had the blow-up with Fowler.'

'How could he? You were blatantly out of line.'

Stevie snorted. 'I thought you at least would support me.

Fowler seems to think he can get me sacked for tampering with a crime scene.'

'Bullshit, it'll just get brushed under the carpet. You're the hero of the hour, the flavour of the month, walking on bloody water in fact.'

Ice clinked as he drained the last of his whisky then thunked the empty glass upon his bedside table — more than a little drunk, she suspected. He shouldn't have been drinking so close to his operation, but she couldn't chastise him now, not when he was saying things she needed to hear. 'There's not much you can do wrong at the moment,' he went on. 'Milk it while you can, it won't last.' He said it with no bitterness, despite the uncertain direction of his own career.

She snuggled into his back. He was a large man who carried his weight well. She had always thought he was fit too, despite the cigarettes. Until the onset of angina last year, he had jogged along the beach most mornings. It was hard to reconcile this outwardly fit body with its inner frailties.

'I managed to get a bit more from Trotman when Fowler finally climbed back under his rock,' she said. 'According to the people in the street, neither of the Pavels has been seen for four days.'

'The baby can't have survived alone for four days.'

'I know that. But the date corresponds to when Jon Pavel was last seen at work and Delia was seen at the supermarket. It doesn't necessarily mean that was when they last tended to the baby, though going by the state of him I'd say he'd been on his own for some time. '

'What does Jon Pavel do?'

'Businessman.'

Monty grunted. 'That covers a multitude of sins.'

'Runs a couple of restaurants in West Perth and a nightclub in Fremantle.'

The phone by their bed rang. Monty swore. Stevie groped for the light and leaned over him to answer it.

With no preamble, Skye gave her a rundown on baby Pavel's condition. She said he was improving and the doctors were cautiously optimistic he'd get through the physical ordeal with no lingering ill effects. 'But what about his mental condition?' Skye said with a hitch in her voice. 'That's what I want to know. Can you imagine the psychological effect this will have on him? I mean, the poor kid was obviously adopted in the first place, so who knows what hell he's already been through?'

Stevie sat up in bed. 'Adopted? Who told you that?'

'I don't need to be told, it's obvious. I noticed it straight off, didn't you? The kid's Asian.'

Stevie paused and thought back to their discovery. Yes, come to think of it, she had noticed Asian features under the dirt and grime. But as she hadn't known anything about the child's parents at the time, she hadn't given the matter much thought. The penny should have dropped when the deli woman mentioned that the parents were eastern European. She chided herself—she was usually more on the ball than this. Just as well this wasn't her case, that her leave was almost due. Monty, the cyber-predator case, the house; the stressors were adding up. She was more tired than she'd thought.

With her hand over the receiver, she told Monty Skye's news. He lay on his back with his hands under his head and stared at the ceiling, his face mirroring her own perplexed look.

Stevie listened to Skye a while longer and tried to reassure her that everything was being done to locate the baby's parents. 'She's not handling this very well,' she said to Monty when she finally extracted herself from the phone. 'This baby business has really upset her, she's a sensitive soul.'

Monty turned and raised an eyebrow as if to say: and you're not?

'At least I can detach,' she said, flipping the light off again. Despite almost half an hour under the hot shower, she could still detect the sour odour of the baby on her skin. In some ways, she reflected, its associations made it worse than the scent of decay.

Monty said, 'You've always said Skye was a bit, what was it, unbalanced?'

'No, not unbalanced, just highly strung and with a keen sense of moral justice.'

'Sounds like someone else I know.'

She didn't rise to the bait. 'I get the feeling Luke Fowler and Skye know each other. She certainly doesn't seem to have much faith in his abilities. There's some history there, I'm sure of it. He strikes me as a bully—he'd better not be giving her a hard time over this.'

'I've come across him once or twice; did a course with him in Adelaide. He seemed okay to me.'

'He might be okay to prop up a bar with after a day of lectures, but you've never had to actually work with him.'

'True. He must have seriously pissed off someone to land Peppy Grove. Never mind, if it does turn out there's a homicide behind this case, it might end up on my desk at SCS, which means Peppy Grove can be ousted.'

'You're not on active duty,' she reminded him.

'But at least I'll be able to find out what's going on and you won't have to rely on gathering information by devious means.'

The conversation faded; they lay in silence. He rolled over and she spooned into his solid back once more. His pragmatism, though sometimes an irritant, was a comfort tonight. She wondered again why it had taken her so long to agree to set up house with him, wondered how she'd ever thought she could do without him.

But then her thoughts drifted to the negative, the dialogue in her mind of 'what ifs' that refused to shut down. Monty's upcoming heart procedure was a dangerous operation. The blockage was in the left anterior descending artery, the one the doctors called 'the widow maker'. What if the operation was a failure? He could become an invalid or die under the anaesthetic; which was something he'd probably prefer, she contemplated morbidly. And they weren't married, even though they were engaged and they lived together—would she still qualify as a widow? She wondered if she'd ever be able to revert back to the old Stevie, the one who didn't need him or any other man in her life. The thought of being without Monty grabbed hold of her and shook her like a pitbull.

His muscles began to relax, his breathing to deepen. She breathed with him. Images of neglected babies, lonely old women, letters of dismissal and flatlining heart monitors faded. Finally she began to drift off.

Then Monty started awake with a sharp intake of breath. 'Stevie, I'm so scared,' he said.

did I ever tell you
I was born into a family with
a wealthy family

you probably can't imagine

how that was

WEDNESDAY

CHAPTER SIX

Like any member of the public, Stevie followed the Pavel case through newspaper articles and the TV news, bolstered by the occasional reports from Skye on the baby's condition. After an official complaint from Fowler, Inspector Veitch—her boss at Sex Crimes—told her in no uncertain terms to lay off, and, as Monty had predicted, disciplinary action was taken no further. As Stevie's own cases and the courtroom finale were dominating her every working hour, she backed down with little reluctance.

A couple of days had passed since their disturbing discovery and Skye's calls became less frequent. But then Stevie received a call from Skye just as court was adjourning for lunch. The impeccable timing was soon explained by Skye's appearance in the anteroom, phone still clamped to her ear, resplendent in full body armour: nose stud, eyebrow ring and multiple ear piercings.

Well prepared for battle, she would not take Stevie's no for an answer. 'Skye, I can't, I've been warned off.'

'C'mon, girlfriend, I'll buy you lunch,' Skye said, linking her arm through Stevie's.

Stevie cringed at the loudness of her friend's voice

amongst the muffled whisperings of those leaving the court. 'Skye, what the hell are you doing here?' she shot back in a stage whisper.

'Like I just said, I want to buy you lunch.'

'I don't have time for lunch. I have to go back to Central and grab some notes in time for the next session.'

'You *so* do have time for lunch. I asked one of the bailiffs while I was waiting and he said you have an hour and a half. Are cops sub-human, don't they need to eat? I have my Vespa—I can scoot you over to Central for your notes after we've had a snack and a talk.'

When Stevie continued to make noises of protest, Skye lowered her voice. 'I've just come back from the hospital, went to see the kid. There's still no sign of his parents and the police haven't been able to trace any relatives. The ward social worker says at this rate he'll have to be fostered out when he's discharged. There's some other stuff too, stuff we need to talk about in private.' The way her eyes slid toward a group of bewigged lawyers waiting for the lifts, suggested something furtive.

Soon Stevie would be commencing three weeks of leave and she had more than enough to do than get involved in a case she'd been warned to step away from. This was to be an important family time for them. Monty needed her; Izzy needed her even more. She would be the perfect mother: school runs, excursions, sitting through assemblies, helping with reading classes ...

When she didn't get the desired response, Skye raised her voice to an unnaturally loud pitch. 'Okay, Stevie, it's like this, the police are handling this case like DICKheads ...' The lawyers at the lift ceased their murmurings, all heads turned.

'Did you get that? D—I—'

A bailiff caught Stevie's eye and frowned.

'Okay, you win.' Seemed there was no choice. If she didn't want to be evicted from the building, she'd have to hear Skye out. Stevie took Skye's arm and guided her firmly toward the stairwell. A tall, fair-haired man stepped out in front of them as they were about to make their way down, deliberately bumping her on the shoulder. 'Watch where you're going, Stevie Hooper,' he said, disappearing into the crowd outside the courtroom before she could get a good look at him.

Did she hear him correctly?

'Hey, what's that supposed to mean?' Stevie started after him, only to find herself held back by Skye.

'Stevie, we don't have much time.'

Stevie pulled against her friend's hand, but not enough to dislodge her grip.

'Who was that guy?' Skye said. 'Hey, are you okay? You're white as a sheet.'

Stevie absently touched her cheek, stared back into the whirlpool of people and shook her head in disbelief. 'I'm not sure; I think the case is getting to me. I must be imagining things.'

Stevie hitched her skirt and climbed onto the pillion behind Skye. Dodging traffic and parked cars, they caught more than a few gaping stares and whistles as they sped down the terrace, to which Skye laughed and raised her middle finger. They arrived at the wine bar more than a little out of breath, Stevie laughing despite the annoyance at allowing herself to be so easily manipulated. The incident with the man on the stairs was forgotten. They ordered cheeseburgers and settled into a corner table, Stevie nursing an orange juice, Skye a vodka and Red Bull—it was her day off, after all.

'How's Monty? Do you think he'll go through with the op this time?' Skye asked.

From anyone else, the question might have been contrived, something off-topic to ease into the intended subject matter. But Skye had shown genuine concern for Monty's health problems when they'd first come to a head last year, even offering to come over and talk to him about the operation if it would help.

'Maybe he'll go through with it if Wayne—he's a guy Mont works with in Serious Crime—keeps his mouth shut this time,' Stevie said. 'He insisted on showing Monty his own scar, said the operation was like boning a duck with a pair of poultry scissors.' She scissored her fingers. 'I mean, it used to be dick length, now it's bypass scars. What is it with guys growing older?'

Skye laughed. 'Jeez, no wonder he's been put off. But it's really not that bad these days. Cook me dinner and I'll come over and explain it a bit more gently. Better not make it poultry, though, just to be safe.'

'Or rare beef.'

Skye took a swallow of her drink, smacked her lips. 'That's hitting the spot.' Then she casually said, 'I guess he's also worried about sex.'

Stevie put her glass down. 'What?'

'Don't be coy, he's a man; sex is never far from his mind.'

Stevie broke into a smile, 'Well, now you mention it ...'

'When he gets home from hospital, he's got to find some stairs to start practising on.'

Stevie laughed.

'No, not that, you dag; I mean once he can climb two flights of stairs with no pain or breathlessness he can get back into it again.'

'I'll pass on your words of advice. I'm sure he'll find them very comforting.'

Their burgers arrived and Stevie was running out of time. 'Okay, Skye, spill it, what have you been up to?'

Skye's eyes took on a worrying gleam. 'Well, for a start, I think a lot more is going on with this Pavel case than Luke Fowler is capable of handling.'

Stevie frowned. 'You and Fowler know each other, right?' Whatever Skye thought of Fowler, Stevie got the feeling it was mutual.

'No time to explain the sordid details of my life right now, but let's just say we have a history and he hates my guts.'

'Okay,' Stevie said, 'Change of topic. You said before you thought the baby was adopted.'

Skye swallowed one bite of burger and took another, speaking with her mouth full. 'Yeah, it's the obvious explanation seeing as both parents are Caucasian.' She pulled a crumpled newspaper photo from her bag to remind Stevie what the Pavels looked like. The images were grainy, but Jon Pavel's high forehead and blunt features spoke of an eastern European heritage. While not quite so obviously European, Delia's small, mousy face could never have been mistaken for Asian.

'Yes, Romanian, they've been in the country for about six years,' Skye said. 'I've no idea if the police are going any further with this, or if they've just given up and chucked the matter into the too-hard basket. A mate of mine in the DCP tried to dig up the adoption papers but hasn't been able to find a thing.'

'He's probably telling you a furphy—what you asked him to do is a serious, sackable offence. Still,' Stevie added thoughtfully, 'I suppose the baby *might* have been adopted from overseas.'

'That's what I'm getting at. He *was* adopted overseas and the papers burned in the house fire last year. But is there any way you can follow through with Fowler on this? Just so we know all the bases are covered. I feel this might be important.'

'No way, I'm keeping away from this.' Stevie eyed her friend suspiciously. 'Wait a minute, how did you know about the fire last year? The newspapers haven't mentioned it.'

'Just a bit of, er, networking.' Skye's gaze dropped to a sprinkling of crumbs on the table and she pushed them around with the stub of a black-painted fingernail.

'Go on,' Stevie prompted.

Skye took a breath. 'Yesterday Mrs Hardegan's phone was out of order. I needed to visit the neighbours on the other side to see if theirs was working—and it was by the way.'

'And Mrs Hardegan's was never broken anyway, you just needed an excuse for a chat.'

'Muriel and David Blakeman are nice, friendly people, but they don't like the Pavels at all. David said Jon Pavel was a slimy, inconsiderate wanker—my words—who he wouldn't trust as far as he could throw. The Blakemans told me about the house fire, an electrical fault apparently. Jon Pavel was obnoxious even when they put him and his family up for that first night when they had nowhere else to go. The baby was only a couple of months old then.'

Stevie remembered the deli woman telling her how

unpopular the Pavels were with the neighbours, although she wasn't about to let Skye know she'd been doing some undercover snooping herself.

'But I still got a lot more from Mrs Hardegan than I did the Blakemans.'

'Hang on, tell me more about the old lady: she can't be a reliable witness, surely?'

'Oh, you'd be surprised, there's not much escapes her, don't be fooled by her crazy speech.'

'So she understands what's going on?'

'You bet she does.'

'Then why does she talk like that?'

'The stroke was in the language centre of the left side of her brain, meaning it effects the right side of her body.'

Stevie's mind stretched back to school biology lessons, something about the nerves crossing as they left the brain. 'That's why she's weak down her right side?'

'That's right,' Skye said. 'She's lucky, the stroke could've been a lot worse. Her speech difficulties aren't as bad as they could be, difficulty with naming things mainly, confusing pronouns, et cetera. Her auditory comprehension and understanding are preserved, although her reading and writing are very much impaired. Every case is slightly different though—even with lesions in exactly the same place, no two people have quite the same symptoms.'

'What about thought processes?'

'Pretty good; but there can be personality changes. I didn't know her before the stroke so I can't say if her personality has been affected or not. She sure as hell doesn't suffer fools, but I suspect that's nothing new.'

'Whatever, it must be very frustrating for her, she's bound

to get narky sometimes—I sure would.' Stevie paused, took a sip of juice. 'So, what did she tell you about the Pavels?

'Seems she knew Delia Pavel quite well, was one of the few people in the street who got on with the both of them. Before the stroke she used to help out by watering the indoor plants when they went away—that's why she still had the key to their front door. From what I could gather from Mrs H, they were unhappy because they couldn't have children. Then an overseas agency organised a child for them and they were over the moon. But after they'd had Joshua for a couple of months, Delia seemed to fall into some kind of depression. Mrs H couldn't explain it, but I reckon it must have been the reason behind the badly kept house, although she assured me the baby continued to be loved and well looked after. It wasn't long after that Mrs H had her stroke and her memory of that time is a bit hazy. I tried to tell Fowler all this but he wouldn't listen, even when I said I understood the old lady more than most. He's just dismissed her as a loopy old woman and he already thinks I'm an interfering cow. He said he couldn't see that the overseas adoption had any relevance at all. He even threatened me with a restraining order—can you imagine that?'

Stevie speculated on the reasons why a restraining order hadn't been served already, or Skye charged with interfering with police business. Had this been her case, she certainly would have opted for one of the two. She wondered again about the history Fowler and Skye shared.

'I can't afford to let that happen,' Skye went on. 'I'm the only one who has any inkling what the poor old dear is saying. On top of all this drama with the Pavels, she's really upset with her son who wants to sell the house from under her and put her in a Z-grade nursing home—her block's worth a bomb, apparently. Pressure like this could easily cause another stroke. The long and the short of it is: in order for me to stay in contact with Mrs H, I'm going to have to hand the investigative reins over to you. '

Stevie almost choked on her burger. 'Oh no you don't!'

'But you've got so many resources at your fingertips. We found the baby together, for God's sake! You can't tell me that this affected you less than me. How can you not be interested?' Skye hesitated. 'And there's two other things you need to know about, very important things that might make you more willing to help.' She paused for breath, took a large swallow of her bile-coloured drink then rummaged in her handbag for a moment, producing a paper lunch bag. 'I found it on the other side of the taped driveway quite close to the house, but in an area the police hadn't searched. It might be important; then again it might be nothing, but if I were you I'd get it DNA tested.'

Stevie gaped at the bag Skye dangled like bait between her black-tipped fingernails.

'Christ, you shouldn't have this Skye—you shouldn't even have touched it! If it is something important, the only DNA that would be on it now is yours, and the remains of a cheese and ham sandwich by the looks of it.'

Skye looked hurt. 'I've seen how they do it on CSI; I used sterile forceps from my medical kit and the paper bag was clean. I didn't give it to Sergeant Dickhead because I found it just after he'd finished screwing me over and told me to get lost, and I sure wasn't going to go putting any feathers in *his* cap. Bugger him; he should have found it himself.'

Stevie tried to stay calm, wishing she had something

stronger than orange juice on the table in front of her. 'Okay, so what's in the bag?'

Skye made as if to reach into it.

'No, don't touch it,' Stevie warned. 'Just open the bag up and show me the contents.'

Skye opened it so Stevie could peer inside.

'It's a button,' Skye responded, oblivious to Stevie's horrified look. 'Silk-covered—very unusual and very pretty; I found it just outside the Pavels' front gate the day after we discovered the baby. It has a small piece of pale green material still attached, as if it was snagged on something, the gate maybe, and ripped off. '

Stevie pressed her hands to her eyes, feeling the onset of a headache. It was the same button she'd pointed out to the crime scene tech and he obviously hadn't bothered to do anything about it.

'Shit, Skye, what the hell did you think you were doing?'

Skye's unprofessional handling of the button, the lack of a photograph and no other documentation to prove where it was found meant that it could never be used as evidence—but evidence of what? Stevie had no idea how seriously the local police were taking the possibility of foul play behind the disappearance of the Pavels. The newspaper reports suggested they were pursuing the original accident theory, though she knew this could easily be a blind to lull any possible offenders into a false sense of security—if only she knew the angle Fowler was working this.

There was only one thing she could do. She took the paper 'evidence' bag from Skye and put it in her briefcase. 'I'm afraid I'm going to have to show this to Fowler.'

'Now why doesn't that surprise me?' Skye pulled a face

and turned her head away.

'You said there were two things I needed to know. What's the second?'

For a moment Stevie thought Skye might refuse to tell her, but after shooting her a petulant look, continued. 'One of my mates works on the ward where the baby is and knows all the medical tests the poor little bugger's had.' Skye licked dry, guilty lips. 'And all the results.'

'Go on.'

'You know how no one had seen the Pavels for four days before we found the baby?'

Stevie nodded.

'Well, didn't you think it was amazing that the kid was still alive?'

'It did cross my mind, but just because the parents hadn't been seen for four days, doesn't mean they'd been missing that long. One of them could have been hiding in the house for at least some of that time. Plus the baby was confined to the cot, couldn't expend much energy, the weather was mild ...'

'Quite. Medical tests showed he'd only been deprived of food and fluid for two days max. But who was it who fed him and why did they stop? Stevie, can't you see? We have to find out what the hell's going on here.'

I had lots of brains no looks,

good for university, but not romance!

but then of course
there was the War

THURSDAY

CHAPTER SEVEN

Stevie needed time to prepare for the confrontation with Luke Fowler and it wasn't until the next evening that she'd managed to arm herself with some relevant facts. She decided not to change out of her court clothes, putting her faith in the menacing effect of the dark suit and heels that made her taller than most men.

She was relieved to find him alone in the large open-plan office he shared with several detectives, and gratified to see his blue eyes widen with surprise when she pushed through the swing door unannounced.

'Good evening, Sergeant Fowler.' She slapped a single file upon the desk in front of him and sat on the visitors' chair with her long legs crossed. His suit jacket hung over the back of his chair, his tie pulled loose at the collar of his creased white shirt and the skin around his eyes was dark and pouched. On his desk sat a grubby computer monitor and a keyboard with letters worn to smudges.

He looked at her across a barricade of mugs, each holding a residual smear of coffee. 'Ms, er ...' He recognised her, she could tell, but was too stunned by her sudden appearance to put a name to her face.

'Senior Sergeant Hooper, Central,' Stevie reminded him.

'Ah yes ...' he made a searching movement with his hand.

'We met a few days ago outside the Pavel house. You filed a complaint against me, said you'd get me dismissed. Don't tell me you've forgotten who I am already?'

'Of course not.' He regarded her closely. 'A grim business — on all counts.'

'Very grim.'

'So what is it I can do for you?'

Stevie put her hand into her pocket and removed Skye's paper bag, carefully placing it on his desk. 'This is a button found by Skye Williams just outside the taped crime scene and given to me. I thought you should have it.'

Fowler peered gingerly into the bag as if it might have a snake in it. His pink face turned violent red. 'Good God, the vindictive little cow; she's withheld this from me deliberately and now it's completely useless — I can't use this.' He shoved the paper bag back at her. 'I'll have her charged for this.'

Stevie returned the button to her bag and snapped the clasp. 'Yes, I suppose her actions could be seen as vindictive,' she said, 'just as your handling of the Pavel case could be seen as incompetent. You've been letting an incident between yourself and Skye Williams from nearly three years ago colour your dealings with her now, and you have ignored vital evidence from her as a result.'

Fowler slapped his hands upon his desk. 'Jesus Christ, what the hell is it you want?'

'Not your case, if that's what you think. I've enough on my own plate. I want you to find the Pavels and I want you to show some respect for Skye.'

'Your friend's a whore. Are you aware of that, Hooper?'

Stevie expelled a breath: my God, this man had women issues. 'She *was* a sex worker, and of course I'm aware of it. I've read the file. As far as I'm concerned it makes no difference to our friendship, just as it should have made no difference to you when she reported her rape to you almost three years ago. She was turning tricks to finance herself through uni. It might not be everyone's idea of gainful employment, but it pays a lot better than flipping burgers.'

'She's a junkie.'

'That's a fabrication.'

'She denies it?'

'Skye hasn't told me anything.' Stevie tapped the folder on Fowler's desk. 'It's all in here, including your negligent investigation of her case. Skye has never been a user; she wouldn't have coped with the nursing curriculum if she had been. Christ, Fowler, no wonder you were transferred to Peppermint Grove. If it was me on the internal affairs panel I'd have dismissed you altogether.'

Clearly shaken, he didn't answer, got up from his desk and turned his back, suddenly taking great interest in the drops of rain coursing down the window.

Stevie wasn't enjoying this as much as she thought she would, but now she'd started she had to continue to the bitter end.

'Skye was brutally assaulted by one of her customers and you refused to take her allegations seriously,' she said. 'It wasn't until a sex worker was murdered months later that some bright spark pulled the file and linked the man to Skye's assault. True to form, Skye didn't stay silent. She went to your boss and told him how you'd treated her, which resulted in you being busted down to Peppermint Grove. And what a place.' Stevie waved her arms around the tatty office with its dented desks and faded green walls. 'One of the most affluent suburbs in WA, yet its cop shop is struggling to stay afloat. I guess the powers that be don't think the occasional luxury car theft, home burglary and drug deals between private school kids warrant much of a budget. This place can hardly be a challenge to someone with your record.'

Fowler continued to stand at the window, his only movement the clenching and unclenching of fists at his side. Stevie hadn't just hit a nerve, she realised—she'd severed a spinal cord.

'You could have gone far, Fowler, your record was exemplary until then. You'd probably be an inspector in a specialist division if it weren't for Skye Williams. No wonder you hate her guts.' Stevie paused. 'I guess you must have had friends in high places, keeping a lid on it, maybe out of respect for your late grandfather, the Commissioner.'

Stevie's implication wasn't lost on Fowler. Pull your finger out or I'll start spreading it around further. *You'll never work in this town again ...*

Fowler cleared his throat and slowly turned to face her, the scar on his cheek red and angry against his skin. 'So, what is it you want me to do?'

'You can listen to what Skye has to say: for a start, she's the only one who knows what the old lady is talking about.'

He stared at her for a moment. 'Okay,' he said, barely above a whisper.

Stevie hesitated; she hadn't been expecting him to roll over quite so quickly. Her threat to spill the beans on him was no big deal; cops had done far worse and still maintained face with their colleagues.

'Apparently Mrs Hardegan thinks there's a lot more behind this than a tragic accident,' she said, still trying to suss him out. 'From what Skye can decipher, the old lady thinks it might have something to do with the baby's adoption. I notice that was withheld from the newspapers, as was the house fire. Is that because you're taking these as serious leads?'

'I can't dismiss either of them.' He sank back into his desk chair.

'Then why haven't you referred this to a specialist crime squad? Are you still trying to redeem yourself, Sergeant Fowler? Do you think you can manage all this on your own?'

'I didn't think it necessary to bring in specialists at this stage. We still don't know for sure if we're dealing with a homicide or not.'

'Then I suggest you talk to the old lady, using Skye as interpreter. What she says might help you make your decision.' Stevie rose to leave. 'And you can also do me the professional courtesy of keeping me informed about the investigation.'

She was at the door when Fowler's subdued voice made her turn. 'Foul play hasn't been eliminated,' he said. 'You were right; there was blood under the couch. We think it's Delia Pavel's—at least the DNA matches various other samples taken from the house.'

Stevie walked back towards his desk, her interest in the case now piqued more than her desire to stamp him further into the ground. 'I heard someone had been feeding the baby—for some of the time anyway.'

Fowler's jaw dropped. 'You heard? How?'

Surely it was obvious to him who her source at the hospital was. When she failed to elaborate, he said, 'Yes, the doctors think that's the case.'

'Any idea who had been feeding him?'

'There's some speculation. As we've only found Delia's blood in the house, it could mean Jon Pavel killed his wife and returned to feed the baby himself. On the other hand, neighbours did report seeing a woman around the house on two separate occasions. They didn't know the Pavels were missing at that time and took her to have been a visitor.'

'Description?'

'Vague.'

'But why would this person quit after two days?'

'Well if it was Pavel, or a woman he was in collusion with, they might have known the baby would survive because they knew when it would be found.'

'But how would they know that?'

Fowler shrugged. 'Pavel was going to call us himself after he'd skipped the country?'

They both paused for thought; the theory did make a certain amount of sense. Finally Stevie said, 'I'd like to look at your phone log.'

'Why?'

'Just bring it up on the computer please, Sergeant.'

Fowler frowned at his smudged monitor. 'System's a bit slow at the moment—I've got someone working on it.'

He rang for the log and it was brought up to his office by a uniformed constable. Stevie leaned into the desk and carefully traced her finger down the computer printout of a month's worth of calls.

'I can see Skye's call listed, then mine after we found the baby; apparently Mrs Hardegan's son Ralph also rang on behalf of his mother, but there's no record of his call here,' she said.

Fowler asked her to hand the printout over so he could have a look for himself. 'Christ,' he exclaimed after a moment of sifting through the wide ribbon of reports. 'Ralph Hardegan might not have cracked a mention, but read this.'

Stevie left her chair and looked to where his finger pointed, to a day dated two days before the baby's discovery.

'Anonymous female,' she read, 'called 1345, very distressed, unintelligible, officer could not understand complaint.' Stevie paused. 'The same message was repeated the next day. And you mean to tell me your guy didn't report this to his supervisor?'

Fowler smoothed his hands over the wheat stubble on his head. 'Shit.'

'What is it with you Peppermint Grove people—are you *The Misfits*, *The Dirty Dozen* or what?'

'I'll have the desk sergeant's head on a platter.'

Stevie puzzled over the problem aloud: 'But who can this anonymous female be—Mrs Hardegan perhaps? Her speech is pretty unintelligible at times, some might think she has an accent.'

'Or this could tie in with the theory that Pavel killed his wife to be with someone else. Can another Romanian woman who couldn't speak English have been feeding the baby? Can she be the one who made the phone call?'

Their speculation was put to a halt by the ringing of the phone. It was a courtesy call from Swan Detectives. A body had just been found in the river at Middle Swan. They knew Fowler had been searching for the missing Pavels—would he be interested in joining them at the scene?

In the station's ladies room, Stevie changed into spare clothes stored in the boot of her car, then accompanied Fowler in his own car, a silver-green vintage Bentley.

Stevie sank back into the soft leather seat, appreciating the walnut dash, the leg room, the smooth slap of the wipers as they headed into the rainy night.

'Belongs to my old man,' Fowler said somewhat self-consciously. 'He wants me to buy it so it stays in the family. Thinks if I drive it for a while I'll get to like it. I wouldn't normally have it at work, didn't think I'd be going out tonight ...'

They said little else on the drive, settled into an uneasy truce, Stevie luxuriating in the car's opulence, Fowler sitting stiffly behind the wheel. By the time they arrived at the riverbank the rain had weakened to a drizzle but the wind had become a gale, bending the red gums on the riverbank into the shapes of poor distressed souls. This stretch of the river at Middle Swan was familiar to Stevie, close to the hostel where she'd boarded as a high school student.

Powerful lights erected at a parking area near the scene reflected on the choppy water, a moving palette of glaring brightness and sinister shadows.

Low voices, muffled shapes.

A burst of lightning morphed into the flash of a police photographer's camera.

The wind blew fresh and moist against Stevie's cheeks. Turning up the collar of her waterproof jacket she followed Fowler to the police vehicles clustered near the river's edge. His shape was illuminated in the yellow cut of headlights as he walked, his hands deep in the pockets of his Drizabone, shoulder flaps blown by the wind. They picked their way across the slippery grass, the scent of mud and algae stronger with every step. A tree grew on the riverbank, one branch stretching across the choppy water, a swinging rope dangling. They used to play truant at this stretch of the river, Stevie remembered, swinging from the bank, their tanned bodies plopping like sinkers into the brown water.

But the tree hadn't seemed sinister then.

Next to the four-wheel drives a group of police, in yellow coats with luminous armbands, were gathered around the bundled body. One man left the group to shake Fowler's hand. Stevie wasn't introduced to the Swan detective, Joe Burridge. She knew she should be appreciating this feeling of unlicensed distance, the lack of responsibility, but with no procedural guidelines and no fixed role to play in the investigations, she found her emotions heightened, drowning the objectivity on which she usually depended.

The photographer, having finished his task, stepped back to give Fowler some room.

'Is it her?' Burridge asked Fowler who squatted down next to the sodden form. Stevie looked for a moment and then averted her eyes.

'Not decayed enough if you ask me,' Burridge said.

'It's impossible to tell.' Fowler sighed as he looked at the pale, almost translucent head of the corpse. 'Longish hair, could be a woman.'

'Bodies decay a lot slower in cold water than on land; with so many variables at play, it's almost impossible to tell at this stage how long the body has been in the river.'

The female voice belonged to the pathologist, Melissa Hurst, who emerged from behind the white coroner's van acknowledging Stevie and Fowler with a nod of her curly grey head.

'You've already examined the body?' Fowler asked Hurst.

'No, only got here a few minutes before you.'

Hurst beckoned him back to the body. The other officers stepped aside. Fowler shone his torch at the slurried face and empty eyes. Decay and aquatic scavengers had eliminated any hope they had of a visual identification. The view from the forehead up told its own story.

'A shotgun to the head,' Hurst said. 'See the peppering of shot on either side of the wound?'

Stevie forced herself to look. The top of the woman's head was split down the middle, the skin on either side of the wound peeled back, exposing the remnants of waterlogged brain tissue and ripped blood vessels. Fine shotgun pellets formed a smoky rash along the torn sides of the pale skin.

And then something moved.

'Oh, fuck.' Fowler turned his head and expelled a sharp breath. Hurst lost no time scissoring her gloved fingers into the cranial cavity. Stevie stepped back, horrified to see the yabby flicking back and forth between the pathologist's thumb and finger.

'Bag!' Hurst snapped and dropped the small crustacean into the hastily proffered bag. 'Okay put it in with the body bag,' she told the constable.

'Like something from fucking *Alien*,' Burridge muttered.

As if this was their call, two hovering mortuary attendants took a step closer. Fowler held up his hand. 'We're not ready yet.' He turned back to Hurst. 'Was the wound inflicted before or after death, doc?'

'I can't tell for sure, not until I open her up. Information from bruising would be inconclusive after more than a day or two in the water. How long has Delia Pavel been missing?'

'Last seen a week ago,' Fowler said.

Hurst said, 'Let's have a look at the rest of her. We'll have to remove this covering.'

The body was wrapped in a waterlogged doona secured by thin wire ties around the ankles, waist and chest. 'This'll be the missing cover off her bed,' Stevie said under her breath to Fowler. She wondered what had led to the gruesome transformation of something so domestic and banal. Though discoloured by river slime, the small blue flowers on the fabric stood bright under the spotlight's beam, undoubtedly matching the pillowcases on the Pavels' bed.

Fowler nodded and took the pliers a constable handed him. 'Okay, here goes.' He carefully snipped the lengths of wire wrapped around the torso and ankles. Hurst peeled open the sodden doona. The woman wore jeans that swelled at the belly from the build up of bodily gasses. A long-sleeved T-shirt stretched tight across the distended abdomen. The exposed skin of her neck, hands and bare feet was pale and loose; her fingernails, barely keeping a grip upon her skin, looked like fakes about to come unstuck. Stevie caught a whiff of putrid gas, took a step back and pulled the neck of her jumper over her nose and mouth.

'Washerwoman's skin,' Hurst remarked, pointing to the dimpled flesh on the feet. 'How was she found?'

'A couple taking their dog for an evening walk saw what they thought was a log floating near the bank,' said Joe Burridge. 'The guy reckoned it might be a danger to small boats and attempted to pull it ashore. Then he realised it was a body—she'd been weighted down with this.' He shone his torch on what appeared to be a car axle next to the body. 'It was tied on with a length of old rope. The river level's risen over the last few days because of the rain. The body must have been dislodged by the increased water flow and floated free.'

Hurst sighed. 'There's not much else I can do here. Let's get her back to the lab.'

Fowler agreed with the pathologist. 'We've collected some of Delia Pavel's DNA from the house.'

'Good,' she said. 'I can use it as a comparison.'

Lights from an approaching vehicle cut through the darkness. The divers had arrived to search the river for more evidence and potentially the body of Jon Pavel.

'Have you seen enough?' Fowler asked Stevie.

Stevie nodded, cold to the bone. Clasping her arms across her chest, she followed Fowler back to the car. She looked back at the decaying mass on the riverbank. Delia Pavel had been a wife and mother of a young child. Stevie wondered what she had done to deserve this.

My parents
Were most disapproving
did'nt like my joining the navy
one little bit

I lied about my age

I Was a nurse you See
should have been a doctor
and they never liked that

FRIDAY

CHAPTER EIGHT

An emergency hospital admission and several new patients on her round meant the more independent Mrs Hardegan had been bumped to the end of Skye's afternoon list. Technically speaking, she barely qualified to be on the list at all, but Skye knew the old woman looked forward to her visits and had promised to keep them going as long as she could. At the recent case review meeting, Skye had emphasised the point that although Mrs Hardegan had improved physically, she still needed to be monitored for signs of depression, a common occurrence in recovering stroke victims.

When dealing with her patients Skye always strove to see the person behind the disabilities. They all had stories to tell which reflected their lives and well-being and consequently influenced their nursing care. But other than the barest biographical details gleaned from her son (at best, disinterested, at worst, sleazy), Mrs Hardegan's story remained a mystery. According to Ralph, his mother was born in Perth in 1923, served as a naval nurse during the war, was married in 1950 and widowed in 1955, his father dying not long after his birth.

He'd told her that his mother had worked in various

hospitals around the state when he was growing up and had attained some senior positions—exactly what, he couldn't say. When Skye had asked if she had ever been a matron—she seemed the type—Ralph shrugged. He remained indifferent when she questioned him about the crisscross pattern of scars she'd noticed on the old lady's back.

See-through frail, but her wits as sharp as ever, there was a lot to admire about old Lil, and a helluva lot more to find out if Skye was to give her the emotional support she required. Barely able to talk any kind of sense when they'd first met after the stroke, the old lady had answered Skye's questions about the scars with strings of neologisms—nonsense words of her own invention, a typical characteristic of many stroke patients with expressive dysphasia. Even though her speech had improved greatly, Skye still couldn't understand everything the old lady was saying, and encouraged her to practise her speech whenever they were together.

They were chatting away now as Skye placed the weekend's medications into the plastic pill tray. They'd been discussing Ralph who had gone away on business and left no forwarding phone number.

Busy with her parrot, Mrs Hardegan seemed not the least bit concerned about Skye's dilemma about who to leave on the contact list. After filling up the seed bowl, she replenished the bird's water supply, using a jug with a long spout. Skye assessed the way she carried out these tasks, noting how barely a seed or drop of water was spilled. The old lady's fine-motor skills were improving daily, she noted with satisfaction.

'Our good boy, our little feathered friend,' Mrs Hardegan muttered to herself as she put the feeding paraphernalia back in the drawer of a heavy oak sideboard at the far side of the room. 'We are the same age as the feathered one. We were given him by a sea captain when we were just a boy.'

'I know, and he's very beautiful,' Skye said; she'd never seen anything more endearingly ugly in her life. The old lady seemed a lot fonder of Captain Flint than she had ever been of her son. But Skye could hardly list a parrot as the emergency contact.

'Is there anyone else we can put on your list, Mrs H?'

'Liar. Not beautiful, ugly as sin.' Mrs Hardegan must have noticed the exasperation on Skye's face and answered her question with a shrug of her bony shoulders before shuffling back to her chair by the window. Still saying nothing, she pointed to the Pavels' house.

'I know, it's a shame they've gone,' Skye said. 'They could have gone on the list. They were good neighbours to you, weren't they?'

'Used to be. Not now.'

'Well ... no, not now.' Stevie had rung Skye the previous night and told her about the discovery of the body in the river, which she said more than likely belonged to Delia Pavel. Although Mrs Hardegan hadn't mentioned it, she couldn't have missed it; it had been all over the TV news. The news didn't seem to have affected her. She sat as she usually did, rigid in her chair, hands clasped, buttoned tight as a pair of winter combinations, as Skye's gran would've said. When she was dying in hospital, Gran had said how strange it was to be old and sick on the outside, yet still feel twenty-one on the inside. Mrs Hardegan was very much like her gran, Skye decided.

'The boy told us all about the snoodle pinkerds. Now we

know. We know what happened,' Mrs Hardegan said in her no nonsense, matter-of-fact tone.

Snoodle pinkerds. Skye hadn't heard her use that term since the early days of the stroke. She wondered what it meant, but was reluctant to bombard the woman with questions that might only lead to more frustration. For that same reason, she didn't want to raise the distressful topic of Delia Pavel just before the weekend when there wouldn't be anyone around to keep an eye on her.

On the phone Stevie had mentioned getting together for a meeting with Mrs Hardegan and Luke Fowler on Monday. Hopefully, between the three of them, they'd be able to work out what she was talking about. It surprised Skye that Luke Fowler had agreed to this. She certainly wasn't looking forward to dealing with him again, and was sure he felt the same. They reminded each other of things they'd both rather forget.

Still poised over the empty emergency contact list, she nibbled the top of her pen and worried about the coming meeting—he'd hardly say or try anything stupid with Stevie standing as a buffer between them, would he? Skye didn't usually care what anyone said or thought about her, but her 'holiday job' was one thing she didn't care to broadcast, especially to Stevie. She wasn't sure why she didn't want her friend to find out—it wasn't like Stevie was 'conservative country', like her folks. Even though she knew Stevie was not judgemental, she worried that knowledge of her past might diminish her value in Stevie's eyes. Their friendship wasn't worth the risk.

'Have you any plans for the weekend, Mrs H?' she asked, putting the pen, Mrs H's notes and her disturbing thoughts away.

Mrs Hardegan pointed to her cross-stitch, then to the TV.

'Don't just point Mrs H; you've got to practise your talking. That's what the speech therapist said, isn't it?'

'Tripe, the boy talked utter tripe, getting us to look at all those stupid picture cards. We know what a teapot is, we know a car when we see one, an apple with an *aaaaaa* — we're not at kindergarten.'

'I hope you weren't rude to her.'

'No. We just told him to fuck off.'

Skye grinned back. 'Bet you didn't.' She picked up the TV guide and slowly read the weekend TV listings aloud. She could sense the old lady taking it all in, committing her weekend viewing schedule to memory. Mrs H could no longer understand numbers, so Skye had stuck small coloured dots on the TV remote to signify the channels. Next, she took the coloured wool Mrs Hardegan pointed to, and threaded enough needles to last the weekend. The tapestry was a laborious task, something Mrs H had taken up after the stroke when the screen-printing had proved too messy.

'I'm going to visit my folks. They live on a farm near Wyalkatchem,' Skye told her as she finished the threading.

'Lucky parents to have a boy like you. Better than our cowardly waster.'

'I don't think my parents would agree if they knew what I'd been up to a few years ago.' Skye got up from the footstool. 'Anyway, I'd better get going if I want to miss the city traffic.'

But she was too late to miss the evening traffic. Skye rang her mother from her car to say she'd be late and not to hold dinner for her. In the evenings the corner store often cooked fresh Asian dishes to go. She'd had them with Mrs Hardegan before and they were always delicious. She'd get a container and eat in the car on the way to the farm.

Heading to the deli, she tried again to make sense of Mrs Hardegan's words: *The boy told me all about the snoodle pinkerds. Now we know, we know what happened.* There was something there, she knew it, something she'd failed to grasp. Ralph Hardegan had disappeared, supposedly on business, and the Pavels, or at least one of them, had been murdered. There had to be a connection between the three of them—but what?

She started to call Stevie on her mobile, then decided against it. Monty was having his operation tomorrow and Stevie would probably be sitting with him in the hospital while he went through the last minute preparations for surgery. Even if she did get through on the phone, she doubted her friend would be in the right frame of mind to listen. Never mind, maybe she could work it out for herself while she was up at the farm. God knows there wasn't much else to think about in that barren, sand-blasted place.

She ordered the nasi goreng, a fully-leaded Coke and a packet of smokes she'd have to hide from her mother. In her head she heard her mother say, 'Still smoking, and with your asthma as bad as it is? Skye, you must have a death wish.' She smiled to herself. If her mother knew what else her little girl had been up to since she left home, she'd probably be overjoyed at the insignificance of her one remaining vice.

Skye stepped from the shop onto the footpath, thinking again about what Mrs H had told her. Maybe she should call Stevie. It was an intriguing mystery and she might appreciate the diversion after all. Putting her purchases on the roof of her car, she reached into her uniform pocket for her phone. Predictably, Stevie's phone was switched off so she left a voice message. 'Hi Stevie, it's me. Hope all's going well with Monty, give him my love and luck. Listen ... I've just had another talk with Mrs Hardegan. There seems to be some kind of a connection between her son and the Pavels, and I think you should know that Ralph, the son, has also gone missing. I thought you might like to mention it to Luke Fowler, now that you're so palsy walsy with him. I'm spending the weekend with my folks in Wyalkatchem. Give me a ring on their landline if you can, there's no mobile reception up their way.' She rattled off her parents' number. 'Ciao for now, see you Monday at one ...'

Skye made herself comfortable in her white Hyundai, the radio on Triple J, the tray of nasi goreng safely wedged on the front seat between her bag and an old towel positioned to catch any dropped rice. She cracked the Coke as she pulled into the street, cutting off a shiny posh car about to pull out behind her. The driver didn't so much as offer a finger or even a honk of annoyance. What a suburb, she thought with disgust: leafy green verges, proximity to river and ocean, palatial mansions, graffiti free bus stops—who in hell would want to live here? It was almost as dull as Wylie.

With the traffic and the silky grey of the city far behind now, Skye entered the other world of country driving. The clouds, if they'd been here at all, were gone, the night sky clear and star-sprinkled, the road long, straight and mind-numbingly boring. With no decent radio reception she turned to her iPod and slapped her thigh to John Butler, agreeing with his political rants, laughing out loud at the crazy irreverence of Tim Minchin.

It looked like someone was tailgating again—it had been happening off and on since she'd left the city. Once more she caught the dazzle of headlights in the rear view mirror. If she continued the journey like this, she thought, she'd end up blind. She scrunched her eyes, wound down the window and flipped him the bird: *get lost, tosser.* He probably wouldn't even see the gesture, but it made her feel better.

She slowed and veered into a truck stop, expecting to see the impatient vehicle zoom past. To her dismay it slowed too, so close on her tail she could hear the gravel pinging on the undercarriage.

No way was she going to hang around here to find out what this creep wanted. Flooring the accelerator she shot a spray of gravel at his windscreen and fishtailed toward the exit, hammering her way back onto the open road.

Her relief was short-lived. Two silver-blue eyes dazzled in the rear vision window and the car closed in once more. The roar of its engine told her it was a helluva lot more powerful than her little Hyundai; she'd never be able to out-drive it here on the open road.

Her mouth went dry; she swallowed painfully. Was she being road-raged? She gripped the steering wheel until her knuckles glowed and wondered what the hell she'd done to deserve this.

Her gran would've said her sins were catching up with her at last.

She tried to work out where she was on the road and if she knew anyone in the vicinity. The farms here were wide and isolated. Every few kilometres there might be an entrance, but the driveways were often several kilometres long. Turning down one of these was no option; the car following her had shown in the truck stop that it could stick to the gravel a lot better than she could.

The police, she must phone the police, they would intercept this prick and give him the what for. She scrabbled for the phone on the passenger seat, panicked when she couldn't find it. The skidding and pitching on the gravel at the truck stop must have knocked it off. Then, after some frantic searching, she spotted it peeping out from under the empty food carton at the far corner of the floor.

She drove now at breakneck speed, struggling to keep the car on the road while she stretched for the phone. Finally her fingers closed around it and she straightened behind the wheel seeing no sign of the tormenting headlights. Lost him — *Yessssssss.*

Her jubilation evaporated into the stifling air of her car as the sinister, streamlined vehicle pulled out of her blind spot. This time she recognised it as the wanky car she'd cut off outside the deli.

What a jerk. He must really have a hair up his arse to follow her all this way. But knowledge didn't make the situation any easier to take. People had been killed in road-rage attacks.

She grabbed the phone, fingers jabbing at the keys. No service. *Shit*! But if she was lucky, the emergency numbers might still work. She risked a glance at the adjacent car as she punched 000 and saw the shadowy figure of a man behind the wheel.

Fuck, fuck, fuck — still no service. With a yell of abuse she hurled the phone onto the passenger seat.

Should she slow down, confront him, what should she do?

If she continued at this speed she'd surely end up wrapped around a tree.

The driver buzzed his window open. A pale hand flapped, indicating her to slow down.

No way, José.

She caught a green face shimmering in the light from the dash and felt the air leave her lungs with a whoosh.

She knew that face.

Oh God. It's you.

Fear grabbed her like a python's coil around the chest. When she breathed out, the coils tightened. It was a familiar, horrible feeling. With asthma, she knew, if you try to fight it, you only make it worse. She tried to stay calm, lifted her foot a fraction off the accelerator and slowed down a little. The other car slowed too. Now it was only a few centimetres from her door. It gave her car the smallest of nudges, not much more than a scrape, but it was enough to do the trick. She panicked and swerved to the left, just missed a tree and attempted to straighten. Then her oxygen-starved brain over-compensated and she veered into the centre of the road.

My dear
have you ever been in love

how odd
how strange that love
Should find

come to me in the
middle of a War

SUNDAY

CHAPTER NINE

'I'd kiss you only I've just washed my hair,' Monty slurred around the ET tube. Well, that's what it sounded like, Stevie thought as she reached for his hand among the morass of lines. She didn't ask him to repeat it; doped to the eyeballs he immediately fell back into a deep sleep.

Despite the several months she'd had to psych herself up for this, nothing had prepared her for the shock of seeing Monty post-op. His face was that of an old man, his skin the colour of a corpse. It was as if after draining his blood they'd forgotten to put it back again.

Thank God kids were not allowed in the ICU. Izzy would have had a fit if she'd seen her father looking like the living dead.

They could have been on a brightly lit tanker moored with several others on a quiet black sea. Night time in the ICU: raised, oversized beds with lifeless people buried somewhere amongst the bleeping machines and wires, the tread of crepe-soled doctors and nurses, the scratching of pulled curtains, the clanging of stainless steel and the low rumble of trolleys. How she hated hospitals.

Yesterday's operation had been an unmitigated success,

the surgeon had told her earlier. Monty would remain in the ICU for another day or so until the breathing tube was removed and then transferred to a single room in the coronary care unit. Barring complications he should be home in just over a week.

Barring complications. Stevie had made the mistake of looking up the complications on the Internet: thrombosis, infection, myocardial infarction; the list went on and ended with 'death'.

Some complication.

The glass-panelled nurses' station glowed like a captain's bridge. Behind the glass she saw a tall man with wiry hair like a mad professor talking to one of the nurses. A strange time for Wayne Pickering to visit, she thought. Didn't he know that only close family members were allowed in the ICU?

He saw her looking his way and indicated for her to step outside the ward. They met at the lifts.

Wayne clasped her arm. 'How is he?'

'He's doing fine. They won't let you see him though, the nurse in charge is tougher than Central's desk sergeant, she —'

'No,' he cut her off. 'It's you I need to see. C'mon, I'll buy you a coffee. You look terrible, the bags under your eyes could pack for a family of five.'

Wayne had always been a charmer.

A few minutes later they were sitting in the hospital canteen with cappuccinos and an oozing jam and cream doughnut for Wayne.

'You shouldn't be eating that,' Stevie said, 'think about your arteries.'

Wayne ignored her. 'Do you know someone called Emily Williams?'

'Emily Williams,' Stevie repeated, thought for a moment. 'No.'

'She's a nurse.' Wayne took a bite of doughnut.

'Oh. I know a nurse called Skye Williams.'

Wayne swallowed before he'd chewed his mouthful properly and appeared to be in pain. 'That would be her.' He patted himself on the chest. 'Her mother calls her Emily.'

A cold stone dropped in Stevie's stomach. 'Wayne, what's this about?'

'Your name was in her phone. MCI called Sex Crimes trying to contact you. Sex Crimes knew your phone would be off so they called me, knowing Mont was off sick.' Wayne reached for Stevie's hand across the plastic table. 'I'm afraid your friend was killed in a car crash on Friday night.'

Stevie shook her head as it filled with discordant thoughts. 'No, you said Emily, not Skye. I don't know an Emily.'

Wayne continued to squeeze her hand.

'She called herself Skye. According to her mother she thought *Emily Williams* far too pedestrian.'

Stevie did not immediately respond. She sat still, her gaze switching from Wayne's hand to a blob of cream on his psychedelic tie. Skye had changed her name, she would. It would be her way of distancing herself from her conservative farming family. When she was older she'd probably change it back again. But she wasn't going to get older now.

'They think she had an asthma attack while she was driving, lost control and hit a semi,' he murmured.

'She was only twenty-five,' Stevie whispered to the air between them. She couldn't cry. Like wheatbelt rain, the tears evaporated before they fell.

'I'll drive you home,' Wayne said.

Stevie pushed hair from her face. 'No, I have to stay with Mont.'

'He's out of it Stevie. He'll need you later, but not now.' Wayne would allow no further argument. He pulled her up by her arm and guided her towards the exit.

Twenty-five; the thought would not leave her head. You'd think she'd get used to it, in her line of work, but it was a different thing altogether when you knew the person, were friends with the person. And then her thoughts shifted to Monty: if The Old Man Upstairs could take Skye, He could take anyone.

in the middle of a War on a Ship to PNG
he was called Percy

he was young handsome and a naval
always say naval not navy
lieutenant

the war kept us apart
but I loved him

MONDAY

CHAPTER TEN

For much of the next morning, Stevie went through the motions as if her mind were disconnected from her body. She had breakfast with Izzy who was temporarily staying with her mother, Dot; she told everyone Monty was doing fine and dropped Izzy at school with a kiss and a smile as tight as stretched leather.

When she arrived at the ICU, she discovered a wizened old monkey of a man in Monty's bed. She clung to a hunk of curtain, staring at the unconscious man as the pressure inside her began to build. She found herself gripped by an unreasonable sense of rage. How dare they move him without telling her!

The nurse responded to Stevie's snapped enquiry with a flinch.

'Mr McGuire is doing extremely well,' she said nervously. 'We moved him to the ward first thing.'

Stevie attempted to pull herself together, tried to make it up to the nurse with a deep breath and an awkward smile of apology. She mustn't let Mont see her in this state and on no account would she tell him about Skye. If she tried to explain, she knew she'd lose it.

He was high as a kite on painkillers when she at last found him on the ward. He wouldn't have known anything was wrong, even if she'd thrown herself on his pillow and sobbed her heart out—which was what she felt like doing. But soon he'd be back to his perceptive self and she had a lot to sort out before then. She stayed with him in his room for the rest of the morning, helped him eat an unappetising bowl of green jelly for lunch, put up with some moaning and a lot of swearing, then hurried off to meet Luke Fowler at Mrs Hardegan's. On the way she remembered she'd volunteered to take a reading session at Izzy's school. She rang the teacher and cancelled.

Fowler was napping in his unmarked police car when she pulled up alongside him in front of the Californian bungalow. She tapped on his window.

'You're late,' he said buzzing the window down to look at her through cool blue eyes.

'I've been at the hospital. My partner's recovering from surgery.'

He grunted out a stock reply of sympathy, attempted some small talk. It seemed he did remember doing the course with 'Inspector McGuire' in Adelaide. 'Where's Skye?' he finally asked.

'She's dead.' In a tone as emotionless as a police report, she told him what happened.

He gave her the same stunned look she must have given Wayne.

'We'd better go and see Mrs Hardegan and tell her about Skye,' Stevie said briskly, giving him no time to absorb the news. She hurried on bubble-soled trainers toward the house, anxious to get the next unpleasant task over and done with.

She stopped when she realised he wasn't following.

Fowler hadn't left the car. He turned his face away when she opened the passenger door and leaned in. 'Are you coming?' She paused, regarded the turned back and hunched shoulders and let out a sigh of impatience. 'Is there something you're not telling me, Sergeant Fowler?'

He put on his mirrored sunglasses and released a heavy sigh of his own. 'Just a shock,' he said as he climbed from the car.

The old lady took the news better than either of them, though it was hard to tell quite what was going on behind the thin skin of the veined forehead. Every now and then though, Stevie caught a glimpse of something in her eyes, a look she'd only noticed in the eyes of the very young or the very old. She couldn't have explained what it was, but it spoke of some kind of privileged, hidden knowledge.

'Silver Chain will be organising someone else to come and see you soon,' Stevie told her.

Mrs Hardegan pulled her gaze back from the window. 'They murdered him,' she said in her forthright way.

'Bloody Japs, bloody Japs!' The parrot in the corner screeched. It ruffled its sparse covering of feathers, making the dust motes fly, releasing a sweet, seedy smell.

Fowler ceased his search of the kitchenette for tea making equipment and met Stevie's eye.

'Tell the feathered one to shut up,' Mrs Hardegan said, glowering at the cage.

'Who murdered who?' Gripped by an urgent state of panic, Stevie had to hold herself back from shaking the old lady into some kind of coherency. 'Skye? Someone killed Skye—who?'

Mrs Hardegan responded to Stevie's impatience with a

sharp snap. 'How the hell should we know? Don't want tea.' She turned to berate Fowler. 'Brandy, need brandy!'

'What makes you think Skye was murdered? It was a car accident.' Fowler moved to the tall cupboard to which Mrs Hardegan pointed a knotted finger. When he opened the door, Stevie glimpsed rows of unopened bottles of cheap brandy.

Mrs Hardegan caught Stevie's look. 'We're saving them for the Big Push.' She took the glass from Fowler, her hand a lot steadier than his. 'The boy knew about the snoodle pinkerds, we told him and they killed him. Now you know about them and they might kill you too.'

Snoodle pinkerds? Stevie shook her head in exasperation.

'Now, go. Leave us alone. We have a headache. And you ...' As if with an afterthought, Mrs Hardegan thrust her glass towards Fowler's chest. 'Take one of our bottles, go and get drunk.' She turned to Stevie. 'In love with him, stupid boy.'

PNG was hot and steamy
maybe you'd like it
too hot and steamy for me

the dead and dying trickled in
like rain through the hospital roof

I thought of Percy on his ship
somewhere.

it kept me going

CHAPTER ELEVEN

'She speaks like the fucking Queen: we this, we that ...'

'She can't help it, Fowler. She's not in control of the words that come out. It's the stroke she had. Expressive dysphasia. Skye explained it to me.'

Fowler flinched.

Stevie noted it, and wondered why. 'I'd like to see what you're like when you're that old,' she said, a bit more gently. 'What'll you have? My shout.'

'Perrier.'

She ordered the water for him and a Crown Lager for herself—he might not need the pick-me-up, but she certainly did.

The barman tilted her glass to the tap and she watched the amber liquid rise. 'I've just started three weeks leave,' she said though this hardly felt like a celebration.

'Time off so you can look after Inspector McGuire?'

God he was irritating. Why did he have to call Mont 'inspector' all the time? 'Yes, if he lets me,' she said, scooping the beer from the counter. The delicate green bottle of water looked incongruous in Fowler's thick hand.

They carried their drinks to the only free table in the lounge, rammed against a sidewall near the loos. The place was more crowded than usual, many of the clientele fixated on a soccer game on the wide-screen TV above the bar. Fowler poured his Perrier into a glass and Stevie checked her missed calls, an emergency call from the hospital foremost in her mind. There was nothing from the hospital, she discovered to her relief, but she did find a voice message from Skye.

Stevie stared at her phone. The message had been sent the day Skye died. The illuminated screen swam before her eyes. Her first tears for Skye could not have come at a worse time. Swivelling in her chair she turned her back on Fowler, took a steadying breath and dialled 101. After listening to the message she placed the phone on the table and slid it toward him.

'Are you okay?' he asked stiffly.

Stevie sniffed, swiped her eyes with a table napkin. 'Do I look it?'

Frowning, he picked up the phone and glanced at the screen. 'From Skye?'

'Have a listen,' Stevie said, lifting her glass and swallowing several mouthfuls of beer.

He listened, unmoving, then put the phone back on the table. The sparkling water in his glass ticked through the silence between them.

'She said she thought there was a connection between Ralph Hardegan and the Pavels,' he said at last.

Stevie kept her eyes on her glass of beer. 'And Mrs Hardegan thinks she was murdered.'

There was another long silence as they considered Skye's last words, both floating in their own private bubbles of misery. Everyone else in the tavern seemed to be laughing and flirting, roaring at the soccer game, getting on with having a bloody good time. Someone put a coin in the jukebox. The noise hammered at her ears and sank into her chest.

'I thought the old lady was talking crap,' Fowler shouted above the racket. 'But I'm not so sure now—she might be right.'

Stevie pushed back her chair and stood up. 'I can't think in here. Come outside.' He followed her into the street where she turned and asked abruptly. 'You still on the Pavel case?'

Fowler leaned into the brick wall of the tavern as if he needed it to stay upright. 'Only helping out now. When the pathologist IDed the body and confirmed that it belonged to Delia Pavel, I handed the case over to the Serious Crime Squad. The officer in charge is an acting DI called Angus Wong; he seems very efficient. I've been delegated some *tasks*.'

Stevie ignored the bitterness of his words; she had enough problems of her own without worrying about Fowler's shattered career and flimsy ego, although she did agree with his assessment of Angus's efficiency. 'He's Monty's right hand man, "acting up" while Monty's on sick leave.' She paused, rested her hands in the back pocket of her jeans and considered the possibilities. 'What tasks have you been given?'

'Mainly reinterviewing the neighbours and the people Jon Pavel worked with. I think it's worth mentioning the disappearance of Ralph Hardegan to Wong, even though the man might just be away on business. He was interviewed when Pavel first disappeared, but not by me. I don't think he was able to shed any light on it. I'll see if I can get clearance for an APB and a nationwide search. We need to talk to him again.'

Stevie nibbled at her bottom lip; maybe it was time to put

aside some pride. Through the closed tavern door she heard The Panics singing 'Don't Fight It' — maybe they had a point.

'Need a hand with these tasks?' she asked, keeping her gaze fixed on the dirty slabs of the pavement.

Out of the corner of her eye she saw Fowler pull away from the wall and straighten. He looked at her suspiciously, as if she must have another agenda, as if maybe she'd organised this whole thing for the sole purpose of spying on him — some people, *Jesus*.

'You're on leave,' he said.

'Mont's officer in charge of the SCS, I know the guys there well — used to work with them.'

'Going to pull some strings?'

Stevie gave a non-committal shrug.

He relaxed slightly and reached inside his jacket pocket. 'Well, you're not the only one with contacts. There's got to be some perks to the job,' he muttered as he punched numbers into his phone.

Stevie listened as he spoke to a mate in the Major Crash Investigation Squad, one finger in his ear to lessen the din from the tavern. When the phone was back in his pocket he pointed in the direction of their parked cars at the back of the building. 'C'mon, I've made an appointment to see someone about this.'

It occurred to Stevie that Fowler was as determined to get to the bottom of Skye's death as she was. Like her, he seemed to believe what Mrs Hardegan had said about Skye being murdered. As she followed him along the pavement to their cars, she recalled what else the old lady had said. *In love with him, stupid boy* — maybe Mrs Hardegan had been right about that too.

This is a merry-go-round I
cannot stop
Cannot get off

She's dead
that nice young nurse
because of something I told her in
with the wrong words

the same way I could not
tell you.

CHAPTER TWELVE

Senior Constable Tony Pruitt met them outside the locked yard. The blue police overalls with the single stripe on the shoulder did nothing to complement his physique. Short, fat and balding, he looked about ten years older than he probably was. Perhaps this is what working in the MCIS did to a person, Stevie reflected. God only knew it was a joyless branch of The Job.

Pruitt unlocked the gate and she and Fowler followed him into the yard, threading their way through the morgue of wrecked cars: countless, inanimate reminders of death. Over the years, she'd seen her share of grisly and unusual forms of death, and more murder investigations than she cared to count. But there was something about the very randomness of death through car accident that made her bones turn to jelly. You might be the safest driver in the world, but if fate puts you on the same stretch of road as someone over the limit, or whacked out, or asleep at the wheel, or simply not concentrating, there's not one single bloody thing you can do about it. And most people faced these risks on a daily basis without giving the matter a second thought.

If she were Pruitt, she probably wouldn't drive at all.

'The wrecks in here have all involved fatalities,' Pruitt explained in a tired voice, the oily gravel crunching under their feet as they walked. The spring sun had quite a kick today, a taste of the coming summer. Stevie peeled off her denim jacket and slung it across her shoulder.

'We conduct our investigations on behalf of state or district coroners,' Pruitt went on. 'And keep the wrecks until the investigations are finalised and the cause of death determined. Once we're finished with them, they're usually released for scrap.'

They reached Skye's crumpled Hyundai lying next to a burned out Lamborghini. The strip of cartoon graphics on the side panel of the small white car stood out jolly and bright from the twisted metal surrounding it. Stevie swallowed hard, reading the Silver Chain logo: 'Every minute, every hour, every day.' Not any more, she thought, not for Skye.

'I'm sorry,' Pruitt said awkwardly, looking from one to the other of them. 'She was a friend, yeah?'

Stevie nodded. Someone had tied a large white label to the crumpled bumper and it reminded her of a toe tag.

Fowler put on his mirrored sunglasses, not only to protect his eyes from the glare of metal, Stevie suspected. 'What happened, Tone?' he asked.

'She was driving fast, but the speed, according to the intermittent skid marks, was pretty erratic. It was a dark night, but the road was dry. According to the truck driver, one minute her lights were on the correct side of the road, the next they were heading straight for him.'

Stevie noticed then that the roof of the car was missing, sliced through like the top of a boiled egg.

Oh, Christ, no, not that. She felt herself begin to sway.

Pruitt put his hand out to steady her. 'It would have been very quick,' he said softly.

Fowler kept his face like a mask. 'Any other witnesses?'

'The truck driver did see another pair of headlights, but the other car didn't stop,' Pruitt said. 'We've put out a media bulletin with no luck so far.' The Senior Constable regarded them through brown, hound-dog eyes. 'Let's get out of the sun, have a cuppa. I've got some other things to show ...'

'Wait on,' Stevie said. She'd moved to the other side of the car while he was talking. 'What's this from?' Squatting on her haunches she pointed to a slash of green on the driver's door. The surrounding dent had been circled in black marker pen.

'Yes, we thought the dent looked recent, last couple of weeks, anyway—that's why we highlighted it,' Pruitt said.

'Can you take a paint sample?' Stevie asked.

'Not at this stage, no.'

'Why not?'

'Because everything points to this being an accident. Tests like that cost money.' He hesitated. 'Let's get out of here, continue this in the office.'

Stevie and Fowler exchanged glances and followed him to a demountable in the middle of the yard next to a large tin-roofed workshop with open sliding doors. 'That's where we do the inspections,' Pruitt explained. A pair of booted feet stuck out from underneath a jacked-up concertina of metal. The frenetic sound of a horse race from the radio followed them into the adjacent office until the closing door cut it off.

The air in the room was oily and close. It would have been more comfortable outside. Stevie flopped into a worn swivel chair.

With the flip of a wall switch an air conditioner rumbled

to life and Stevie took a gulp of musty cool air. Pruitt poured them tea from a thermos flask. 'Kettle's broke,' he apologised as he rested the thermos on a grey filing cabinet. An out-of-date calendar hung on the wall above it. Faded and flyspecked, Miss November 2001 had seen better days.

Pruitt must have seen Stevie glancing at the nude. 'The public don't get to come in here,' he said, colouring slightly.

The tea tasted of unwashed thermos, the milk suspect. Pruitt, sensing her squeamishness, slapped his thigh as if to say bad luck and all that, and gave her a look as suffocating as the office in which they sat. She knew the man meant well, but like any morgue technician, he wasn't used to handling grieving friends and relatives.

He hefted a cardboard box from the floor and placed it on the grey metal desk. 'These are the possessions retrieved from the boot of her car.' Professional once more, he was easier to take. Stevie watched him closely as one by one he withdrew an assortment of items from the box: a clipboard with patient files, a medical bag with an inventory of contents, all appearing to be there, he said. A small overnight bag held jeans, T-shirts, underwear and toiletries.

'And these,' he placed a large evidence bag upon the table, 'were in the front of the car.' He began to extract the bag's contents, placing them on the surface of his desk. 'We have a handbag found with the clasp still closed. In it were some cosmetics, a purse containing credit cards and ten dollars twenty-five cents in cash, a hairbrush, a near full packet of cigarettes and a Ventolin inhaler. The phone we got your number from, Sergeant Hooper, was on the passenger side floor, along with a takeaway food container, a towel and an empty can of Coke.'

'The Ventolin was in her handbag you say?' said Stevie..

'Um, yeah.'

'And where was the bag found?' Fowler asked.

'Also on the passenger side floor, though it could have easily fallen from the seat during the impact.'

'And the autopsy clearly stated that an asthma attack was the cause of death?' said Fowler.

'No, not exactly, just that her lungs indicated she was having an asthma attack when she died—that's what caused the accident. Her phone shows that she had attempted to call emergency services, but couldn't get through. Death itself was by ...' he stopped, slapped his thigh again and sighed. 'Well, do you want to read the report yourself?'

Stevie made eye contact with Fowler and they shook their heads simultaneously. She attempted to detach, to force herself to think like a detective. As she sat on the swivel chair in the poky office, she swung from side to side, running her ponytail through her fingers. 'I've seen her have asthma attacks before. As soon as she feels one coming on, she reaches for her inhaler.'

'But the inhaler was still in her bag,' Fowler said. 'And the bag was found closed. It's like she didn't even attempt to reach for it.'

'Why didn't she pull over to the side of the road and get it? Surely she would have done that before dialling 000?' Stevie directed the question to both men.

Fowler shrugged. Despite the cool air rattling around them, crescents of sweat stained the underarms of his white shirt.

Something caught Pruitt's eyes from the demountable's window. He got up from his desk and peered through the security screen. Stevie followed his gaze. A police four-wheel drive towing a mangled wreck pulled up outside the locked gate. 'Make yourselves at home, folks,' Pruitt said as he thumped across the hollow floor to the door, opening it to a stream of sunlight. 'Another delivery; I'll be back shortly.'

The detectives sat for a moment in silence after he'd gone. Stevie's mind travelled back to the mild asthma attack Skye had suffered in the Pavel house just before they'd discovered the baby. 'Why would Skye have a sudden, severe asthma attack when she was driving?' she asked.

Fowler shook his head. 'I guess people get asthma for a variety of reasons: allergy, exercise ...'

'But she was in the car; there can't be too many allergens in there. And driving could hardly be called strenuous exercise.'

'What are you getting at, Hooper?'

'Skye had her attacks when she was frightened or anxious. Something must have frightened her out of her wits when she was driving, making her too scared to pull over to get the inhaler from her bag. That's why she had the crash.' She looked Fowler in the eye. 'Pruitt's a mate of yours, right?'

Fowler opened his hands. 'Well ...'

'Reckon you can get him to delay that report to the coroner for a few days?' She eased off the swivel chair and felt in her jeans pocket for her penknife. The demountable's floor bounced under her feet as she headed for the door, not waiting for Fowler's answer.

'Hey, wait, Hooper, where are you going?' He moved to follow.

She indicated for him to stay put. 'When he comes back, just tell him I've gone to find the ladies room, okay?'

Where was I

oh yes   the war in New Guinea

a letter came
from Percy's mother

his ship was sunk
no one knew if he was dead or alive

CHAPTER THIRTEEN

Surprisingly enough Stevie's parking spot at Central hadn't been stolen in her absence. Things must be looking up, she told herself as she jogged the short distance to the Chemistry Centre, the envelope of paint scrapings burning a guilty hole in her pocket.

The Chemistry Centre was a long, low building of concrete blocks and curling pipes. Blood, tissue and urine samples, gunshot residues, suspect drugs and anything else requiring detailed chemical analysis were all delivered to the laboratories here. The facilities were available to the private sector as well as the police, but despite this knowledge, Stevie felt jittery and furtive. It would be typical to bump into anyone she knew, or caught in a tangle of red tape before she got where she wanted to be. She started to rehearse what she'd say to her boss if she were hauled before her again. This is an entirely different case ma'am, she'd say. I had no idea the death of Skye Williams and the Pavel cases were connected.

Bullshit they weren't.

By the time she arrived, she'd managed to smooth some of the jagged edges of her nerves. She took a calming breath and pushed her way through the door into the poky reception area. After explaining the reason for her visit she presented her driver's licence for scrutiny and filled out the request form in her small untidy hand. Nowhere did it ask the reason for the requested tests. Stevie bounced from one foot to the other as she waited to be processed. She should have expected this. You couldn't get into any kind of government institution in a hurry these days.

'I'll take the sample down now if you like,' the receptionist said at last.

'Um, I'd like to speak to the scientist myself, if that's okay.'

'Sorry, civilians aren't allowed near the labs.'

This time she produced her police ID, casually dropping the name of the chief forensic scientist as she did so. After consultation with her supervisor and a phone call, the receptionist granted Stevie entry.

With the *Get Smart* tune thumping in her head, Stevie followed a security guard down a warren of corridors and clanging fire doors, until she found herself in the paint analysis department. The young man at the reception desk told her Mr Douglas would join her soon, if she wouldn't mind just waiting for a moment.

Mark Douglas pushed his way through the double door within a couple of minutes. Stevie leapt to her feet. 'You *are* still here!'

'Where else would I be, Stephanie Hooper, working on a cray boat in the Abrolhos?' Despite the gruff tones, the warm kiss on the cheek told her he was glad to see her. Years ago they had dated casually, but with little in common to keep the spark going, the relationship had broken up without animosity. All he'd ever wanted to talk about was his job, she remembered. As she sat on the chair with him now in the reception area, she hoped nothing had changed.

They both refused the receptionist's offer of coffee; Stevie's nerves didn't need any more stimulation.

She saw Mark glance at the wall clock above the desk. 'You have a child now I hear?' he asked to be polite.

'Yes, Izzy's seven.' In a minute's time, if she were to ask him to repeat the name and age of her daughter, she knew he wouldn't remember.

'Cool.' He paused. 'How did you manage to wangle yourself down here? Police samples are usually left up top.'

'This isn't exactly a police job. I needed to see you personally about this.' She handed him the envelope. 'This needs to be analysed asap. I have no signature from the OIC of the case because the tests are unauthorised. I'll pay from my own pocket. I know private sector jobs are usually put way down the priority list, but I was hoping these tests could be done quickly.'

He examined her request form. 'For old times' sake?' he asked without looking up from the paperwork.

She felt herself colour. 'Well ...'

'I'd have been offended if you hadn't come to see me about this. I'll do my best. You understand what the tests involve?'

By the time he looked up again, her colour had returned to normal. 'I have a vague idea.' She braced herself for the lecture she knew was to come.

'The PDQ is a searchable database developed by the Canadians. It contains information on more than 13,000 makes of vehicles and 50,000 types of paint.'

Stevie stifled a yawn and made some appropriate noises of awe.

'A car paint job is usually comprised of four layers.

Four layer samples are collected worldwide, from car manufacturers, paint shops and junkyards, analysed by their chemical composition and coded into the database. These can then be used for comparison against paint samples taken from crime scenes or from suspect vehicles, providing an accurate picture of car manufacturer, make and model — I can show you how it's done, if you like.'

Feeling herself beginning to sag, Stevie made an effort to straighten in her chair. 'Sounds fascinating, Mark, but I mustn't take up any more of your time.' She stood to leave. Mark's look of disappointment provoked a twang of guilt. Jeez, recently she'd been on enough guilt trips to open a travel agency. 'So, the bottom line is can you tell me the exact make and model of the suspect car from this paint sample here?'

'Provided it's in the database. Vintage cars and custom jobs aren't. Individual layers can be identified, though they are of course not necessarily an indication of model and make ...'

Stevie cut him off. 'And when will I have the results?'

'Within the week.'

'Sooner?'

'I have to liaise with the PDQ in Canada.' He smiled; dimples pricked both cheeks and she remembered her attraction to him all those years ago. 'But I'll do my best.'

He escorted her to the exit, turned as they passed through the heavy door. 'I got married a couple of months ago. Jane's a blood-spatter specialist in E wing.'

'Congratulations,' Stevie said and pecked him on the cheek. She hoped he'd be happy. He was a nice guy; he deserved it.

after the War I found out that Percy
had been taken
prisoner by the japs

not dead at all
but he was gone
and I never really got him back.

CHAPTER FOURTEEN

Something was crushing her, she couldn't breathe. She fought for air, arms flailing, striking flesh and provoking a sharp cry of pain. 'Jesus Christ, Stevie, be careful, you nearly cracked me in two!'

Monty! Christ, what was she doing? She sat up, pushed the hair from her face, and looked around, trying to get orientated. She was in the chair next to Monty's bed, alongside a bunch of green curtains. She must have dozed off, head resting on the bed. With a hand against her chest, she willed her heart to stop pounding.

'I'd give you some of this,' Monty pointed to the morphine pump by his side. 'But with you thumping around on top of me like that, I think I'll need every last drop.' To prove his point he pressed the button and administered another relieving dose.

'I'm sorry,' she shook her head and tried to shake the memory of the bad dream. 'Are you okay?'

'Better than you I'd say.'

She looked at her watch; she'd been at the hospital about two hours. One of the last things she remembered was helping the nurse assist Monty to the bathroom, supporting his elbow with one hand, the other pushing his drip, while the nurse carried the drains. The ordeal had been too much for him—and her too. She'd eased him back into bed and must have fallen asleep too.

'Bad dream?' he asked.

She nodded, passing him a glass of water from the bedside locker. 'You've been told to drink more water,' she reminded him.

'Then bring me something to flavour it with.' He sipped from the bent straw, examining it longingly. 'Christ, I'd kill for a cigarette.'

'You've got to be joking.' Stevie took the glass from him and drained the rest of the water.

'You were talking in your sleep,' he said.

'Was I?'

She said nothing more, concentrated on the noises from the passageway. A rattle, a rumble and a clink of spoons on china told her the tea trolley wasn't far off. She was about to welcome the interruption when the sound continued past Monty's room, receding into the background.

'The trolley lady's passed you by. You must have really pissed her off,' she tried to joke.

Monty looked at her for a moment, unsmiling, then tilted his head to a rumpled newspaper on the visitor's chair. 'The accident was written up in Saturday's paper.' He collapsed back upon his pillows with a heavy sigh. 'What a waste,' he murmured, closing his eyes as if a wave had broken over him. 'And here am I, old enough to be her father with years to go before my use-by date—if my surgeon is to be believed.'

Depression was a common side effect of heart surgery, and one of the reasons she had been sheltering Monty from the news. She searched his face, looking for signs of grief beyond grief. Thankfully at that moment, the morphine kicked in and he fell into a light doze. She continued to study his face, pale and drawn. Her gaze fell to the dressing down the centre of his shaved chest. As she envisioned the zipper-like scar beneath, crusted with dried blood, she began to tremble uncontrollably.

And then, as if from a blow to the stomach, she couldn't seem to find her breath. With difficulty she tried to concentrate on drawing a steady stream of air into her lungs, but it seemed to slam against an invisible, impenetrable barrier.

Is this how it was for Skye during the last moments of her life?

Stevie panicked as she fought for air. Slipping off the bed, she bent at the waist, one hand on Monty's mattress, and struggled to breathe. A paper bag, she needed a paper bag. She found one on the tray table, grabbed it with shaking hands and tipped the grapes from it. Several rolled to the floor. After a couple of inhalations the relief was almost instantaneous.

'Are you all right, Mrs McGuire?' A nurse carrying a clipboard strode to the end of Monty's bed and inspected his chart. Stevie didn't care about the incorrect title, said she was fine despite feeling like a popped balloon.

'I sometimes think this is harder for the loved ones than it is for the patients,' the nurse said as she checked Monty's vital signs on the monitor, glancing down as a grape popped under her foot.

'Sorry, I'll clear those up,' Stevie said, dropping to her knees to pick up the grapes and bumping the side of the bed as she did so. Monty woke up with a startled grunt. The nurse smiled and placed the thermometer in his ear. Stevie would have liked a longer delay, wanted the nurse to stay longer, but the thing didn't take long to cook, beeping after only a couple of seconds. Monty's eyes met hers, his searching expression telling her he'd not forgotten their earlier conversation.

When the nurse left the room, he said, 'So, what you going to do about it?'

Stevie feigned ignorance. She sat on the side of the bed and gave him a puzzled shrug.

'Skye's death. Tell me what the hell's going on and stop treating me like a piece of cut crystal.'

As it happened, talking to Monty provided as much relief as breathing through the paper bag. She told him she thought Skye's death was connected to the death of Delia Pavel and the disappearance of Jon and Ralph. In trying to protect Monty from this, she reflected, she'd been damaging herself. The more she spoke the more objective she became. The spark of interest she saw in his eyes jumped into her own, re-kindling the old investigative feelings on which she thrived: the flutter of nerves through the stomach, the thrill of the chase.

She explained what she'd discovered from the MCI officer, Tony Pruitt, and the streak of green paint on Skye's car. 'With Pruitt otherwise occupied and Fowler in the office, I went back to Skye's smashed car and took a paint scraping and dropped it off at the lab on the way over here.'

'That'll cost money.'

'I'll pay from my own pocket. Even if it can't be used as evidence in court, it'll help guide me in the right direction. The guy in the lab reckons he should be able to get the make and maybe even the model of the car.'

Monty paused. 'That guy at the lab—that wouldn't be Mark Douglas would it?'

Stevie looked away. 'Maybe.'

'Jesus, Stevie, despite evidence to the contrary, you're not above using your feminine wiles, are you?'

'I'll do whatever it takes.'

'And then what?'

'I'll do my best to help out.'

'You mean you'll go round treading on people's toes, pissing them off and carrying out your own investigation. Angus won't go with it. You know how he plays by the book.'

'Me? Tread on people's toes?'

Stevie slid from the bed and kissed his cheek. 'I've got to go, have a date.'

Some of the sleepiness left Monty's eyes; he straightened in the bed as much as he was able. 'What, where, who?'

'Clubbing.' She turned from the door and shot him a Marilyn Monroe wink. He was muttering about feminine wiles when she left the room.

Fowler opened his door wearing a torn rag of a T-shirt and faded, baggy board shorts. For a moment Stevie thought she'd stumbled upon the wrong apartment.

'Hi there,' she said, masking her surprise at his more than casual attire. 'Can I come in?' His eyes widened. If the startled look was anything to go on, he was as surprised at her change in image as she was of his.

She loomed above him in her seldom worn, thigh-high boots. She'd had to lie on the floor to do up her straight-legged jeans. A hip-hugging broad white belt and a see-through flimsy shirt and diamante camisole completed the outfit. This wasn't her usual style of comfortable grunge, but it had been appreciated by the various men she'd come across on her journey across the city: the overly attentive cashier, the leering man in the queue at the counter, and the guy in the flash wheels who'd crawled the kerb to get a better look when she alighted from her car.

She heard the roar of laughter from a TV in the room behind, eased her way past him and turned the sound down. The apartment was clean with minimal furniture, mostly white and mostly Ikea. An ironing board with a white shirt draped across it stood next to a basket of more crumpled white shirts. The iron clicked, it was on and the air was tinged with the fresh odour of spray-on starch.

'What do you want?' Fowler said with more puzzlement than hostility.

'How about grabbing something groovy from your wardrobe and hitting the town with me?'

He looked from the pile of ironing to Stevie. 'Groovy? But I only have these white shirts.'

He was joking; he had to be. She looked at his mask-like face and tried to search for some humour in it. About to give up, she noticed the corners of his mouth rise with the flicker of a smile.

'Where are we going?' he asked as he headed to a closed door off the main room.

'You mentioned you were going to reinterview the staff at Pavel's restaurants and club,' Stevie said. 'I thought now would be a good time to do it, when the staff are preoccupied and not concentrating so much on their answers.'

He thought for a moment, agreed, then disappeared into his room for about five minutes. He re-emerged in suit pants and a cream shirt with no tie.

When he saw Stevie's barely concealed amusement he said, 'I didn't think they'd let me in wearing jeans.'

Shit, he hadn't been joking.

Changi
Have you heard of it?

even the word
to write the word
or even think it

Changi
still makes my blood
go cold.

CHAPTER FIFTEEN

Like many inner city venues on a weeknight, the two Pavel restaurants, one Thai and the other French, were less than half full. 'You can see why this town gets called Dullsville,' Fowler said. An interesting comment from Mr Dullsville himself, Stevie thought.

They spoke to the managers in each restaurant, receiving no new information, just repetitions of what the previous investigating officers had been told: that Jon Pavel rarely put in an appearance at these establishments, his interests were more focused on his Fremantle nightclub. Both managers stressed that highly respected certified accountants managed their books. Fowler told them not to worry, that the confiscated books would soon be speaking for themselves. At the mention of an audit, the male and female managers had respectively squirmed inside their business suits.

'Come on, let's go find some action. We might have more luck at the hip-hop club in Fremantle,' Fowler said as they crammed themselves back into his highly polished white WRX. 'Pavel runs his businesses from an office in the same complex and spends most of his time there.'

'Has the office been searched?' Stevie asked.

'Yeah, some papers and a computer were confiscated, but I'm not sure what they're about yet. There's a team briefing tomorrow at Central.' Fowler hesitated before taking off from the curb and turned to her. 'Why don't you come? With your contacts you should be able to wangle yourself in.'

Was he being sarcastic? If he was she decided to ignore him. 'Thanks, Sergeant, I will.' That'd teach him. 'Any more news about Ralph Hardegan?'

'Same thing. His home and businesses have been searched and his records are being combed, but there's still no sign of him. A couple of his staff at the veg shop in Mosman Park—where he has his main office—did mention how he'd seemed unusually anxious recently, though they couldn't say why. SOCO found blood traces in his apartment. Someone had attempted to clean it up with bleach, but missed a few spots.' He eased his car into a patchy line of traffic.

'What do we know about him?'

'Divorced, no current lady-friend, expensive unit in East Perth. Established the Fresh'n'Tasty chain about ten years ago. Met Jon Pavel when he was setting up one of his restaurants. The men hit it off and began investing in each other's businesses. Both businesses boomed with the new input on both sides. According to the neighbours, Ralph Hardegan found the house for the Pavels next door to his mother. The neighbour, Mrs Blakeman, reckons he must have seen Delia as a soft touch, getting her to keep an eye on his mum and easing his own conscience—he apparently hardly ever visited her.'

'A man with his own key visited the other night,' Stevie said, thoughtfully. 'Do we have a picture of Hardegan?'

'In the glove box.'

The photo showed a man in his fifties, good looking in a designer way, with a neat beard and wavy hair—not Stevie's type at all. 'How tall is he?'

'About six foot.'

Stevie replaced the picture and thought back to the shadowy figure she'd seen from the window when she was trapped in the room. 'About the right height, it could've been him.'

They crossed the bridge. Lights bobbed on the water below. Hulking silhouettes of docked cargo ships were lit up like apartment blocks. Unlike Perth on a weeknight, these city streets throbbed. There was always something to do around Fremantle provided you had the money for it, and those that didn't had plenty of ways of getting it. Like its neighbour, Perth, Freo was bright by day, but once night fell its shadows were long and dark.

Parking spots were scarce, but eventually they pulled down a one-way street, not much wider than an alley, and parked with two wheels on the curb. It was a short walk to the club.

Crowds wearing arty black spilled from a nearby cinema. A group of youths in torn jeans lounged on fold-up chairs outside the market's entrance, selling their wares: cheese-cloth skirts and kaftans, brass water pipes and tinkling wind chimes made from knives and forks.

A living statue of Captain Cook spookily illuminated by lamplight shot Stevie a cheeky wink as she walked past. Next to him a bearded busker sang duets with his howling dog. Stevie flipped a dollar into the busker's hat; the dog stopped howling and wagged its tail.

Situated in the middle of a busy street, the Vertex offered

more than hip-hop and expensive drinks. Enticing smells wafted from the Italian restaurant below where well-dressed groups of young people dined and drank before heading for the club upstairs. The dining area was filled with rattan chairs and tables with polished glass tops; one wall taken up with a bad imitation of the ceiling of the Sistine Chapel. Fowler went to find the club's manager while Stevie scrutinised the menu tacked to the rag-washed pillar at the restaurant's entrance, her stomach growling at the thought of peppered squid and Mediterranean salad.

'Can't get a decent feed anywhere these days,' Fowler said, looking over her shoulder at the menu. 'All grease and garlic.'

'Looks great to me — I missed out on dinner.'

'Won't do you any harm.'

Prick. Stevie spun to face him, saw he was holding up a key. 'Mr Marius told us to wait in his office,' he said, oblivious to her clamped jaw and narrowed eyes. 'Said he'd join us when he'd finished dealing with some customers.'

Fowler led the way up the stairs to a closed safety glass door where bright colours flashed, shadows bobbed and weaved. A couple of men in black muscle shirts stood outside. Fowler showed them his ID and Stevie beamed her best Colgate smile — she wasn't technically supposed to be here and didn't want anyone making a note of her name. Fowler showed them the key and asked where the office was.

'Down the corridor, on the right,' the smaller man pointed. They followed his instructions, the odours indicating they were also heading in the direction of the toilets.

Fowler opened up a door next to the gents and turned on the light. The office was decked out in a style befitting a successful young businessman: antique partner's desk, framed hunting prints, a silk oriental rug.

'Doesn't look very Romanian to me,' Stevie remarked, realising as she said it that she wasn't quite sure what a Romanian's office was supposed to look like. Gothic towers and screeching bats sprang to mind: strings of garlic, wooden stakes and men with very pale faces.

Stevie examined a picture of the mousy Delia on the desk. Fowler said, 'We've already taken his computer and account books, there's not much left in here to go through, but I think it's worth talking to the manager again. He said about five minutes.'

Dominic Marius arrived sooner than expected. Stevie replaced the picture of Delia Pavel and turned to face him. He was as short as he was broad, his laboured respiration from climbing the stairs causing the pinstripes of his waistcoat to wave to and fro. Tiny droplets of sweat burst along his hairline. He mopped his brow Pavarotti style, and indicated a studded leather couch to the detectives. He relaxed more as he settled into the matching seat behind the desk and his eyes lit with a small, satisfied gleam: he looked very much at home in his boss's chair.

Marius looked from one to the other of them and opened up his hands. 'I really don't think I can help you any further. I've told you everything I know about Jon Pavel.'

'Which didn't amount to enough, I'm afraid, Mr Marius,' Fowler said.

'I know very little about his personal life, if that's what you mean, never even met his wife.' He nodded to the picture Stevie had been studying. Delia stared back with deep-set mournful eyes.

'Do you know a businessman called Ralph Hardegan?' she asked.

'Of course, he runs the fresh fruit and vegetable markets, he's Mr Pavel's partner. He supplies our restaurant downstairs as well as several others we have an interest in. You must have heard of Fresh'n'Tasty?'

'Has there been any trouble between the two of them recently that you're aware of?'

'No, not as far as I know. I saw them dining downstairs together about a week before Jon disappeared. They seemed friendly enough.'

'And Delia Pavel has never joined them at the restaurant?' Stevie asked.

'Never when I've been around.'

'What about Ralph Hardegan—when did you last see him?' Fowler asked.

'At the same time, with Mr Pavel in the restaurant a couple of weeks ago.'

'Mr Hardegan seems to have disappeared too. Would you know anything about that, sir?'

Marius looked shocked. 'No, of course not—have you questioned his staff?'

'Yes, the story seems to be similar to that of Jon Pavel, only Hardegan disappeared several days later. One evening he was at his main shop in Mosman Park, where his office is, the next day he was gone and hasn't been seen since. His car was still in his apartment garage.'

Marius swallowed. A look of fear replaced the gleam in his eye. Fear of the police, Stevie wondered, or fear of someone else? 'You think it's something to do with their business?' he asked.

'More than likely, Mr Marius,' Stevie said. 'I'd like to know more about this partnership of theirs.'

'I've already been asked all this.'

'Not by us.'

Marius gave in with a weary sigh. 'Each man holds the majority of shares in the businesses they originally established, so their interests are closely connected. They go to Asia frequently to negotiate for fresh produce.'

'Any specific country?' Stevie asked.

'Thailand, mostly — we import a variety of tropical fruits, mandarins, asparagus, garlic, potatoes et cetera. Both men believe in quality control and choose only the best.'

'Ever been with them on one of these jaunts?'

'No.' Marius looked away from Stevie, keeping his expression rigid. Maybe he was pissed off because he'd never been invited. Maybe he knew there was more to these trips than fruit and veg.

'We can check your passport,' she added.

Marius, summoning up his indignation, leaned heavily on the desk on flattened palms. 'Be my guest. I'm *only* the manager, there's no need for me to go, I just see to the running of the shop floor. I have very few dealings with Ralph Hardegan. Until now I didn't even know he was missing.'

And now he is, Stevie thought, you might at last get your slice of the pie.

As if sensing that Stevie had seen through him, Marius made an effort to relax into the padding of his chair and tried for a look of respectful calm. 'Of course I'm devastated by Mrs Pavel's death and as mystified by Jon and Ralph's disappearances as you are. I—I just can't see Jon as the type to murder his wife.' He shook his head from side to side. 'And

I also can't see why you think I'm somehow involved.'

'We never implied you were,' Stevie said, responding to his aggrieved look with a deliberately unnerving smile.

'We just need to eliminate you from our enquiries, sir,' Fowler added.

'Is there a type who murders his wife, Mr Marius?' Stevie asked, not smiling now.

'You know what I mean,' Marius blustered. 'I only said that because the officers who spoke to me before implied it.'

'What about girlfriends? I imagine in this kind of business the temptations must be pretty strong,' Stevie said.

Marius manufactured a chuckle, directing his reply to Fowler. 'Any red-blooded male would be tempted.' He couldn't have made a worse choice for some man-to-man bonding; Fowler's return expression was less animated than the living statue's they'd seen earlier in the street.

Marius touched the knot of his tie. 'Yes, he had girl-friends, Mr Fowler,' he said as if it was the most natural thing in the world. 'Most of the girls behind the bar obliged him at one time or another.'

And they probably oblige you too, you greasy toad, Stevie thought. 'Is there one he saw more than most?' she asked.

Marius moved as if to get up from his chair, but she put out a hand to stop him. 'It's okay; I'll find her myself. Just tell me who to ask for.'

'Her name is Rodika, she should be behind the bar now. She doubles as Jon's secretary.'

Versatile woman.

'Rodika,' Fowler rolled the name on his tongue. 'Is that a Romanian name?'

'I believe it is, Mr Fowler.'

Stevie headed for the door.

'Please, have a drink on me, madam,' Marius called out.

Stevie needed something to eat before she could risk a drink. She pushed her way through the bodies on the dance floor, the sticky surface like velcro under her feet. At the circular central bar, finding no evidence of bar snacks, she plunged her hand into a bowl of nuts, which tasted like old cardboard — so much for quality control.

A bottle of water cost six dollars. She took one from the young barman and shouted above the din to chalk it up to Marius. She asked where she could find Rodika and he pointed to a woman wiping down a table next to the DJ's set up. If Stevie had known the song blasting forth, she would never have recognised this remixed, pounding version, which burrowed deep into her chest and stayed there.

And boy was it hot. She swallowed several mouthfuls of water and began to push her way through the writhing bodies. She glanced at the people around her. It looked liked she'd chosen the wrong outfit again; never seemed to be able to get her dress style right these days. Sometimes she wished she really could pull off strappy and frills. Most of the women dancing under the flashing mirror ball wore skimpy dresses. The guys flashed luminescent smiles back, assorted bling bouncing to the beat.

She tapped the barmaid on her bony shoulder. The woman swung around with an exaggerated startle response, looked ready to plunge her dirty dishcloth into Stevie's face. Stevie stepped back and smiled and put her palms up. 'Sorry, didn't mean to give you a fright,' she shouted above the music.

Rodika responded with a wide smile of relief. One of her

side teeth was missing, Stevie noticed; others flashed with gold. Her hair was platinum blonde and fluffy as an exotic chicken's, her false eyelashes long enough to bat over a wineglass.

'I'm with the police,' Stevie said. 'Can we go somewhere quieter to talk?' Rodika glanced toward the club's entrance. 'It's okay,' Stevie told her, 'Marius said I could talk to you.'

The woman indicated the fire exit with a tilt of her feathery head.

It was blissfully cool in the stairwell, though not as quiet as Stevie had hoped. Music still pounded in her ears and chest.

'Is this about Jon? Have you found him?' Rodika's English was hard to decipher, her accent guttural. Stevie thought back to the police phone log. Yes, Rodika might sound unintelligible down a bad line if the cop on the other end was harassed enough or lazy enough not to give her his complete attention.

'No, I'm afraid we haven't found Mr Pavel yet,' Stevie said.

The woman let out a sigh. Stevie examined her closely in the bright light of the stairwell. Despite her trim figure and scanty clothes her age was ambiguous. The delta of creases around her eyes, the deep marionette lines of her mouth, suggested anything from a worn out thirty-five to a well-preserved fifty.

'Were you told about the baby found abandoned in the house?' Stevie asked.

'Yes, poor little Joshua. I feel sorry for him. How is he?' There was concern in her voice, even though her look remained distracted and flickering. What was she frightened of, Stevie wondered: the police? Rodika had come from a country with a history of repression; fear of the police was ingrained. But Ralph Hardegan, Marius? The same virus of fear seemed to have infected them all.

'He's fine now,' Stevie said, still searching Rodika's heavily made-up face. 'Fully recovered and being looked after by a foster family. But he wasn't left alone in the house as long as we first thought. It turned out that someone had been coming into the house to feed him.' Stevie saw surprise in the woman's features, fear still, but no evidence of guilt. 'Would you know anything about this, Rodika? Did you feed the baby after his parents disappeared?'

Rodika shook her head and clutched at Stevie's arm. Bordering on hysteria she said, 'No, not me, I have nothing to do with this! I no kill Delia, I no feed the baby!'

Stevie tried to calm her down. 'It's okay, Rodika; no one's accusing you of anything. If I thought you were responsible, I'd be arresting you now and taking you down to the station, wouldn't I? Have you visited the Pavel's home at all over the last few months?'

'No, I never go there. Jon always keep me away from Delia, he says we separate.'

Made sense to keep the wife and mistress apart, still, Stevie didn't trust this woman any more than she did Marius. She'd make sure to get Fowler to take her prints and see if they matched any in the Pavel house.

Rodika took a calming breath and nodded her fluffy head.

'Were you intimate with Jon Pavel?'

'Intimate?' Rodika paused as if pondering the word. 'Oh, you mean sex? Yes I had sex with him, many times,' she said, looking down absently and pulling at her strappy top.

'Did his wife know?'

Rodika shrugged, as if the matter was irrelevant.

'Did you have sex with Ralph Hardegan too?'

'They partners, they share,' she said, still attempting to cover some cleavage.

'Did you like Ralph as much as Jon?'

'Lady, like don't matter—they both arseholes. But Ralph was more, how I say, stingy. He always want something for nothing.'

'But Jon paid you well?'

'And give me good job. I help in his office.'

'What about Mr Marius, do you sleep with him too?'

The woman put her hands on her hips, and looked at the concrete floor of the stairwell as if contemplating spitting on it—by the looks of the slippery surface, many already had. 'He try, but I no have him. Maybe if he was partner I have him.'

'He wanted to be a partner though, didn't he?'

Rodika made talking motions with both hands. 'Always go on and on, very jealous of Ralph I think—but you don't tell him I say that right?'

'Jealous enough to want to kill him?'

She shook her head vehemently. 'No, Marius is a big fat coward. He would trick you, yes, but he would not kill you.'

'Did you ever go to Thailand with Jon and Ralph?'

Rodika's mouth turned down. 'No, there plenty other young girls in Thailand. I have holiday when they away.' Then her demeanour changed, as if everything she'd said and the way she had said it, had just been a tease. She clapped her dishcloth between her hands and stretched her mouth into a wide smile. 'Now I need go back to work.'

Stevie placed her hand on the woman's arm. 'Just one more thing; I've only ever seen one picture of Jon, and it wasn't very clear. Did he have any distinguishing features—special marks? Is there anything else important about him that you forgot to tell the police before?'

Rodika gave the matter some thought. 'He wore big thick gold chain and matching bracelet, also big ring. I told them that.'

It figured. 'Would you recognise the jewellery if we found it?'

'Yeah, I think so.'

'Anything else you can tell us about him?'

She didn't answer straight off. Stevie waited. After some lip chewing Rodika said, 'I always think there was something funny on his hand. He had had funny marks here.' She pointed to the web of skin between her thumb and forefinger.'

'What kind of marks—tattoos?'

'Yes, tattoos I think, like little tiny dots in little tiny colours. You can hardly see them.'

This reminded Stevie of something she'd seen or read of recently, something she couldn't quite put her finger on. She became aware of her heart pulsing above the thump of the music and knew that whatever it was, it was important.

'Thank you Rodika, you've been very helpful.'

While Stevie had been interviewing Rodika, Fowler had been talking to the younger bar staff. Stevie met up with him on the street outside the restaurant while staff inside cleared tables and vacuumed. The restaurant had closed for the night but people still entered and exited the club through the side door.

Fowler hadn't got anything of interest from the barmen, but like Stevie he had his suspicions about the manager. 'We need to bring Marius into the station for a formal interview,' he said. 'Get both his and that Rodika woman's prints. He's hiding something, I'm sure of it.'

'He's also shit-scared, and so is the woman. That place is slippery with sleaze. I feel like I need a shower.' They left the noise of the club and coffee district behind them and headed down the almost deserted street. 'According to Rodika, Marius was jealous of Hardegan,' Stevie said. 'We saw it for ourselves in the office. Marius was very put out that Pavel chose to team up with Hardegan and not him. Rodika said he was hoping to make partner himself.'

'But it makes sense for Pavel and Hardegan to pool their resources. What does Marius think he could bring to the equation? Could he be behind all this, wants to get his hands on the business?'

'Pavel and Hardegan have made quite a gravy train for themselves. Money, girls ...' Stevie stopped mid-sentence and came to a halt under a streetlight.

'What is it?' Fowler asked.

'According to Rodika, Pavel had a discreet tattoo, here.' Under the light she pointed to the web of her hand. 'It was made up of a series of coloured dots.'

'Doesn't ring any bells.'

'Fresh produce ... Thailand, girls ...' Stevie thought aloud. 'Monty's been doing research on human trafficking for the CCC—I recently read something he'd written about the east European crime gangs.' She rubbed her eyes as she tried to think clearly, the lateness of the hour beginning to take its toll. 'They have tattoos like the Asian gang members, only much more subtle. You'd have to be a gang member to recognise them—often just a dot on the skin.'

'As soon as I hear mention of these kinds of gangs, I think of that shipment of illegals found dead in the container at the Dover docks. Horrible.' Fowler paused. 'You think Hardegan and Pavel were in the skin trade?'

'Rodika's certainly not one of the vestal virgins, and I'm sure Marius takes his share of anything he can get.' Stevie pulled at her ponytail. 'But I reckon this might be more than straightforward prostitution—they're old hands. Ralph and Marius wouldn't be this scared if that was all they were up to.'

They continued their journey in near darkness to Fowler's car, possible scenarios jostling for space in Stevie's tired mind. The busker had gone home long ago. A salty breeze played with a discarded newspaper in the middle of the road until a hotted-up Holden growled past and squashed it flat.

'Remember when I got locked in the Pavel's upstairs room?' Stevie said.

'I won't forget that in a hurry. Of all the stupid, interfering—'

'Shut up and listen to me, Fowler! The room was decked out like a dormitory—no, make that a prison cell, completely self-contained with no inside doorhandle and locked safety-glass windows. And I'm pretty sure it wasn't like that because they were redecorating.'

They continued to head down the pavement, both thinking this through. Finally Fowler said, 'People held as prisoners? You're right, it does sound a lot more than prostitution.'

'While it's unlikely that Pavel would've been using his own place as a brothel, it could easily have been used as a halfway house for girls imported illegally into the sex industry.'

'I didn't think there was much of that kind of thing going on over here.'

'That's Monty's argument. People seem to think it's an Eastern States phenomenon, that it isn't relevant to us in the west. Over here the problem tends to be more of smuggling people for illegal labour or immigration than for human trafficking. That's why the trafficking that does happen doesn't get the attention it should—because no one expects it.'

'I don't know much about this kind of thing, never had any experience with it,' Fowler said.

A rare admittance of ignorance, Stevie guessed.

'So what's the difference between people smuggling and human trafficking?' Fowler said.

There were no lights down this end of the street. They didn't realise they'd reached Fowler's WRX until they almost stumbled into it. Fowler unlocked the door with a beep of his key and leaned on the frame from the footpath, without getting in, waiting for Stevie's answer. Light seeped from his car, illuminating one side of his face while the other side was cloaked in the shadow of the narrow alley.

'Trafficking and smuggling share some characteristics,' Stevie explained, standing with him beside the open car door, 'but it's the voluntariness than sets them apart. In both scenarios people are illegally taken across borders and exploited. But those who are trafficked, as opposed to smuggled, are taken against their will and used as sex slaves: women, girls, young males—'

The squeal of tyres cut Stevie off. They whirled to face the noise. A car barrelled out of the darkness towards them, headlights on full beam.

It wasn't going to stop.

The street was narrow; the open car door took up most of its width.

'Get in!' Stevie yelled at Fowler who'd frozen to the spot. She gave him a shove, heard the side of his head crunch against the doorframe.

She scrambled onto the roof of Fowler's car using the door sill as a springboard. The hurtling car slammed into the WRX, knocking it further up the curb. With a shriek of tearing metal, the door was severed like a limb.

The impact rocked the car and it teetered on two wheels. Shock waves coursed through Stevie's body as she clung to the roof, throwing her weight toward the raised side to balance it.

It was over in a few seconds. The WRX wobbled and righted itself, vibrations ceased.

The other car continued to charge down the street. Lodged on its undercarriage, Fowler's ripped door scraped along the road leaving an electric pattern of sparks in its wake. The car's rego was indecipherable and so was the make; all Stevie caught was its long, low shape swerving towards the end of the road. It rumbled to the end of the street and took a sharp right. The door dislodged on the curb and bounced onto the pavement. The sound of the powerful engine roared toward the docks until darkness swallowed it.

My dear
at the hospital there was
typhoid dengue rain heat
More men died there
than in battle

I threw myself into my work
not Careng
I did'nt Care if
I lived or died

TUESDAY

CHAPTER SIXTEEN

The man gave one last grunt of satisfaction and hefted himself off her, his flaccid penis leaving a wet trail along her thigh. Was he number six or number seven tonight? Mai counted on her fingers. First there was the man in the wheelchair who Rick had helped onto the bed, then the sour-smelling truck driver friend of Rick's. The drunken boys from the eighteenth birthday party had all looked and behaved the same: embarrassed, fumbling, reeking and, in a couple of cases, non-functioning. Mai realised then that she'd lost count. This was unusual for her, seeing as she was paid per customer—not that she ever saw much of the money she made.

Soon she and the other girls would be leaving the city. Her mind was numb with the thought of the journey ahead. Perth had been her prison for nearly a year, but at least it meant that she had been close to Niran. This time next week she would be in a place so far away, they might just as well be in another country.

They had renamed her son Joshua. She could hardly get her tongue around the western name. When she tried, the white men, the *farang*, laughed and mocked. They did their best to confuse her. They didn't want her to learn any English words other than what she'd been taught to say to the clients; words and phrases such as *sexy big boy, handsome man, I fuck you silly, you like it doggie?* But she found she could understand a lot more of their language than she could speak. You could learn a lot in a year.

The man hauled himself from the bed and patted her on the head. In Thailand the head was an object of holiness. Once she would have cringed under his touch. She used to think a man touching her there was worse than anything he could do to the rest of her body.

Now she knew different.

Now she didn't care.

He drew the curtain closed behind him. She heard his heavy tread on the stairs. The sound of laughing and shouting men reached her from the bar. She stripped the bed and wrapped herself in the soiled sheet and opened the curtain.

The pungent scent of ganja wafted into the cubicle and mingled with the bleachy smell of sex. She picked up the used condom from the floor — at least this guy had agreed to wear it — and flushed it down the toilet in the bathroom opposite. The curtains in the other cubicles on the upstairs landing remained closed. From behind them she heard the fake laughter of the girls and their mechanical moans of pleasure.

Clients milled around the bar below — they often needed alcohol before partaking in the pleasures upstairs. Beer, wine, spirits or worse: their breath made Mai feel sick, though she never showed it; she never showed any of the revulsion she felt. She was good at her job and she knew it. At the top of the stairs she stood for a moment and listened to what was going on below.

With little effort, she could pick out Rick's voice: he sounded excited and Mai had trouble deciphering his rapid speech. He was probably talking about the journey—she heard him mention that place called Broome again. She tried silently to curve her mouth around the sound. He said something about the money he would make and how he would spend it—on pills probably. Sometimes drugs were used on the girls to make them more compliant, but they were always forbidden to the guardians. Rick shouldn't be speaking like this.

Another man spoke; she recognised Jimmy Jack's higher tones. He seemed to be giving Rick some kind of warning, probably reminding him of what happens to those who abuse the Mamasan's trust, what The Crow had done to Jon Pavel. Rick fell silent; there was no more talk of pills and parties. Even he had been shaken up by the events he'd witnessed.

Over a week ago, just before dawn, the other girls having only just got off to sleep, Mai had crept down to the kitchen to look for something to pop the blisters on her sore feet.

Rummaging through the kitchen cupboards she heard strange noises coming from the basement and decided to investigate. As she limped toward the closed door the sounds became clearer: dreadful screams of unspeakable agony. The Crow was at work again. She fled back up the stairs and vomited into the toilet. When she recovered sufficiently to move, she peeped from the landing and saw Rick and Jimmy Jack hauling Pavel's charred body through the door that led to the garage.

But she would not dwell on it now. To do so would make her crazy, and there were enough crazy people in this house.

Her brain had to stay clear and uncluttered; she had things to do and plans to make.

Still wrapped in her sheet, she made her way across the upstairs landing to the room she shared with five other girls. Four beds were empty, which meant the girls were still working. All except the youngest, fifteen-year-old Lin, who lay on her bed curled into a ball, hiccoughing between sobs.

Mai sat on the edge of the bed and rubbed the girl's back.

'I can't take any more of this, Mai.' The girl spoke with the accent of a northern peasant—her complexion was still quite dark. Mai was of peasant stock too, but she had lived in Bangkok long enough to smooth some of the rough edges from her voice and allow the city's shadows to lighten her skin.

'Work hard and you will soon pay off your debt,' Mai said. Both Lin's parents had died last year. Seduced by tales about the golden roads of the city, Lin had left her village and found work in a Bangkok foot-massage parlour. A few months later Jon Pavel had introduced himself to her. He told her he was going to set up a similar kind of place in Perth, Australia, and asked if she would like to manage it for him. He said it was a chance to make more money than she'd ever seen in her life—all she had to do was pay back the money he would spend to get her there.

On her first night Lin was hired to an Australian businessman who took her to a swanky hotel where he paid five thousand dollars for her virginity. When she tried to run away she was fined more than she'd been allowed to keep from that night. And then she was fined again for arguing with another girl. The cycle continued, the debt mounted. In some places girls had to pay for the drugs used to control them and that too was added to their debt. That was the thing Mai worked hardest to protect her girls from—once the drugs got hold of you there was no going back.

'But you haven't paid off your debt yet,' Lin said, 'and you've been doing this a lot longer than me.'

Mai sighed. 'I will never pay off my debt. Besides, it is different for me; I was doing this long before I was brought to Australia—I knew what was in store for me. My mistake was in believing they would let me keep my baby.' Sometimes it's need that makes you do certain things. Mai wasn't ashamed of anything she'd done. What made her ashamed was that she had been taken as a fool. When she was a child she believed her good fortune was the result of a previous life of virtue. Now she realised it was the opposite. She must have been very bad in her former life to end up here, trapped in an Australian brothel.

Lin broke into her thoughts, '"Do good receive good, do evil receive evil."' It was a Buddhist saying they'd all learned by rote at school.

'You think there is nothing you can do to change things here,' Mai said, 'and that is why you can sit back meekly and accept what has happened to you? I am not so sure I feel that way any more. I don't see why we can't seek to improve our lives now.'

Lin shook her head. 'Things will change, everything is temporary— we just have to wait.'

'When you've been doing this as long as I have, you might not want to sit around and wait for things to change. You can help things change for yourself, you know.'

Lin's voice rose, 'I don't know what you mean or what you are planning, Mai, and I don't want to hear it.' She put her hands over her ears like the *hear-no-evil* monkey. 'They said they will kill your baby if you try to escape. You can't risk that.'

Mai paused. 'Who says I will try to escape?'

Lin looked back at Mai, first with incomprehension, then panic. She shook her head vigorously. 'I'm not listening, I'm not listening!'

Mai slipped off the bed, straightened Lin's sheets and plumped her pillows. 'You don't need to. Forget about it. Maybe things will be better in Broome. You never know, you might meet a nice man who will take you away from this.' She'd been doing her best to convince the girls that better things lay ahead and it seemed to be working. Who knows, some of them really might be able to pay off their debts and return home — it did happen sometimes.

Lin's eyes followed Mai around the room as she turned down the other girls' beds. Finally she began to calm. 'Little mother,' she whispered. And then, 'Mai, what does it feel like to have a baby?'

It feels as if you are being split in two, Mai thought. Then, when the baby is taken from you, you are split in two all over again. 'There will be plenty of time to talk on the bus, but not now. Now we must sleep. We are going a long way tomorrow with several days of driving.'

'I'm in trouble with Rick,' Lin said, finally getting to the cause of her tears. 'My last client complained to him, I think. I couldn't act for him, my body turned to ice when he touched me. He had red scaly skin and long dirty hair with bugs in it — I saw them sprinkled like pepper on the white pillow.'

As if on cue, Rick called to Lin from the bottom of the stairs. Lin clutched at Mai's hand. They heard the sharp slap of his thongs upon the wooden boards of the landing. He walked like an elephant, the floor shaking under his tread. He flung open the door. 'Get out,' he snarled at Mai.

Grabbing her toilet bag from her nightstand, Mai fled to the bathroom without looking back. She turned the shower on as high as it would go to block the sound of Lin's cries. As she stared at the water trailing down the shower screen, she noticed how each tear-shaped drop obediently followed the course of the preceding drop. It doesn't have to be like that, she thought.

'Jai yen yen,' she whispered words of comfort to Lin, as she stood there, rigid under the pricking spray. Cool your heart.

Like me.

i never told anyone
what those days were like

day after day
soldiers and civilians suffering

I worked very hard
to feel nothing at all.

CHAPTER SEVENTEEN

After they'd called the incident in to the local police and filled out the report, they caught a cab to Stevie's house. She gritted her teeth as she stood in the kitchen and dabbed antiseptic at the angry graze on the side of Fowler's head. 'Try and hold still, will you?'

He flinched. 'You didn't have to push me quite so hard.'

'I didn't push hard enough. Your fat arse did such a good job at blocking the door I couldn't get in.'

That shut him up. It annoyed her that he still hadn't thanked her for saving his life. He'd spent most of the journey back from Fremantle whingeing about his wrecked car. He started on it again. 'That's two bloody cars in the panel beaters now,' he grumbled.

'But you've still got your father's car haven't you?'

'No. Had a bingle in it the other night, nothing major. I just hope to hell it's fixed before he finds out. With any luck he won't notice. I don't want the damn thing anyway, it's too old, too expensive to maintain. I can't see the point of buying someone else's problems.' He paused. Stevie followed his gaze around her dilapidated kitchen and, tacked onto it, the skillion-roofed lean-to they used as a temporary family room.

The real estate agent had called it a 'sunken lounge.' Izzy's toys lay strewn across the floor, and a sagging bright orange couch Monty had picked up from someone's front verge fronted the brown veneer TV. Their new old house might seem like Buckingham Palace to them, Stevie conceded, but through a stranger's eyes it probably did have a few shortcomings. Fowler waved his hands around to further his point. 'I mean, look at this place—what were you thinking?'

She replied without words, making the last dab harder than necessary, causing him to hiss out a breath. Collecting the soiled cotton wool balls, she tossed them in the bin and began to pack up her first aid box.

His mobile phone rang. He listened to an update from the Fremantle police, spoke a few succinct words and hung up. 'My car's been towed away and the door collected,' he told her. 'They tell me it's scarred with streaks of green paint.'

Stevie hadn't told him about the scraping from Skye's car she'd sent to the lab. She reminded herself to give Mark a ring tomorrow to see if the results had come through. She looked at her watch: today, she amended. 'Green paint, like on Skye's,' she said. 'They'd better damn well take a paint sample this time. What kind of car does Marius have?'

'A dark blue Audi, undamaged and not driven recently. The Fremantle cops say he hasn't left the club since we saw him.'

'That doesn't discount one of his thugs in another car.'

'All the cars in the staff parking area have been checked and an alert put out for a green car with a freshly crumpled bumper. I'll organise someone to pick up Marius and the woman for questioning tomorrow, let them stew at home over night.'

'But if it's not Marius, who else could it be? That attempt on us must mean we're getting close to something. Could Pavel and Hardegan be behind all this?'

'We don't even know if they're still alive.' Fowler pressed his fingers into his temples. 'Wait a minute. What colour was Pavel's missing Jag?'

Stevie paused, looked back at him as she tried to visualise the shape of the car in the alley. 'Green. Shit. It could easily have been a Jag that rammed us—maybe Pavel's still alive after all?'

'I guess we won't know for sure if it's a match to his car until the paint results come back.'

Sooner than you think, Stevie thought to herself.

Fowler got up from the table, swayed slightly and put a hand on it to steady himself. 'Well, hopefully more will be revealed at the briefing.' He looked at his watch. 'It'll be light in an hour, guess I'd better go.'

'Is that wise?'

'I've had worse cracks on the head than this.'

Oh, Lord, spare me the macho crap. 'I didn't mean that—I know you've got a head tougher than a macadamia nut. I meant someone tried to kill us tonight and it might be safer for you to stay here.'

'What—you going to protect me?' he said with a slight curl of his lip.

Stevie rolled her eyes at him. 'Yeah, you seem to need it. Don't be a dickhead; stay here. I have a spare room made up. It's on the right of the passage near the front door; help yourself. I'll drop you home when you've had a couple of hours rest and then you can put on a clean white shirt and we can go to the meeting at Central together.'

Fowler agreed without further persuasion. 'I'll need to touch base with Angus before the meeting though, tell him about all this.' He yawned, his gaze wandering again over the primitive kitchen. 'I suppose this might scrub up okay, if you can bear to put the work into it—very different to mine.'

Stevie shrugged. 'Horses for courses.'

'Guess so.' He moved over to Monty's tropical fish tank, temporarily placed against a wall that would one day be demolished for a walk-in pantry. He stared for a moment at the frantic movements and flashing colours of the darting fish, going nowhere, never stopping for rest. 'I never understood what people mean when they say looking at fish is relaxing,' he said. 'These hyperactive little guys are doing nothing for me but increasing my headache.'

'Monty's prized possessions. He breeds them.'

'Remind him of you, do they?'

Jeez, Stevie thought, the man not only had the hide of a rhino but the tact of a farting bull elephant to boot. She set about putting the first aid box away in one of the high kitchen cupboards. When she turned around again, she expected Fowler to have made a move, but found him still staring at the fish.

'Are you sure you're okay?'

He nodded. 'I just saw a fish eat one of its babies.'

'Generally the fish with the biggest mouth wins.'

Fowler muttered something she didn't catch.

'I'm going to make an omelette—do you want some?' she asked.

'May as well, I'm tired, but too tired for sleep.'

Stevie knew how he felt.

Stevie had planned on picking Izzy up from her mother's and taking her to see Monty for the first time since the operation. But after the night's drama, it was paramount she attend the briefing at Central if she was to get any inkling about what they were up against. Izzy was not impressed when she rang to cancel. She would probably store the disappointment and hurt away, Stevie thought, use it for ammunition when she was a teenager. Stevie let out a heavy sigh and replaced the phone.

Fowler had also been on the phone, talking to Angus. 'He wants me to fill the team in at the briefing,' he said with a noticeable edge to his voice.

They arrived at the Serious Crime Squad's incident room with plenty of time to spare. Angus had not yet emerged from Monty's office. Officers milled around the room sipping coffee from corrugated cardboard cups and pulling up chairs.

Wanting to remain unobtrusive, Stevie perched on her old desk at the back of the room. Wayne Pickering wandered by without seeing her, but spotted Fowler immediately. 'Hey, what happened to your head?' the older detective said.

'I was picking flowers,' Fowler replied.

'Picking flowers can be a dangerous occupation; just ask Little Red Riding Hood,' Wayne said, heading to the front row of seats.

Stevie jumped down from the desk and grabbed Fowler's arm before he could sit down. 'Christ, you sure know how to win friends and influence people, don't you? You might have to work closely with that man, but there you are, antagonising him before you've even started.'

'My mother always told me to be wary of men in purple and pink plaid sports jackets,' Fowler said dryly.

'Wayne's a personal friend of mine. Just because he's an eccentric dresser ...'

'With breath like a komodo dragon.'

Someone told them to shut it. Stevie retreated to her perch at the back of the incident room and folded her arms just as Angus stepped out from the office.

Monty's office.

Stevie thought of Marius waiting in the wings, ready to fill the vacuum Pavel had left behind, but stopped herself before it went any further. Angus wasn't like that.

As Angus summarised the case, Stevie recalled her days with the SCS: this briefing was a lot more organised than when Monty ran the show. It was almost as if Angus had stood in front of the mirror and rehearsed for it; he looked as dapper as a presidential candidate in his dark suit and striped tie. There were no tension-relieving jokes or ironic putdowns, and even Wayne and Barry were being less competitive with each other than usual. Officers raised their hands before they asked questions and Angus managed to keep his cool, no matter how idiotic some of the questions were.

A small specialist group, the SCS seconded officers from other divisions when the need arose. As Stevie watched the proceedings she found herself putting names to many of the backs, uniformed and non-uniformed, before her. Angus, Wayne Pickering and Barry Snow sat in the front row near the whiteboards and overhead projector and ran the show.

Angus moved to the board near the wall and the officers reached into the files of information they'd been provided. Stevie hadn't been issued with one because she wasn't supposed to be here; she'd have to have a gander at Fowler's later. On the wall next to the whiteboard hung a corkboard with pinned pictures of Jon and Delia Pavel, baby Joshua and Ralph Hardegan. As yet Skye's name or photo hadn't been posted. By the end of the meeting, she hoped they would.

Angus summarised the events leading to the discovery of Delia Pavel's body in the river, then ran through the time line. It had been twelve days since the Pavels were last seen, eight since the baby had been found and five since the discovery of Delia's body. He also presented Melissa Hurst's pathology report, which delivered no surprises—cause of death: gunshot wound to the head.

A SOCO sergeant stood and addressed the team. 'As well as fingerprints from both parents in the baby's room, we found several sets of unidentifiable prints which don't match any others in the house except on one of the back windows. The window was unlocked. We think this might be where the woman—we're assuming either a woman or child as the prints were relatively small—accessed the house to feed the baby.'

Stevie hoped Rodika's prints had been taken by now. No mention was made of a match.

'Upon searching the perimeter of the house,' the SOCO officer went on, 'we found two shotgun casings in a ventilation gap in the wall parallel to the ground, just below the kitchen window.'

Stevie shifted in her chair and wondered how close she'd been to the casings when she'd been scrabbling amongst the weeds. It was unlikely the perpetrator had placed them in the gap deliberately—she might even have inadvertently knocked them into the ventilation gap herself. Shit! Her stomach dipped. Better stay silent on that one.

But if her error was grave, Fowler's was even worse; he

hadn't bothered to have the area near the window searched at all. Stevie saw his white shirted shoulders stiffen; he knew this was another black mark for his file and she felt almost sorry for him.

Angus took the floor again and explained how a gun using the same or very similar ammunition to that found in the gap had been used to inflict the wound to Delia's head.

A young female officer put up her hand. 'A shotgun's a bloody noisy weapon. Didn't anyone hear the blast?'

'During the second round of questioning,' Wayne's tone emphasised the fact that this was missed the first time around, 'some of the neighbours reported hearing a car backfiring that night.' He paused and looked directly at Fowler. 'But I guess a shotgun blast is the last thing anyone expects to hear in Peppy Grove.'

'A backfiring car's not likely to be heard in that area either,' Barry said. Someone sniggered. Angus silenced the offender with a look. He asked Fowler to tell them about his recent findings. Stevie saw Barry's elbow dig into Wayne's side. Other members of the team shifted in their chairs, squirming for the man from Peppermint Grove.

Fowler's back moved as if he was taking a breath to bolster his courage. He rose from his chair. Stevie felt a tightening in her stomach. Fowler looked at the crowd, his gaze travelling over every face in the room except Stevie's.

'The old lady next door who raised the alarm has speech difficulties and seems to know a lot more than she can tell,' he explained in a level voice. 'I arranged to interview her with a Silver Chain nurse present who I hoped might be able to help interpret. Sadly, the young nurse was killed in a traffic accident before she could attend the meeting.'

At this, Wayne turned his head to the back of the room and raised his eyebrows at Stevie, drawing a ripple of attention from the others, including Angus. Stevie felt herself colour. *Just bugger off why don't you, Wayne?*

Fowler cut to the chase as if hoping to redirect everyone's attention. 'But recent events have led me to believe that the nurse's death might not have been accidental.' He moved over to the board and added Skye's name. He explained how he and his nameless colleague—at which Wayne turned around again—visited the Vertex nightclub to reinterview staff, and then he filled the team in on the attempt on their lives in the alley.

Angus told the group that the staff at the club were being requestioned, with the manager, Marius, and barmaid, Rodika, waiting downstairs to be formally interviewed. The barmaid's prints were being compared with those in the baby's room. Both Marius and Rodika's prints were also being run through the National Database to see if they could be linked to any other crimes.

A detective Stevie didn't know asked if the audit results had come through from the club, restaurants and fresh-produce shops.

'I spoke to the money boys first thing,' Angus said. 'They hadn't finished the audit, but the books are hot, with several anomalies detected so far. It seems the lifestyles of Pavel and Hardegan don't match the bottom line of their legitimate incomes.'

Angus turned back to the team. 'I want the door knocking to be continued, and anyone with anything interesting to say the first time around is to be reinterviewed. We want to jog memories. We have vague reports of a woman sighted around the house at the time the parents were missing—I want this pursued further. The baby is thirteen months old. Tests reveal that he was given canned baby food as well as milk formula. The woman in question must have been carrying a bag, bulky with feeding equipment, food and clean nappies. The image of a bulky bag might just be the memory jogger we need.'

Angus indicated for Wayne to take over and Stevie assumed they'd discussed the information Angus had received from Fowler earlier. Wayne mentioned their suspicions about Pavel and Hardegan being involved in a people-trafficking operation. He said he was waiting for Interpol to get back to him on anything they might be able to scratch up about Jon Pavel. The AFP had also been notified. This meant that if they didn't play it right they could lose the case altogether. The news was not well received; no one wanted the Feds on their patch.

Angus stood for a moment like an actor playing for the right dramatic timing. When Wayne had returned to his seat, Angus reached into his jacket pocket for a typed report and stopped the murmuring of his audience with a raised hand.

He read directly from the police report: 'Last night, at approximately ten p.m., fishermen discovered the body of a naked man face down in the Swan River at Bassendean. The back part of his skull was missing.'

Jon Pavel? Stevie's mind latched hold of the idea and ran with it. The body was found further west than Delia's, but that would make sense given the pull of the current. And he was naked, which must mean no identifying jewellery. She wondered if the hand tattoo was still visible.

Angus Wong put an end to the direction of Stevie's racing thoughts. 'The pathologist did the autopsy first thing this morning,' he said, 'and found the COD to be a shotgun wound to the head, inflicted by a similar, if not the same weapon as killed Delia Pavel. The body has been in the water for about two days, and though it's not been formally identified, it seems to match the description of missing businessman, Ralph Hardegan. Someone from one of his shops is coming in this afternoon to identify the body—that's something I don't want his elderly mother to have to do.'

Stevie closed her eyes for a moment. Mrs Hardegan's neighbour, Skye, and now her son: just how much could one old woman take?

an isolated village asked for
medical Supplies
I Volunteered With others from
the base
to take them

With Percy missing
What did I have to lose

CHAPTER EIGHTEEN

The official part of the briefing came to an end with Angus answering individual questions while other officers added notes to their files. Barry and Wayne were busy delegating jobs to the various members of the task force and making sure procedures were in place for all the necessary gathering of information. Fowler was assigned the joyless task of breaking the bad news about her son to Mrs Hardegan and re-questioning her if possible. Stevie overheard a uniformed officer remind Angus that he was due for a press conference downstairs.

Wanting to avoid Angus for as long as she could, she was the first to slip from the room. She caught the lift downstairs hoping to wangle her way into the observation room to watch the Marius and Rodika interviews. She sensed that Pavel and Hardegan had been the victims of some kind of internal power struggle, but between whom? Marius had been uptight over something, and while Rodika had appeared ignorant of the circumstances behind Jon Pavel's disappearance and his wife's murder, there was no hiding her fear. But was it fear of the known or fear of the unknown? Stevie was anxious to find out.

On her way to the interview rooms, she called into the ladies off the central foyer. In it she found a middle-aged woman wearing a colourless skirt and thin grey cardigan, bent over the sink scrubbing at her face. She looked up and Stevie caught the spark of recognition in her puffy red eyes. The woman tried to hide her grief by reaching for the paper towels and pressing a wad into her face.

'Mrs Williams?' Stevie placed her hand upon the woman's arm.

Skye's mother gave her face a last dab, sniffed and threw the towels into the bin. 'I know you, don't I? Sorry, I'm no good with names.'

Stevie smiled. 'That's okay; we've only met the once, when I dropped something off for Skye, I mean Emily, at her flat. I wouldn't expect you to remember me. My name's Stevie Hooper.'

'You were Emily's policewoman friend, the one she met when she was a volunteer at the Rape Crisis Centre?'

'Yes, that's right.'

Someone banged through the door and disappeared into one of the cubicles. Stevie placed her hand again on the woman's arm and said in a whisper. 'Are you all right, are they looking after you?'

'As well as can be expected I suppose.'

'Look, there's a coffee shop just down the road. Why don't we go and get a cuppa?' Stevie changed her mind about watching the interviews. Talking with Mrs Williams might prove more beneficial to both of them.

The woman hesitated. 'I wanted to talk to someone about the accident, that's why I'm here. I was told to see someone called Angus Wong.'

Stevie wondered who had told Mrs Williams to talk to Angus. Did she know that Skye's death was now being regarded as suspicious? 'Angus is tied up with a press conference at the moment,' she said. 'But I'll take you up to him after we've had a coffee if you like.'

'Okay,' said Mrs Williams, her eyes filling with tears again. 'It's been a long drive.'

Stevie held the door open for Mrs Williams then walked with her down the road to a coffee shop near Central. This was one of Stevie's favourite boltholes, a place rarely visited by anyone on the Job, most cops preferring to hold their meetings in the local pubs and bars.

They ordered coffee and settled into a table near the window. Mrs Williams rarely met Stevie's eye. Even when reminiscing about Skye she spent most of the time watching the smartly-dressed office workers striding purposefully up St George's Terrace, holding skirts down, coats closed, battling the perpetual wind. 'Did Mr Williams come with you?' she asked.

'He's seeding. You know what it's like; we have to take advantage of the rain.'

Stevie knew too well. Mrs Williams probably envied her husband locked away in the cabin of his John Deere, cutting himself off from everything around him.

'Emily had a younger sister, didn't she?'

Mrs Williams nodded and ladled three teaspoons of sugar into her coffee. 'Gillian. She's really upset of course; she's at a difficult age. Never as focused as Emily was. I can only hope this isn't going to tip her over the edge.'

'I'm sure you and Mr Williams will be there for her.'

'Terry, his name's Terry; and I'm Irene.' She began to cry,

silently. Stevie passed her a napkin and she wiped her eyes. 'I'm sorry about this; I'm just so tired. Luke phoned about four this morning and it felt as if I'd only just got to sleep. He said I should leave early if I wanted to catch this Inspector Wong bloke—Luke knows full well how long the drive is.'

'Luke?' Stevie couldn't hide her surprise. 'You mean Luke Fowler?'

'That's right, he's been terrific about all this. I don't know how I would have coped without him. He rang as soon as he heard the news, sent flowers, even offered to come and help with the seeding.'

Stevie frowned. Was this the 'sordid' history Skye had been referring to? 'How well did Skye know Luke, Irene?' she asked.

'They were only together a few months. She brought him to the farm a few times. He was a bit odd, but we still liked him enough.'

Stevie shook her head with amazement. While Mrs Hardegan had flatly stated that Fowler had been in love with Skye and she had seen for herself how committed he was to finding the truth behind her death, she hadn't thought for a moment they'd actually been an item. She'd assumed it must have been some kind of unrequited infatuation on his part. Although her experience with him in the Fremantle alley did suggest he wasn't quite the Action Man she'd first pegged, it was still almost impossible to see a connection between the girl she'd considered her friend and the man she could barely tolerate. Eccentric, flighty, impulsive, Skye would have run a conservative, finicky man like Fowler ragged.

'I didn't know that. I can't ... I just can't imagine them being suited at all,' she said.

'He was quite a bit older than Emily, and very different, but they do say opposites attract, don't they? But I know what you mean. It wasn't really much of a surprise to Terry and me when Emily told us she'd broken up with him. She wasn't one to take relationships too seriously; she was way too young for that. I think he was in far deeper than she ever was. He didn't take the break up at all well, apparently. I did feel sorry for him. Emily was a wonderful, kind girl and everyone loved her, but when it came to relationships with men ...' Mrs Williams shrugged. 'She didn't seem to really care; they were just a bit of fun. She got bored so easily.'

Stevie had always known Skye to be a love-'em-and leave-'em type of girl, too young for a serious relationship she always maintained, and oblivious of the trail of broken hearts, or 'fuck buddies,' she left sinking in her wake.

'How long ago did they break up?' she asked.

Irene looked to the ceiling. 'Three or so years ago.' Her absent gaze returned to the window.

In her head, Stevie began to click together the background pieces of the relationship, using what she knew and adding some creative imagination. Fowler and Skye had been an item. He probably had no idea about the nature of Skye's part-time work. She must have decided to tell him or else he found out for himself. He would have been horrified; a job like that would have been hard enough for any regular guy to accept, not to mention a man like Fowler.

When Skye was assaulted by one of her customers she made the mistake of seeking his help, probably thinking that going to a cop she knew would make it easier. Wrong. Fowler would still have been smarting over their broken relationship, hurt and humiliated. He'd not listened to Skye and brushed her allegations under the carpet. Stevie could almost hear his voice in her head saying that Skye had brought this trouble upon herself. If he had taken Skye's complaint seriously, the next victim might have been alive today. That was quite a weight to be carrying about on those starched white shoulders; no wonder he was so cut up about Skye's death. Why though, Stevie continued to puzzle, had Skye told her he still hated her guts? Maybe she was mistaken. Maybe it was more a case of Fowler hating himself.

'He was too old and too serious for her anyway,' Mrs Williams broke into Stevie's thoughts. Stevie couldn't have agreed more. But she also knew from the errors of her own past, that sexual attraction alone rarely followed conventions and good sense.

Stevie pointed out to Irene Williams the office on the other side of the incident room, planning on leaving Barry to introduce her to Angus. Her timing couldn't have been worse; the door opened just as she was about to beat her retreat. Several officers looked up from their phones and computers when Angus barked, 'Stevie, a word.'

'This is Emily Williams's mother, Irene,' Stevie said hurriedly, smiling at the woman. 'She'd like to talk to you about her daughter. I'm afraid I've got to rush, Irene, my partner's in hospital ...'

'I'm sure Mrs Williams won't mind waiting for just a minute,' Angus said. 'Barry, look after Mrs Williams please, put the kettle on. Excuse me for a moment, ma'am. Stevie, come in.'

He closed the office door behind them. The office was on the fifth floor of the Central Police building, with views across the WACA and the Swan River. Not that Stevie was paying much attention to the view outside the window. Her gaze flitted about the room. It already looked and smelled different from when Monty had been using it: no overflowing bin surrounded by misfired balls of screwed up paper, no dry-cleaning on the back of the door, no clandestine cigarette smoke leaking from the small attached bathroom. The photo of her on the desk was gone too, that was a relief; she'd always hated that picture. Her hair had been especially unmanageable that day, as if she'd just been pulled backwards through the Terrace wind tunnel—which she doubtless had. She wondered where Angus had put it. At the bottom of a drawer along with Monty's name plaque, probably. She noticed that the clay dinosaur Izzy had made for Monty was still on the desk, holding down a stack of papers.

Angus ground at the loose change in his pockets. 'Stevie, what the hell have you been playing at?'

'What do you mean?'

'That innocent look won't wash with me. You're messing around where you don't belong. Haven't you got better things to do than gatecrashing a team meeting? Shouldn't you be with Monty and your daughter? Surely a child needs her mother at a time like this.'

How dare he. She felt a rush of anger, clamped her jaw and said nothing.

'If it wasn't for the incident in Freo last night I might not have realised you were playing such an active part in the investigation,' he went on. 'Some peripheral interest is understandable—you found the baby after all—but actually participating in witness interviews is out of the question. I won't allow it. It's paramount the case is only run through official channels. There's the insurance for a start; you could have been hurt last —'

She interrupted him. 'Izzy's at school and Monty tends to sleep at this time of day. I'm taking her in to see him later after school, which will be out soon. So unless you need me for anything else, I'd better get going.'

'I'm serious, Stevie. This is your last warning. I know Veitch has already had a word with you.'

Stevie made a move toward the dinosaur paperweight, but stopped herself. Taking it would be childish; besides, its presence here on the desk meant that Monty was still coming back. 'I'll send your regards to Mont,' she said as she turned on her heel and left the office.

We were still hacking through
the jungle
when they caught us

the japs
they killed the men
I was saved for
better things
you can guess what
human nature is my dear
it doesn't change

WEDNESDAY

CHAPTER NINETEEN

It was closer to lunch than breakfast, but everyone in the establishment slept late. The girls wiped sleep from their eyes as they sat around the table devouring rice cakes and coconut milk, baked bananas and sweet fish curry left over from the night before. The packets of sugary western cereal standing on the table remained untouched. They were well fed — the assurance of good food was about the only promise of Jon Pavel's that had come true.

Excitement crackled like static through the kitchen. The girls were going to Broome to work as hostesses at the resort where they would make more money than they had ever seen in Perth. Soon they would all be rich, pay their debts and return to their villages as celebrities. That might happen, there was always a chance, Mai thought as she silently shuffled around the table, ladling rice from a large aluminium pot to those who wanted it. She didn't express her doubts about the venture, didn't want to dampen their spirits. At twenty-three she was the oldest by several years, but sometimes it felt like decades.

She'd worked the high end of the market before, the favourite of a wealthy Chinese Catholic, and had enjoyed special favours for a while. When the Chinaman discovered her pregnancy, he'd paid her old Mamasan a small fortune to skip the customary abortion, telling her in the same breath that he wanted no more to do with her. High end like Broome, low end like here, there was little difference.

Unless you owned the business.

Lin refused Mai's offer of rice; she hadn't touched her breakfast, Mai noticed. The girl continuously rubbed at her stomach and seemed to be having trouble drawing her breath. Rick was a clever one; he knew just how much beating a girl could take, where to punch for maximum pain and minimum damage, often hitting them through a thin foam mattress so the skin wouldn't bruise. Mai could see he'd gone too far this time. He was encouraged to beat the girls for bad behaviour, but she knew the Mamasan wouldn't have wanted Lin to be hit that hard.

Seventeen-year-old Nien peeped around the cereal boxes and met Mai with worried eyes. With a tilt of her head she indicated Lin sitting next to her.

'Does the Mamasan know what happened?' Nien whispered through her hand. If Lin heard what she said, she gave no sign of it; she just continued to stare blankly into her untouched bowl of fish curry. The other girls at the table were giggling, speculating on what kind of men they would meet in Broome. They weren't interested in the serious conversation at the other end of the table. Just as well, Mai thought, the fewer who knew the truth behind Lin's injuries the better.

Without waiting for an answer, Nien went on. 'She can't work now; even the drunken *farang* might notice her injuries. No one will want to lie with a girl with broken bones. This will cost the Mamasan money.'

'I can't take her to the doctor; there isn't time,' Mai said. 'I've bound her ribs; that will have to do, but I think some might be cracked or broken.'

'Why can't you get Mamasan to take her to the doctor then? She listens to you. Isn't the doctor being friendly any more?'

They all received regular check-ups from a deregistered doctor who Mamasan exploited like she did everyone else. He was a drug addict and she got him what he needed. In return he never asked any questions other than those that were strictly necessary.

'It's not a question of who takes her, there isn't time; I told you that,' Mai said.

'But what will you do—will you tell the Mamasan what Rick has done?'

Nien's questions were irritating but justified. Mai took a sip of Coke and thought hard. Rick had been walking a fine line recently. He'd been taking more uppers than usual and they were scrambling his brains; he was sure to fall out of favour with the Mamasan sooner or later. But if he didn't destroy himself with drugs, Mai thought, running her finger around the sharp hole in the top of the can, this extra piece of information might.

'If Mamasan asks, I'll say a client beat Lin up. It's not worth getting on the wrong side of Rick.' *Yet*, Mai added silently.

Other than the most junior of the girls who hadn't learnt how to work the system, everyone in this place made it their business to find a weakness in someone else. It was a means of survival for them, instinctive. The discovery of a weakness provided a tiny modicum of control. Because Mai had seen what the Mamasan and The Crow had done to Jon Pavel, and now what Rick had done to Lin, she had a hold, albeit a small one, on all of them. She didn't know what to do with the information, but she knew it would be useful one day. She would store it away like a crocodile with rotten meat and produce it when the time was right.

Rick pounded from the front of her mind and into the kitchen. The chattering stopped. It was as if the door had been slammed shut, not flung open. 'Coffee.' Rick's voice was gravelly with ganja.

Mai handed him a mug and offered to cook him some eggs. She was the most trusted of the girls. She did most of the shopping and cooking for the establishment—that's what the Mamasan called it, the establishment, trying to make it sound respectable, though they both knew it was no different to the Bangkok brothel, only cleaner. It was on these shopping expeditions that she had been able to slip out, catch the bus and travel to the Pavels' house to feed Niran.

Rick had searched her bag when she'd returned and found the baby's bottle, nappies and jars of food. He'd told The Crow and The Crow had put a hot iron to the soles of her feet so she couldn't visit Niran again. The burns were healing, but she still walked with a painful shuffle.

The punishment had not kept her from her work. 'You don't need your feet to fuck,' the Mamasan had said as she'd watched her crazy son pressing the searing iron into her flesh.

But that was before Mai had found out what they'd done to Jon Pavel. Things were different now she'd all but witnessed them murder a man. Before, she was the most trusted because they had the greatest hold over her; now she had a hold over them—although they didn't know it. Soon, she wouldn't just be the top girl; she'd be a top player too.

Rick said he didn't want any breakfast. His grey-brown beard was the same colour as the tawny dogs that rooted through the trash outside the Bangkok brothel. His eyes were bloodshot, his breath rancid with stale alcohol. He was in no condition to begin their long bus journey.

Rick took milk for his coffee from the fridge and slammed the door shut with his foot. Lin looked up from her bowl and gasped, 'My Buddha!' As the head is holy in Thailand, the feet are unholy. Mai smiled to herself and shook her head—Lin still had much to learn about the *farang* way.

Small steps pecked down the passageway and Jimmy Jack entered the kitchen. If Rick was a lumbering elephant, Jimmy Jack was a fighting cock. He kept his dirty blond hair scraped back in a ponytail, emphasising the turmeric colour of his skin and his sharp, pointy features. The girls sometimes laughed about him behind his back, saying that his nose was plastic and stuck on with glue.

Rick smiled at the younger man and offered him a cigarette from the crushed packet in his shirt pocket. He knew he had to be nice to Jimmy Jack, and not only because of the long fishing knife he always carried. He might tell Mamasan and The Crow what he had been up to last night—drinking their liquor, smoking their ganja, fucking and beating their girls. In Bangkok, The Crow had burned one of the guardians alive for abusing his trust, covered him in petrol and set him on fire.

Rick had better watch out.

A ghost of a smile played upon Mai's lips as she hobbled around the breakfast table, clearing up.

Rick ordered the girls upstairs to change and pack. None

of them had many clothes of their own. The good ones, which they shared, had already been stored away by the Mamasan to be loaned out when they entertained the richer clients.

These men liked to see their women well dressed and sipping expensive cocktails on yachts or at private parties in fancy mansions. That way they could pretend it was all real, that they were handsome men who went with pretty girls because the girls wanted to be with them. Only when the bedroom doors were closed did the real games begin. When it came down to it, Mai reflected, these men were no different than the dirty boys from last night — cleaner maybe, but their grunts were still the same.

There was a sign above the brothel door
in Japanese

They made sure we knew what it said
on the very first day

It was a welcome
to courageous soldiers
Who were on duty
for the holy war

CHAPTER TWENTY

The door to Monty's hospital room was shut. Stevie couldn't recall it ever having been shut before. For a moment she hesitated, peering through the grid of the safety glass, anxious for what she might see on the other side. The room looked different, Monty looked different. Most of the tubing was gone and there was only one drip left hanging above the bed. He looked relaxed, propped up with pillows. If not for the drip and the ubiquitous heart monitor, he could have been in bed at home reading the Sunday papers.

A man sat in the visitor's chair, examining the sheets of paper Monty handed him from a pile on his lap. Must be one of his doctors, Stevie decided; she'd spoken to so many over the past few days she'd lost track of them all.

Monty saw her face against the glass, beckoned her in and introduced her to Colin Zimmel from the AFP. She remembered the name although they had never met. Monty and Col had been in the WAPOL rugby team together until Col had joined the Feds and been transferred east. He'd recently moved back to Perth and Monty had been consulting him for the work he was doing for the CCC.

Monty's build could have singled him out as a rugby

player, but his even features showed little evidence of the game. Col Zimmel's face on the other hand was a testimony to every scrum, every boot and elbow to the face, every broken cheekbone and flattened nose – not a face you'd want to come across in a dark alley at night. His voice, however, was deep and mellifluous and he seemed genuinely interested in Izzy's artwork.

'Izz brought these pictures in when she visited with Dot this morning,' Monty explained after he'd introduced her to Col. 'Col reckons she's very talented.'

Stevie made herself as comfortable as she could on the cramped bed beside Monty, a pillow under her back. 'He wouldn't dare say anything else, would he?'

Col laughed. 'I have to admit I've been keeping my eye on the monitor there.'

'Thank God he won't be bringing that thing home with him,' Stevie said. 'Being nice all the time is becoming quite a strain.'

Monty turned to Col. 'I'm drinking it in while I can.' He passed her Izzy's drawings and she stacked them upon his bedside table. 'Stevie, I was thinking about what you were telling me earlier, and I reckon you need to have a talk to Col here.'

Stevie feigned ignorance. 'What do you mean?'

'This people-trafficking operation you seem to have stumbled across.'

'I can't talk to Col about it, Mont. Col needs to see Angus, not me.'

'I've made an appointment to see Angus Wong tomorrow,' Col said. 'It's very important for us to get some sort of information exchange system into place. I just thought …' He pulled at a cauliflower ear and glanced at Monty who tipped him an encouraging nod. 'There are a few things you need to know. Monty told me about the attempt on your life the other night; it sounded like a close shave. I think it's time you knew about the kind of people you're dealing with.'

'We're concerned about your safety,' Monty said before Stevie could get a word in. 'You need to know this for your own protection. Humour me and listen to the man—I'm not supposed to be under any stress, remember?'

Stevie stifled a sigh, slid from the bed and sat next to Col in the other visitor's chair in order to give him her complete attention. 'Go on then.'

'Although human trafficking is primarily a federal concern,' Col began, 'we often work alongside state police. The sharing of data between the states and departments can be abysmal, so I was impressed when Senior Sergeant Wayne Pickering from the SCS contacted me yesterday and filled me in on the Pavel case. I did some extra digging and came up with some facts about Jon Pavel that I think you should know, seeing as you seem to be, er, peripherally involved.'

Monty threw up his hands. 'Peripherally? Ha!'

Stevie ignored the outburst. She couldn't pretend she wasn't interested and found herself leaning towards Col from her chair. 'Go on.'

'Jon Pavel, aka Anton Arcos, aka George Brasov was born in Bucharest in 1973, the son of a petty thief. He followed in his father's footsteps, but took the family firm a lot further. He started dealing in weapons when he was a juvenile and was lucky to escape the harsh punishments of the communist regime of the time. He was apolitical, supplying arms to anyone who could pay. After the fall of the communists he was recruited into a powerful crime ring—guns, drugs, prostitution and human trafficking. Then he got himself involved in a turf war with another gang and was implicated in a drive-by shooting in which two rival gang members were killed.'

Monty stretched for the water jug on the side locker. Stevie reached it first and poured him a glass. 'I'm not totally helpless,' he said peevishly.

Jeez, Stevie thought, the fun and games have already started and he's not even home yet. 'We're still listening, Col,' she said, ignoring Monty's grumbles.

'When you're quite ready ...' Col sighed and waited for Monty to down his water. 'While Pavel was in hiding,' he went on, 'he applied for Australian residency, using a false name and false papers. He had all the contacts he needed to forge the documents and plenty of money. He married a peasant girl, Delia. Perhaps she showed him the light and he decided it was time to go clean, or maybe just nothing he got up to came through on our radar. Whatever, he didn't get any kind of criminal reputation with the Perth authorities. He established several legitimate businesses—a club and restaurants—which you've visited, right, Stevie?'

She nodded.

'It's quite possible he stayed clean for a couple of years,' Col said, 'until he was headhunted by an Asian human-trafficking syndicate looking for Australian-based middlemen.'

'So we have an Asian mob recruiting Australians and Romanians?' Stevie queried. 'I thought these gangs stuck with their own kind?'

'They have in the past; this is a new development,' Monty

said. Stevie sensed from his animated expression that this was in the paper he was writing. 'If there are two or three cultures to contend with, it makes it harder for us to understand how they're working. It's happening in the UK now, with Lithuanians, Chinese and Albanians working together. The Lithuanians bring the girls in and sell them to the Albanians who set the brothels up. The Chinese organise the affiliated drug shipments. This is huge business. According to estimates by UNIFEM, the numbers of women and children trafficked in South-East Asia could be around 225,000 out of a global figure of over 700,000 annually.'

'Good God,' Stevie said. 'And the powers that be think that little old Perth can stay clear of this? Or are they just ignoring the situation over here?'

Monty and Col exchanged glances. 'Not if we can help it,' Monty said.

'Are the girls always kept locked up?' Stevie asked.

'Not necessarily,' Col said. 'Often psychological control and threats to harm loved ones are enough. The more difficult girls are forcibly hooked on drugs and controlled that way.'

'Pavel had a prison-like room at the top of his house,' said Stevie.

Col nodded. 'Pavel had all the necessary skills and experience and was obviously ready and eager to oblige in any way he could. Perhaps he found life in Perth too dreary and missed the action, could be he just needed the money. He was put in touch with a couple who ran the WA side of the operation, a mother and son team.'

Monty raised his eyebrows. 'You never mentioned them before.'

'We don't know much about them. The woman was

originally called Jennifer Granger. She was the daughter of an Australian diplomat who worked at our embassy in Bangkok. She was snatched as a thirteen-year-old when she was out shopping at the local markets with one of the embassy maids.'

'I think I remember reading about it—early seventies, right?' Monty asked.

'Correct. There was a huge furore, an international search, but she never resurfaced and was presumed dead. Years later she was identified through fingerprints as the Mamasan of a Thai brothel where a large stash of heroin was found. By then she was a powerful underworld identity. She escaped prosecution by bribing and threatening the arresting officers. Like Pavel she got hold of false papers and sought sanctuary in Australia. She came into the country under the name of Marion Godwin, though she'd have changed it since. As in Bangkok, her fingerprints were lifted from a Kings Cross brothel during a drug bust a couple of years back. No one the police questioned at the time admitted to having seen or known anything about an Australian Mamasan. She slipped away again and is believed to be in Perth.'

'How old would Granger be now?' Stevie asked, already doing the maths.

'Fifty-one—I have a graphic artist working on it. The last photo we have is of her as a thirteen-year-old, just before she was snatched. The artist is putting together a picture using a computer program that'll give us an idea of how she might have aged. It might take some time though—we have to dig up photos of her parents too and merge them with the last known photos of her as a child.'

Stevie glanced at Monty. Like her, he was probably

dwelling on the hell the parents went through.

Col must have read it in their faces. 'Jennifer's parents split up a year after she went missing, both blaming the other for what happened. The father eventually committed suicide and the mother died of natural causes about five years ago in Sydney. We think Jennifer was back in Australia by then, though she never made contact with her mother. She is now believed to be an important player in the people-trafficking syndicate that recruited Pavel. Like many groups of this type they have other interests too ...'

'The big four: guns, girls, gambling and ganja,' Monty said.

'Not heroin?' Stevie said.

'The works; ganja just makes for better alliteration.'

Stevie flicked her eyes toward the ceiling.

'But despite her various makeovers,' Col continued, 'Granger was getting too well known in Thailand to travel backwards and forwards, so she employed Pavel to go on her shopping trips for her.'

'And once Pavel was established within the organisation, he recruited Ralph Hardegan?' Stevie asked.

'That's what it looks like. Through their businesses they got to know each other. I guess Pavel must have figured Hardegan as a like-minded kind of guy.'

'A sociopath.'

'Could be. With their newly formed partnership, they had all the reason in the world to make frequent business trips to Thailand and procure girls for Australian brothels.'

'"Fresh'n'Tasty,"' Monty said, dryly.

'What about Granger's son?' Stevie asked. 'What do we have on him?'

'He's Eurasian, goes by the name of The Crow, but we don't know much about him.' Col paused, ran his tongue over his lips. 'Other than that he enjoys burning people alive.'

Monty shifted in his bed and reached for Stevie's hand. 'Nice guy.'

'We suspect the pair are probably running some kind of legitimate business in the Perth area, lying low and reaping the rewards while others do the dirty work for them,' Col said.

Monty thought for a moment. 'The Crow, as in "blackbirder?"' he asked Col.

'Top of the form, Mont.'

Stevie raised a questioning eyebrow.

'It's what the old-time slavers used to be called,' Monty explained, shifting further up his pillows, but still clinging tightly to her hand. 'Now, they call 'em snakeheads.'

Stevie knew the term. She turned to Col. 'And you think this mother and son team murdered the Pavels as well as Ralph Hardegan?'

Col paused for thought. 'Jon Pavel's body still hasn't been found, has it?'

Stevie shook her head.

'He's probably copped it too, then. If those two guys were trying to pull a swifty over Mamasan and The Crow, I doubt they'd get away with their lives, they were taken out I reckon. You should hear some of the stories about them from Bangkok. Mamasan is utterly ruthless, and as for her son, well ...'

Stevie looked from one to the other of the men. Col seemed to be waiting for some kind of reaction from her. Monty fiddled with a button on his pyjama jacket. His silence suggested he was trying to think up a tactful way of saying something she might not want to hear.

'So, that's my warning?' she said after a pause. 'You think this Jennifer Granger might have been behind our attempted murder?'

Col nodded. 'Quite possibly.'

'Stevie, I want you to stay at your mother's tonight,' Monty said.

The gentle tone didn't work. Stevie felt herself flush with irritation. 'Oh come off it. I just happened to be with Fowler at the wrong place at the wrong time. Most of the investigating officers don't even know of my involvement in the case, not to mention the possible offenders—not once have I given my name to anyone I've spoken to.'

Monty's voice rose. 'Stevie, it's not only about you. There's Izzy's safety too —'

The beep of the monitor cut off his words, the squiggly green line jumping into a frenzy of jagged movement. Monty groaned and collapsed back onto his pillows.

Stevie's heart almost stopped too. She jumped to her feet and shook Monty by the shoulder, crying desperately, 'Monty, what is it, what's the matter?'

'Christ, where's the nurse?' Col yelled.

It was over within a few seconds, the heart monitor once more showing a regular pattern of beats by the time the nurse rushed into the room.

'Is the machine playing up again, Mr McGuire?' the nurse asked.

Monty casually opened one eye. 'Guess it must be.'

All things come to an end
Somehow

I was liberated
I found that Perey had Survived
We were married as Soon as
We could as
Soon as our health allowed it

CHAPTER TWENTY-ONE

The evening was damp and breezy. Stevie buttoned up her denim jacket and trudged toward her car at the farthest end of the hospital carpark, towards the railway track. Considering how packed the carparks were, there were surprisingly few people about. The lights of the hospital dimmed as she left them behind, the occasional street lamp impotent in the grainy light of dusk. Several years ago a series of attacks on hospital staff had prompted increased security patrols, but she'd seen no sign of them so far this evening.

As she walked, she thought back to the conversation with Col and Monty. Col thought that the Pavels had been the victims of some kind of gangland revenge killing, something to do with their involvement in a people-trafficking racket. It seemed her suspicions about an internal power struggle had been close, but on a much larger scale than any she had imagined.

Col had continued to fill her in once Monty's mal-functioning machine had been seen to. The organisation sounded huge, efficient and structured like a business with primary producers, retailers, suppliers and middlemen. The various hierarchical levels weren't arranged in a logical pattern though, but via a confusing maze of passageways and dead ends, with members linked to those immediately below and above them on a need-to-know basis only. It was unlikely that even Mamasan and The Crow would know who was at the very heart of the labyrinth.

How could their under-resourced authorities cope with something like that, she wondered as she wound her way through the obstacle course of parked cars. How could *she* cope?

And Monty seemed to think that now the Feds were involved, she could simply step back and withdraw. He obviously didn't know her as well as he liked to think he did; didn't know that the only way she could shake this overwhelming feeling of helplessness was to fight it. First the baby and now Skye; she couldn't just get up and leave now even if she wanted to.

Sorry, Mont.

Her first task was to discover the truth behind Skye's death. With the evidence as it stood, they had virtually nothing to prove she had been murdered at all, let alone by whom. There was even a chance that the people traffickers weren't involved at all, that her death was just a fluke accident. All she had to fuel her suspicions were a dysphasic old woman, an unused Ventolin inhaler, and a paint scrape that could have been caused by a carpark bingle.

A carpark bingle. Stevie thought back to the conversation with Fowler when she'd been dressing his head wound in her kitchen. He'd mentioned that his father's green vintage car was at the panel beater because of a 'carpark bingle.' Could Fowler have run Skye off the road that night? Surely not. He may have had an axe to grind with Skye, but he wouldn't have killed her because of it—would he? His father's vintage was green, but so was Pavel's Jag. She shook her head; amazed at how her mind could wander when she was tired and overwrought; this was hardly a logical thought process.

The wind scythed through her thin jacket, the hairs on the back of her neck prickled with cold. She turned up her collar. A distant streetlight illuminated the roof of Monty's pitted Land Rover near the back fence. Monty's car was also green. Note to self: never buy a green car.

She increased her pace.

A man climbed out of a car on her right. She couldn't see his face.

His door slammed.

Instinctively she pulled her keys from her pocket and held one like a shank in her hand. The man beeped his car locked and turned. His face was still indistinct in the darkness. In the next instant he was looming over her. She saw him lifting a blunt object, ready to strike. She made a feint toward him with the key, stopped and drew up short. 'Fowler, what the hell!'

Out of the shadows, the blunt object became a bunch of broken-necked daffodils. Fowler took a step back. 'Jesus, Hooper, you're not going to stab me are you?'

Stevie's smacked a hand against her thigh. 'What the hell are you doing here?'

'Looking for you. Your phone was off so I figured you'd be at the hospital. I was heading up to the ward, hoping to catch you, when I saw your car over there.' He indicated the far fence with the drooping daffodils and must have sensed her incredulity. 'Oh, these are for the Inspector,' he explained.

Stevie pressed a palm to her forehead and gritted her teeth. 'Shit.'

'Jittery, huh?'

'I think we both have reason to be, don't you?' She unlocked the Land Rover, hurled her bag onto the passenger seat and turned to face him.

'*You're* okay,' Fowler said, carefully placing the flowers on the bonnet of the car. 'It's not your name all over the papers and in the case notes—it's me that should be worried.'

Stevie paused and tried to compose herself. 'So ... what is it you want?'

Something in Fowler seemed to deflate. He leaned back against the car. 'Hooper, please—I need you to come with me to see Mrs Hardegan.'

She folded her arms and regarded him coolly. 'I'm not used to this humility; it doesn't suit you.' Then a thought struck her. She looked back at him with surprise. 'Wait a minute. You mean you haven't even *told* the old lady about her son yet?'

'No. That's why I wanted to catch you here.' He pointed to his car. 'This is a hire car, we don't have any spare in the pool,' he said as if that somehow explained everything. His eyes dropped to his shiny shoes. 'I don't think the old lady likes me much. I'm not sure what to say, how to handle her—you're, er, quicker on your feet than I am.'

This was the nearest he'd got to sheepish about their near miss the other night. Guess I should be grateful for what I can get, she thought, rolling her eyes in much the same way Skye might have done. 'And why might she not like you, I wonder?'

Fowler plunged his hands into his pockets and looked toward the railway track. A train hooted and the ground beneath them shook as it slowed toward the station.

'Well?' Stevie prompted.

'I think she knows. Knows about Skye and me, how we used to, er, go out. Skye must have told her about the assault, that I didn't do anything about it.'

Stevie said nothing.

'I'd do anything to make up for that now, you know that?' Fowler shook his head at her lack of reaction, waved a questioning hand. 'You don't seem very surprised about any of this.'

Stevie expelled a breath. 'That's because I already knew.'

'You knew?'

'I'm a detective.

'How ...?'

'I detected it.' She didn't want to go into what she'd discovered from Skye's mother, not when there was still that other niggling matter to sort out. 'Wait here a moment. I need to make a phone call.'

Out of Fowler's earshot, she called Mark Douglas on his mobile number. 'That paint sample,' she said when he picked up.

'Has anyone ever told you you're a terrier, Stevie?'

'Frequently.'

'I thought it could have at least waited till office hours.' A woman laughed in the background—Blood-Spatter Jane?

'Does that mean the results are through?'

'Faxed to me from Canada just before I left work this evening.'

Shit, he knew this was urgent, he could have at least

texted her. It was gratifying to know he was at last getting a life—but did it have to be right now?' Mark laughed down the phone as if he knew what she was thinking. 'Green Jag XK.'

'Definitely not a vintage?' She looked to where Fowler sat slumped against the bonnet of his hire car.

'No,' he said.

Stevie felt her shoulders sag with relief. 'John Pavel had a green Jag,' she said thoughtfully, 'and it's still missing.'

'Same model?'

'Can't remember. I'll have to look it up.'

'Mark, the movie's starting,' the woman called out.

Stevie thanked him, unable to keep the smile from her face. Still smiling she returned to Fowler and tapped him on the arm. 'C'mon, we may as well go together. I'll drop you back here for your car when we've seen Mrs Hardegan.'

As she drove she told Fowler about the paint results and he reminded her of the model of Pavel's Jag, an XK convertible, 2006. 'A match.' Stevie said. 'Pavel might be alive after all.'

'If he is, and he thought Skye was onto him, he'd have reason enough to kill her, wouldn't he? But surely the car would have been spotted by now? There's a statewide search going on for it.'

Stevie shrugged. Number plates were easy enough to swap. A cop would only run a check of the plates if he had cause to be suspicious of the vehicle. 'I'll have to contact Angus, get him to trace every 2006 convertible Jag in the state—no make it country, irrespective of plates.'

'You'll be popular.'

'I'm hardly flavour of the month right now.'

'How the mighty have fallen.'

'Have you always been such a jerk, or has it taken a lifetime of cultivation?'

He gave a small grunt of what might have been amusement.

They turned from Thomas Street onto Stirling Highway. The university's clock tower glowed brighter than the moon. Stevie's thoughts jumped from Jon Pavel to Skye as the car idled at a red light. Perhaps now was finally the right time to ask Fowler what had happened between them. People tended to find it easier to talk in a car, especially when it was dark.

She voiced the question. He turned his head away from her toward a garrulous group of students near a bus stop, playing soccer with an empty beer can. His shoulders moved as he took a breath to speak, stopped, as if changing his mind and thinking better of it.

'Go on,' Stevie prompted gently.

'I suppose you have a right to know, she was your friend after all.' He let out a resigned sigh. Stevie took off from the lights and proceeded down the highway just under the speed limit. Mrs Hardegan's was only a few kays from here and she knew he'd need time for this.

'We'd been going out for a few months,' he said at last. 'I thought we were getting on well. I liked being with her; it was more than the sex, you know? She made me laugh, I always felt, well, lighter when I was with her. I think she liked me too. I helped her with things, boring things she couldn't be bothered with like finance for her first car, tax forms, that kind of thing. Her landlord was giving her some hassles so I had a word with him and got her out of the shit. Even took her to Bali for a short break.'

You were being used, mate, Stevie thought. That was

the contradiction that was Skye—kind, considerate and compassionate to everything and everyone except the men in her life.

'She also took me home to the family farm to meet her folks. I mean, that's a good sign isn't it?'

Stevie kept her eyes on the road, nodded.

'One night I called round to her place on spec and caught her at it with a guy in her flat.' He returned to the view from the passenger window. 'I tried not to yell, asked her calmly who he was. She said she didn't know and then she smiled. The smile triggered something in me that I couldn't help. I lost it, grabbed the guy, was going to beat his brains out, but he pulled a knife from the bedside table before I could get the first punch in.'

Stevie frowned and indicated to the scar on the right side of his cheek. 'Is that how you got that?'

He turned back to her, brushed the scar with the tips of his fingers, seemed surprised by her question. 'That? Oh, no—a dodgy mole. I think the surgeon must've been drunk.'

She hoped the darkness of the car's interior would hide her smile—some Action Man.

'No, I didn't do anything once I saw the knife,' he continued. 'Turned my back on the pair of them and walked out. Skye laughed, I'll never forget that sound, it followed me all the way down the stairwell ...'

Stevie bit her lip and concentrated on her driving.

'But that's no excuse for me ignoring her assault complaint,' he added.

'No, it's not.'

They turned into Mrs Hardegan's long street. Federation mansions, modern reproductions and concrete houses with flat roofs cast shadows over the remaining stunted originals. An architectural survival of the fittest, Stevie decided as she regarded the quiet street. The buildings in it were as competitive for space as trees in a rainforest.

Fowler filled Stevie in on the details of the Marius and Rodika interviews. 'After a bit of prompting they both admitted to suspecting that Pavel and Hardegan were in the skin trade, although both denied any involvement with that side of the business. Legitimately, they were on a pretty good wicket anyway, didn't need to break the law. Rodika was apparently Delia's cousin and an old employee of Pavel's from their Romanian days.'

'No surprises there, an old tart if ever I saw one—I wonder why she didn't speak up and claim the baby: she is his only next of kin.'

'Because she knew she'd be questioned, I guess. She wasn't involved in Pavel's people trafficking, but she was still here illegally. If the immigration authorities found out she'd got into the country on false papers, she'd have been deported. She probably will be now, anyway.'

'If Rodika is Delia's cousin,' Stevie said after she'd driven another block, 'she must know something about the baby's origins. Surely Delia confided in her? The poor woman had no other friends or family in this country.'

'I asked Rodika that, but all she said was that as far as she knew he was legally adopted from Thailand.'

'Are the results back on her prints?'

'Yes, but they don't match those found in the baby's room.'

'Bugger, but it was worth a try. And Marius,' she asked. 'How involved is he?'

'He knew what they were up to all right, but won't admit it, probably just turned a blind eye. He's very keen on the restaurant and club. I get the feeling he'll be approaching his bank for a loan provided he's cleared of any involvement with the traffickers. Reckon he's secretly delighted about all this.'

Stevie tapped her fingers against the steering wheel and thought for a moment. 'Do they have any idea who else is behind the trafficking operation?'

'Only that they are very powerful, unscrupulous operators.'

She told Fowler what she had learned from Col Zimmel about The Crow and Mamasan. He listened with interest. 'So you think Pavel and Hardegan had been doing the dirty on the Mamasan, ripping her off?'

'At first I thought they'd both been singled out for some kind of retribution. Now I'm wondering if Pavel escaped before they got to him, and left Hardegan to carry the can.' She continued to dwell on the matter. 'Did anyone check further into that house fire from last year?'

'Don't think so.'

'Then find out as much as you can, contact the arson squad. It wouldn't surprise me if the Mamasan was behind that too. If Pavel was as valuable to her as Col thinks he was, she might have thought she could just pull him into line with a warning. There's a chance she even let him go this time, just killing his wife instead.'

Fowler paused. 'You always this bossy, Hooper?'

His earlier humility seemed to have disappeared, she noticed. She ignored him, busy concentrating on another thought tugging at her mind, one that hadn't left since the whole business had started. 'And the baby — has anyone found out how they managed to acquire him?'

'Not sure.'

'Then find that out too.'

'Yes, ma'am,' he saluted — still the same old dickhead.

'But what about the book-cooking?' she asked.

'Marius is feigning ignorance, blaming Pavel.'

'He'll probably get away with it too.' Stevie drew up outside Mrs Hardegan's. Someone nearby had been burning leaves in their backyard, filling the air with a smoky tang. She found her gaze drawn to the empty shell of the Pavel's house and thought of The Crow. Her mouth dried. 'I guess there's a lot worse people in the world than Dominic Marius,' she said.

My mother blamed me for
everything

Will that be the same with
your people?
Perhaps things will be different
if you make a success of it
and return home
rich

a success of it   perhaps

CHAPTER TWENTY-TWO

To save Mrs Hardegan the effort of walking to open the front door, Stevie and Fowler approached the house through the neat back garden, down a crazy paving pathway bordered with terracotta pots of blooming geraniums.

Mrs Hardegan appeared to be asleep in her chair, but sat bolt upright at the sound of Stevie's tap upon the glass. Stevie called from the other side of the window and asked if they could come in. The old lady heaved herself up and opened the back door, white hair awry, skin paper-pale.

They apologised for waking her.

'We weren't sleeping,' Mrs Hardegan said, 'We were writing a letter.'

Stevie's heart gave a leap. Could she write after all? If she could their problems would be solved. Her hopes were dashed when she glanced toward the table and saw no sign of letter writing paraphernalia. The sewing table had been rearranged since her last visit. A man in a silver frame looked out at her; a handsome man with a smooth young face and prominent cheekbones, dressed in naval uniform—her husband?

'You remember who we are, Mrs Hardegan?' Fowler asked as she settled once more into the easy chair by the window.

She glanced up at him, a shadow of contempt falling across her sharp features. Stevie sat down on the footstool and took the soft bony hand in hers. 'I'm afraid we've got some bad news.'

Mrs Hardegan pulled her hand away, leaned back in her chair and closed her eyes. 'The boy, our boy ... he's dead,' she said.

Stevie and Fowler exchanged glances. 'You already knew?' he asked.

Her eyes flew open. 'Of course we didn't know!'

'We're sorry for your loss,' Stevie murmured. 'I've spoken to a social worker. She'll be in contact with you.'

'We've brought you some flowers.' Fowler produced the daffodils from behind his back and waited for a thank you that never came. Stevie caught Fowler's eye. Was he really expecting thanks at a time like this? she wondered.

'I'll put them in water,' he said, hurriedly moving to the kitchenette.

Mrs Hardegan shot Fowler a sceptical look and tossed her head with a humph. 'Dead flowers.' Then to Stevie she said, 'They killed him, didn't they? Just like they did the other boys.'

'Yes, we think so.'

'No surprises there, we saw it coming, we told him. Lie down with dogs and you get carrots.'

'Can I get you anything ... brandy?' Fowler asked. He'd put the flowers in water in the sink and was heading toward the liquor cabinet.

'No, get us this.' Mrs Hardegan pointed to her sewing basket, which Fowler dutifully lifted from the table.

'No, not that, stupid boy!'

'This?' Stevie said, extracting the tapestry from beneath the basket and handing it over. A mess of tangled wool, it was almost impossible to see which side of the tapestry was which. 'We know Ralph was involved with Jon Pavel's activities,' Stevie went on, 'and we think we now know what those activities were. They were bringing girls over from Thailand to work against their will as prostitutes.'

'Snoodle pinkerds — we told you that.' Mrs Hardegan didn't look up, carefully pierced the fabric with her needle, her face a lined study of concentration.

Stevie frowned. 'Snoodle pinkerds? You mean girls — prostitutes?'

The soft expulsion of breath said yes, of course that's what she meant.

'Is there anything else we should know about this? Can you tell us anything at all about the people who killed Ralph and Delia?' Stevie asked.

Mrs Hardegan finished her stitch and looked thoughtfully at the picture on the table. Finally she said, 'The Japs killed him.'

'*Bloody Japs, bloody Japs!*'

The sudden racket made Stevie clap her hand to her chest. She'd forgotten all about that damned bird hanging in its cage in the far corner of the room.

'Cover up our feathered friend,' Mrs Hardegan commanded. Fowler placed the blanket over the cage. The parrot gave a squawk of protest and fell silent.

'But it's still our fault,' Mrs Hardegan continued. 'We couldn't help it, couldn't love him — no wonder the boy turned out like he did.' She paused, her mouth was turned down but Stevie could see no evidence of tears in the age-washed eyes.

'We'll tell you soon what happened, we'll tell our story, but only when we're ready. You must have hours and minutes.'

Hours and minutes: patience. This was something Stevie found to be in very short supply. 'But Mrs Hardegan, please, tell us. Do you know who killed your son?'

'The Japs did — didn't we just tell you that?'

Stevie looked toward the parrot cage, waiting for the nerve-grating echo, but it remained silent, thank God, cage gently swinging from the roof beam. She'd better steer the conversation to smoother waters. 'The baby, Joshua, what can you tell us about him?'

Mrs Hardegan began another laborious stitch. Fowler sighed, put his hands in his pockets and started to pace to and fro. Stevie bit her lower lip. 'Fowler ...'

'They stole him,' Mrs Hardegan said at last.

Fowler stopped pacing and met Stevie's eye.

'And when the boy found out about it,' Mrs Hardegan continued, 'he went quite mad. He was always stupid, only a poor uneducated peasant, but nice, we liked him despite all that. But then stupid turned to mad.'

'What boy, Mrs Hardegan? Jon Pavel? Skye? Ralph?' Stevie asked. 'No, that boy.' The old lady pointed to the Pavel house with the tip of her needle.

'Delia Pavel, you mean Delia Pavel went mad?'

Mrs Hardegan stabbed the needle into the tapestry and left it there, as if she'd had enough of her sewing. 'He came to us and told us what the boys were doing and then that boy of mine said yes they were when we asked him. And then we went mad too.'

With a rush of excitement, Stevie sprang up from the footstool and began to speak rapidly to Fowler. 'Maybe Delia didn't know the baby was illegally adopted — although with the upstairs bedroom as it was, she had to have an idea of her husband's other activities. Somehow she found out that the baby was stolen and the knowledge tipped her over the edge. The madness must be the depression Skye suspected Delia of having and the reason for the house being kept in such a mess. Delia must have confided her fears to Mrs Hardegan, telling her about Ralph's involvement in her husband's illegal activities, which Ralph later admitted to his mother when she questioned him.' No wonder the old lady had had a stroke, Stevie added silently.

Mrs Hardegan nodded her head; all her words had escaped her now. The news of her son's death had taken its toll, despite her efforts at hiding it. She put her tapestry back on the table and sank back into her chair.

'Mind waiting for me in the car?' Stevie said to Fowler. 'I won't be long.'

Fowler hesitated before nodding a sombre goodbye to the old lady. He was about to move when she held up a finger. 'No, wait where you are,' she commanded. 'You are to come back another time. We have some books belonging to the boy and we want you to take them to his parents.'

'I can get them now if you like, it's no trouble, I'll be seeing them at the funeral.' Fowler made as if to move toward the book-crowded hallway.

'We said not now. Later. You will have to take them to that place, where they live, that place with all the dust and woolly animals. It's a long drive but you will do it.'

Fowler said he would. They watched him as he opened the back door and stepped into the garden, shoulders sagging under his creased suit jacket. Mrs Hardegan looked at Stevie and let out a breath. 'Stupid is as stupid does. But not a bad boy.'

Stevie agreed, tried again to clasp the old woman's hand. This time she didn't pull away. 'Are you going to be all right?' she asked. 'Can I get you anything, anyone I can ring? A priest maybe?'

'We'll miss the boy.'

Skye, Delia or Ralph?

Stevie didn't ask.

Stevie called in at the deli and paid the girl Leila for the DVD. Fowler curled his lip when she climbed back into the car and tossed *Gone with the Wind* into his lap. 'What you watching this crap for?' he asked as he held the cover up to the interior light.

'It helps me relax. Don't you have a favourite movie you watch over and over again, something you can just veg out to?'

He shrugged. 'I've watched *Saw 3* a few times, I guess.'

Right.

After dropping Fowler back at the hospital for his car, she returned to her mother's house, read to Izzy for a while and then settled on the couch in front of the TV. She'd had little sleep over the last few nights, her mind spinning like a hamster on a wheel even when she did get the opportunity. Tonight she was asleep before Scarlet and Rhett could fall into their first clinch.

Lilly Hardegan continued to sit in her chair well after her visitors had gone. She didn't feel like writing any more of the letter tonight and anyway, the Thai girl knew the rest of it.

She wondered if Mai would see the irony of it all.

As she gazed at the picture of Percy on her sewing table, grief wrenched her to the core. She'd refused the policewoman's offer of a priest, didn't need one. What good was a priest, she thought, if you don't have the religion to go with it? Lilly Hardegan had lost her faith in the jungles of New Guinea some sixty-odd years ago.

despite my unwillingness
difficulty with intimate relations
there was much love in our marriage

Percy understood what I had been through
having also been through
his own kind of hell.

THURSDAY

CHAPTER TWENTY-THREE

After a good night's rest, Stevie felt energised for the first time in days. She dropped Izzy off at school and did some grocery shopping, stocking up the pantry and freezer with Monty's favourites in preparation for his return from hospital. She bought soy sauce and egg noodles, Asian greens and coriander. It seemed a shame to condemn the fresh tiger prawns to the freezer, but she wasn't exactly sure when he would be discharged and couldn't risk food poisoning on his first day home. Wait a minute, prawns were full of cholesterol, weren't they? Vegetable curry with lots of healthy chickpeas, she decided, that's what they'd have, and enough chilli to blow the tongue off a giraffe.

She pulled up outside their house and looked seaward. A row of conifers guarded the coarse lawn of the beachfront near the café. Before their curry, if Monty were up to it, they'd sit there on the bench near the swings and watch the sun set, talk about anything but work, talk about Izzy, talk about their new house.

She found the revised extension/renovation plans waiting in a cardboard tube in her letterbox. The architect must have dropped them off while she was out—God only knew she hadn't been home much over the last few days. There was a note saying that he'd implemented the changes they'd discussed at their last meeting, and as a result these plans would have to be re-submitted to the council. Christ, when was all this red tape and dilly-dallying going to end? Just as well she didn't have a sledgehammer close at hand or she would've been tempted to start the demolition herself.

She spent the afternoon at the hospital with Monty, but omitted to tell him the latest developments with Mrs Hardegan and what she'd found out about the baby's illegal adoption. Under normal circumstances she would have valued his input, but now she wanted him to think she had withdrawn or lost interest. She didn't think she could cope with any more staged heart attacks.

They discussed the revised plans, which lay stretched over his bed like an extra sheet. She'd also brought in some interior decorating magazines and they pored over them together, selecting fittings and furniture, trying to balance the old-world feel to which they aspired with the comforts of modern life.

'We'll need air-conditioning,' Monty said.

'I don't think so, too expensive and not necessary—besides, those things on the walls are a terrible eyesore. I'd prefer ceiling fans and sea breezes.'

'It doesn't have to be on the wall. I have a mate in the business, Frank Caravello, he'll be able to give us a good deal on ducting.'

'You have friends everywhere.'

Monty shrugged. 'All ex-cops who left the job early enough to start again with new careers ...' He broke off and gazed at the blank TV screen above his bed.

Stevie knew the direction his thoughts were going. 'I don't think you should be thinking about that now. The doctor said you should take one day at a time. You're still recovering; you mustn't start making crucial decisions just yet. The house should be giving you enough to think about for the moment.'

'If I'm not working, how can we pay for the house? We can't borrow any more money from your mother.'

Stevie rolled up the plans and slid them back into the cardboard tube, her way of indicating that the conversation was over. Her mother was a wealthy woman, having sold the family cattle station when prices were high. She'd be beside herself if she knew how stretched they were despite her generous loan, and it was something they were both determined to keep from her.

Once more Mont insisted that she and Izzy stay at her mother's for the night. 'And then after that, they'll be letting me out of this place and I can protect you.'

She smiled back at him, 'Sure you can,' and relaxed back into her chair. 'God, I'm looking forward to getting back to normal again.'

'I need to find some stairs.' He wriggled his eyebrows suggestively; money worries apparently forgotten.

'Our house has no stairs. Bad luck.'

'Then I'll practise on the beach steps.' He took hold of her arm and pulled her toward him, cupping her breast in his large hand and giving her a full kiss on the lips. 'Y'know,' he murmured as he continued to knead her flesh. 'I don't think I'm going to need to practise for this at all.'

The door whooshed open. 'Feeling better are we, Mr McGuire?' the soft-faced Irish nurse said as they quickly pulled apart.

'Home soon,' Monty said.

'Only if you behave yourself.'

For many years Stevie and her mother, Dot, had lived on the same street. It was a convenient arrangement that suited them both when Izzy was born and Stevie still very much on her own. Now, Dot's was almost half an hour's drive from their new place near the beach, though it still served as a home away from home for Izzy. Dot had a large backyard with a fishpond and a small gazebo. Her house was immaculate with deep spongy carpets, vanilla cream walls and a tasteful collection of antiques.

As if in keeping with the civilised surroundings, Izzy tended to behave like a model child when she stayed with her grandmother. Sometimes Stevie felt that Dot had no inkling about what the kid could be like at home, as if her tales of horror were exaggerated or made up. Which was why she couldn't help smiling when she opened the front door to the sound of Dot's raised voice and her own child wailing back at her.

'What's going on?' Stevie asked her mother, who appeared red-faced from the kitchen, blowing a loose tendril of silver-blonde hair from her eyes. Stevie gazed into her own clear-blue eyes looking back at her. They had the same colouring, were physically alike in so many ways other than height. Dot Hooper was ballet-dancer petite, whereas Stevie took her height from her father's side of the family. If she aged half as well as her mother, she reflected, she'd be happy. This reminded her of something. She hadn't yet seen the age-enhanced picture of Jennifer Granger, and made a mental note to ask Col if it was finished.

She tuned back in to what Dot was saying.

'She's had a bad day at school; said she got in trouble with the teacher for not bringing her reading book back this morning. She wanted me to drive all the way to your place and get it. I told her no, and now she's refusing to do her homework. The plumber didn't come, you know, the guest room loo is still blocked, and I can't find anyone to cart away that tree branch over the fence.'

'Sounds like you've had a bad day.'

'Tell me about it. About the only good thing that's happened is that one of Izzy's friends' mothers thought I was you. When I explained I was the grandmother, her eyes nearly popped out of her head. Maybe those herbal skin pills really *are* working.'

Or maybe, Stevie thought guiltily, I'm so rarely at school for pick-up, no one knows who I am.

I am a bad mother.

'I'll go and have a word with Izz,' she said, hiding the pang of self-knowledge.

Dot slipped the apron over her head and hung it over one of the hall hooks. 'You do that. I need some fresh air, won't be long—keep an eye on the roast will you? It'll need turning down soon.'

Dot closed the door behind her and Stevie let out a sigh of relief. She never liked disciplining Izzy when Dot was around: Dot who'd raised four children in the middle of nowhere and always knew best.

She found Izzy in the kitchen, head in her arms at the Baltic pine table. The oven sizzled gently, the delicious aroma of roast lamb wafting around the room.

If she hadn't known otherwise she'd have thought her

daughter had sneaked a peak at *Gone with the Wind* — she was sobbing up a storm worthy of Scarlett O'Hara. When Stevie asked what was up, Izzy repeated what Dot had said, and more. 'I left my book at home, that's why I couldn't hand it in. It's stupid living here with Nanna, stupid! I want Dad to come home so we can go back to the beach. I need my reading book and I need to go home now!'

The sizzle from the oven began to intensify, the roast snapped and crackled. Stevie turned the temperature down and swung sharply on her daughter. 'Enough of that — it'll take too long to drive home and get it now. It's getting late and Nanna's put a roast in the oven. Try and calm down, having a tantrum won't help.'

Izzy slapped her palms upon the table. 'But I have to do my reading!'

'Then we'll find something else for you to read.' Keeping her cool, Stevie reached for the Barbie backpack hanging on the back of the kitchen chair. It weighed a tonne, the amount of stuff these kids were expected to cart around on their backs never ceased to amaze her. She took the half-empty lunch box to the sink, binned the mashed contents and gave it a rinse, then dug into the bag again to see what else she could remove to lighten the load. Smelly sandshoes needed for PE tomorrow would have to stay; a Beanie Kid surely not needed at all, she left on the bench top. She reached for a bag of marbles, which weighed a kilo at least. With a petulant look Izzy told her to put them back, marble season had only just started — didn't she know anything?

Stevie pulled out a picture book. 'How about we read this?'

'Too babyish,' her daughter replied. Then she remembered

something and her mood instantly brightened. 'But there's something else down there Mum—here.' Izzy grabbed the bag. Delving to the bottom she handed Stevie a folded magazine. 'Maybe I could read this—it's got some really pretty ladies in it doing funny stuff.'

Stevie snatched the magazine from Izzy's hand and jumped to her feet, knowing immediately what the high-gloss magazine was about. Attempting to hide her fear she unfolded it at the sink with her back to her daughter. Her stomach churned as she leafed through the hard-core porn, the nausea soon replaced by flaming anger. She took a calming breath and put the magazine face down on the kitchen bench

'Izz,' she turned back, trying to keep her voice steady. 'Where did you get this?'

'A man gave it to me while I was waiting for Nan to pick me up from school. Can we read it now? Some of the pictures look *sooooo* weird, there was even a dog ...'

'What did this man look like?'

Izzy shrugged. 'Tall.'

The man who'd threatened her outside court was tall, Stevie remembered. 'As tall as Dad?'

'I dunno. Come on Mum ...'

'Did he give anything to any of the other children?'

'No, he came straight over to me.'

Hairs stood up on the back of Stevie's neck. 'As if he knew you?'

'Yeah, I think so,' said Izzy, 'But he didn't speak so it was hard to say.' She frowned. 'He just *looked* as if he knew me.' She lunged toward Stevie's pocket and tried to snatch the magazine. Stevie sidestepped and caught Izzy by the wrist harder than she'd meant too. The girl whined, more from frustration than the pain of Stevie's fingers. 'But I need to do my reading!'

The journey to their house by the beach passed by in a blur. Stevie could think of nothing but the filth she'd found in her daughter's backpack. The magazine was obviously a message. It told her they knew everything about her, even her daughter's name and where she went to school. It meant they must also know what she did for a living; that she dealt daily with the scum-of-the-earth who got their rocks off by preying on other people's children. They would know the effect this kind of message would have on her.

Now we have our sights on your child, Stevie Hooper.

The stakes couldn't be higher, the message clearly telling her to back off. But who was responsible? She racked her brains. The obvious contenders were the three paedophiles she'd recently helped lock away—but it was a bit late now, wasn't it? Surely the victimisation would have been carried out during the trial and not after. Unless of course, the motive was revenge, acted out by one of the many men involved in the paedophile ring still on the wrong side of the bars—God knows there were enough of them still lurking about. She'd not told her boss about the man who'd approached her outside the courtroom; it had seemed so trivial at the time, and she wasn't sure if she'd heard him correctly, let alone be able to describe him. Tall and fair, that was all she could remember.

Alternatively, this might have nothing to do with her previous case. Could the people traffickers be behind this? Unlikely, when they had no idea about her involvement with the Pavel investigation. The Crow was supposed to be Eurasian, which meant he was probably dark-haired, so he wasn't the man outside court. But he might be the guy who gave Izzy the mag—maybe the people traffickers couldn't be eliminated after all?

As she drove she took the magazine from the passenger seat and locked it in the glove box. She'd have to report the incident to Inspector Veitch and Angus Wong in the morning and cover all bases. Even if the offender turned out to be merely a random perv from the street, the matter would not be taken lightly. No matter how much irritation her interference on the Pavel case was causing, especially to Angus, cops always looked after their own.

It was dark by the time she pulled up outside her picket fence. In the distance she could hear the rumbling of breakers on the shore. She looked around the deserted street as she locked her car and walked cautiously toward the front gate. It was a corner block, the block next door vacant pending building and the neighbouring houses seemed a lot further away than they were. Her house was in darkness. She cursed herself for not thinking of leaving the lights on when she'd visited that morning.

She stopped before she reached the gate. Bloody hell. She clenched her fists as she looked down her front path. How dare they—no one was going to make her afraid of approaching her own house at night! She straightened her shoulders and forced herself to concentrate on what she'd come here to do. Izzy had said her reader was somewhere in the lean-to, maybe on the rug in front of the TV. As she placed her hand on the latch of the gate, she tried to remember if she'd seen the book there earlier.

A flickering in one of the front windows caught her eye. It wasn't there a moment ago. Simultaneously she became aware of an indistinct, smoky odour on the sea breeze. Then the light in the window blossomed.

A bright orange flash blinded her.

A deep boom hammered through her skull.

She dropped to the ground and covered her head with her arms as a sear of pain ripped into her left shoulder. The blast drove the air from her lungs and replaced it with choking black smoke. Shock waves rumbled through the pavement. Building materials whizzed and clattered in the air from all directions, thudding heavily to the ground around her.

The noise ceased as suddenly as it had started. Lights turned on in the neighbouring houses, windows stared at her like unfocused eyes. Dogs barked, doors slammed.

Still curled into a protective ball on the pavement, she heard the sound of running footsteps above the crackle of flames. Someone shouted, 'My God, what's happened?'

A female voice answered. 'Look, there's someone over there!'

Footsteps pounded the pavement towards her.

Stevie slowly began to uncoil, first her legs, then her back. Other than her shoulder she could detect no other areas of damage. Deafened by the explosion she had trouble hearing what the man crouching by her side was saying to her. The roar of flames filled her head. A sudden crash of falling timber made her gasp and crushed the words struggling to leave her mouth. She tried again to gather her breath. 'We need to get away from here … there might be another explosion,' she panted.

Shaking arms pulled her to her feet. She hissed an expletive when a hand was placed on her shoulder. 'Sorry, dear,' an elderly male voice said. 'Needs must.' He guided her wobbling steps further down the street. She looked to the sky. Above them, peeping through a cloud of oily smoke, the moon glowed.

'It's your house, isn't it? Susan and I have been meaning to introduce ourselves,' the old man said, a pattern of flickering flames dancing across the crevices of his face. 'But we never expected it to be like this. I'm Ted. You'll be all right, don't worry. Susan's called an ambulance. The police and fire brigade are on their way too.'

'My house.' Stevie struggled to free herself from the man's grip. *Our house.* She tried to turn her head but pain shot up her neck, causing her to hiss out an expletive. She shook herself free of the man's guiding arms and almost stumbled at the sight that confronted her, her house that was no longer a house. The blown front window was awash with fire, the central part of the roof collapsed. A quick glimpse around told her that none of the other houses in the vicinity had been affected by the blast—she had to be grateful for something, she supposed.

Susan hurried over. 'We must get her off the street.'

Ted agreed with his wife, then said to Stevie, 'Never trust the wiring of these old houses.'

Stevie knew too well it wasn't the bloody wiring, but she'd let the old man think what he liked. Susan gave her a gentle push and attempted to guide her away from the inferno. Anger flooded through her, then an enraging sadness. Ignoring the pain from her shoulder, Stevie shrugged herself free from the fussing woman. She wanted to scream out, had to hold herself in check. *Bloody bastards, look what you've done to my house!*

The police and the fire truck pulled up simultaneously. With her left arm clamped to her side, she ran over to them, telling the firemen which parts of the house to save first, begging them to go easy with the foam. She yelled to the police, telling them her house had been the target of an attack. Her sentences, she realised were running ten to the dozen in a gabble of nonsense worthy of Mrs Hardegan. She fell silent. Froze. Gazed at the sympathetic faces surrounding her. A strong arm supported her waist and she found herself propelled toward the open door of an ambulance. The attendant gritted his teeth and firmly helped her in, probably having already pegged her as one of those silly, hysterical females.

'I'm not going in that,' she yelled before collapsing on the trolley. 'Our house,' she heard herself repeating again and again until the attendant silenced her with an oxygen mask.

What the hell was she going to tell Monty?

but I could never put meat on
those bones of his

Percy died
not long after Ralph was born

CHAPTER TWENTY-FOUR

Just after midnight, against medical advice and with sixteen stitches in her shoulder, Stevie discharged herself from the hospital and caught a cab back to her ruined home. The fire trucks had left, but a police incident van remained. She heard voices, members of the arson squad sifting through the wreckage, looking for clues as to the cause of the explosion, and called to them across her front garden. Yesterday her garden had been filled with lavender, frangipani and oleander; now it looked like something from the Gaza Strip. A man in black police overalls appeared through a hole that had once been the front door.

'I thought you were in hospital,' he said through the rising tendrils of smoke that separated them. He picked his way through the rubble towards her and said his name was Paul Aubin. He squinted back at her through the spotlight. White lines threaded through the soot around his eyes, etching out his concern.

'I had some glass in my shoulder; they pulled it out and stitched me up. There's was nothing more they could do,' she said.

His pause told her he didn't believe a word of it. 'And

you're with Central, yeah?'

She had trouble hearing what he said; her ears were still ringing with the sound of the explosion. She asked him to repeat himself and studied his lips carefully. 'Yes, Central.' After a moment's hesitation she said, 'I think this might be something to do with a job I'm working on.'

'That figures.'

'Why, what have you found out?'

He scrutinised her again. 'Are you sure you're okay? You're as white as a sheet.'

'Halle Berry would look pale in this light.' She shouldn't have shrugged; the local anaesthetic had worn off and the pain in her shoulder jabbed raw again. She masked it with a smile.

He chuckled, became serious one more, absently peeling the charred paintwork from her front picket fence. 'You opened the gate and ...' he smacked his hands together, 'Boom.'

Had she only imagined the flicker of flames in the windows immediately prior to the explosion? She tried to remember as she stared at the gate. Smoke-blackened and blistered on the inside and hanging on only one hinge, the frame was still relatively intact. 'Surely the gate wasn't booby trapped—it would've been blown to smithereens,' she said.

'No. The bomb was in the house. If the gate had been booby trapped, or if you'd been home five minutes earlier, we'd still be scraping you off the rubble.'

Stevie swallowed, rubbed her face with her hands. Despite having been cleaned up in hospital, she could still detect the acrid smell of smoke on her skin. 'I would normally be home at this time, only tonight I was staying with my mother. My daughter would have been here too ...' The ground began to sway. She steadied herself with a hand on the fence.

'You were very lucky,' Aubin said.

She bit her bottom lip until she tasted salty blood and deliberately flexed her shoulder. The pain helped her focus. 'So what caused it?' It was a relief to hear the steadiness of her voice.

'I'll show you if you're up to it. You might be able to help us out with a few things, anyway.'

He offered her his arm and she took it without hesitation. To hell with keeping up appearances—right now she really was a helpless female. They negotiated the rubble of her front path, climbed the singed steps and he steered her around a ragged patch of splintered timber on the front veranda. They entered the black hole where the front door had been. The heavy jarrah door with the colourful leadlight was one of the original features they'd planned on saving. Some of the leadlight had ended up in her shoulder. She wondered where the rest had landed.

In the front passage, the wallpaper—ugly stuff put up by the previous owners—was soggy and smoke-blackened, but the bedrooms and lounge room, apart from water damage, still appeared to be structurally stable.

'It gets worse, I'm afraid,' Aubin said as he led her to where the kitchen had been. She stood in the middle of the crater and turned a slow circle, trying to get her bearings. Some twisted pipes were all that remained of the sink, but the oven and the kitchen furniture seemed to have vanished into thin air. Above them, stars winked through a jagged hole in the roof.

'The stove's in the backyard,' Aubin said as if reading her

mind. 'Funnily enough it doesn't even look damaged.'

'Where was the bomb placed, do you know?'

He walked over to an intact sidewall, bricks peeping through torn plaster, and pointed to the ground. 'You had a cupboard here, right? It looks like the bomb was placed on one of the lower shelves. We've found explosive residue on the ground.'

'A cupboard?' Stevie queried, her mind racking to what was here before. 'No. Monty's fish tank was there.'

Aubin looked to be assessing her for shell shock. 'No way was that bomb in a fish tank.'

'The tank was on top of a cabinet with doors and shelves for the pump and other paraphernalia.'

Aubin relaxed. 'That makes sense, a good place to hide it.'

Someone had been in her house, poking around in the cupboards, violating her home. The nausea rippling through her stomach was the same as when she'd found the porn magazine in Izzy's bag. She gritted her teeth and prayed she wouldn't throw up.

'We think it was an incendiary bomb,' Aubin continued, 'but can't be certain until the chemical tests are back.'

'Incendiary?'

'We've found fragments of a metal tube which had been filled with a chemical mixture. An inverted glass vial of sulphuric acid is put in one end and its hole blocked up with cork or paper. The acid eventually eats through to the mixture of chemicals, resulting in a very hot fire. It's a crude device, but effective never the less, often favoured by Special Forces or arsonists who don't care for the high tech alternatives.'

'Old school?' said Stevie.

'Possibly. Or cocky to the point of stupidity. It's an inexact science.'

'And the explosion?'

'Gas cylinders, wiring, aerosols, pool chemicals, paint tins ... there's all kinds of household things that could have exploded on contact with such a hot fire.'

'But how did the guy know when I'd be home?'

'Maybe he knew you wouldn't be home, it wasn't meant to kill you, just warn you.'

Or play with me, Stevie thought; it was the kind of thing The Crow seemed to enjoy doing, and there was more than one way of being burned alive. There was no denying it now. The attempt on their lives in Fremantle, the magazine in the backpack—they knew exactly who she was and that she was on to them. Mamasan and The Crow, it had to be them. 'They've attempted to kill me before,' she said quietly.

'Well then ...'

'Look,' her voice rose, she gripped Aubin's arm. 'It's very important that this isn't mentioned to the press. Have you given them a statement?'

'No, not yet.'

'We can't have the offenders thinking we're onto them, can we? When you do speak to the press, tell them that it was most likely faulty wiring which caused the fire and explosion—it's what the people in the street seem to think, anyway.' Her grip on his arm was too tight, she realised. She quickly let him go. Right now she couldn't have cared less what the offenders thought; it was Monty's reaction that worried her. She couldn't hide the fire from him, but she would sure as hell try to prevent him from finding out what had really caused it; for the moment, anyway.

She picked her way to the edge of the crater and stood on the edge, gazing across at the blackness of her back garden. Something was missing, but she couldn't work out what. She pointed helplessly into the void. And then a thought struck her. 'It's gone,' she said shaking her head and gazing around with wonder. Aubin moved to stand next to her. 'What is?'

'The lean-to: the most ugly, jerry built structure you could ever have imagined. We were going to knock it down …' Stevie laughed. Aubin gaped back at the tears of anger, shock and mirth rolling down her face.

My poor boy
I was a refrigerator mother
What those American psycho-quacks
call it

no wonder really
no wonder
Ralph turned out like he did

FRIDAY

CHAPTER TWENTY-FIVE

From the bus window Mai watched the spring green of the city slowly merging into the dustier colours of the bush. Then they came upon a swathe of wildflowers, like jewels scattered by a giant's hand, stretching for kilometres along the roadside. The bus followed the path of flowers as they slowly dried and turned to red dust.

Lin dozed and fretted at Mai's side, unable to find a comfortable position, her cheek hot and red from resting against the sticky bus window. Mai changed places with her, gently pulled the girl's head into her shoulder and stroked her hair. When Lin finally settled, her hair tickled Mai's face like a silken net.

The girls in the front of the bus were singing a song by Pumpuang, 'Love is Like Bitter Medicine'. Rick yelled at them to shut up, but the sad melody remained in Mai's head. She found she could recall every word of the song as she sat there, jolting along in the bus.

It was a hit song played frequently on the radio when she still lived with her family. Her mother would bring the battery-powered radio into the rice field and together they would sing the popular songs to distract them from the ache in their stooped backs. She closed her eyes and thought of everything that had happened to her since then. A lot of it was bad, but there was still plenty of good, too. With the Chinaman she'd sampled a world she'd never known to exist outside her father's movies: French champagne, the rustle of silk against her skin, luxury yachts and expensive cars. This was life as it could be, and to this she aspired with a passion almost as desperate as her need to find her son.

No, she thought as she clenched her jaw, blocking the song from her mind. She didn't miss her old peasant life; not one little bit. She hated what she had now, but she hated what she'd left behind even more.

Their stops were kept to a minimum, with just enough time to fill up with petrol and use the toilet facilities. The roadhouses became smaller the further north they travelled, and less busy. Theirs had been the only vehicle outside the pumps at the last one. Rick and Jimmy Jack veered from the main road whenever possible. The drive would take longer, Mai had heard the men say, but it meant they would have less chance of the rusty old bus being stopped by the police. The men carried the fake IDs in a hold-all by Jimmy Jack's feet. Although they were good forgeries, they still didn't want them scrutinised by over-vigilant cops.

Rick had played the fool for most of the journey, his stupid chatter interspersed with crazy laughter and Mai could see he was getting on Jimmy Jack's nerves. A while ago the smaller man had unsheathed his knife, now he blew on it, polished and fiddled with it, muttering obscenities and shooting Rick dark looks.

Oblivious to his companion's sour humour, Rick continued

to rehearse what he'd say to the police if they were stopped. He threw a pill into his mouth and snapped his jaws around it like a dog.

He altered his voice, attempting to make it sound less rough.

'Good day officer,' he practised, slurring his words, bouncing up and down in his seat as he drove. 'Yeah, this is a tour bus and these girls are all members of a touring Thai netball team ... You wanna examine their papers? Sure can. Yeah, that's right, we're going to Hell-an-Back ... You want your dick sucked, officer?' He laughed uproariously at his joke.

Jimmy Jack didn't flicker a smile; seemed absorbed with cleaning his nails with the long knife. He'd told the girls that if they spoke to anyone outside the bus, or tried to escape, he'd slit their throats and leave them in the desert for the dingoes.

They stopped at another roadhouse. Mai, being the most trusted, received permission to take a short walk on her own. She scuffed along the red dusty road until the roadhouse generator became no more than a distant throb. The air seared her lungs; the wind on her face scorched like a hair dryer. She'd never imagined that air could feel so dry, the earth look so red or the sky appear so huge and blue. The baked ground felt like concrete under her tender feet, yet all around her, the clumps of grass looked as soft as cotton wool.

She wondered what it would be like to just keep on walking through this desiccated landscape of stunted shrubs and red dust. Maybe if she walked far enough, she'd come across a farmhouse where kind people would take her in, the woman plump and motherly, the man strong and protective.

They would help her get Niran back, help her settle and make this place her home.

She continued to daydream as she walked against the wall of heat, slowing down in the small patches of shade and fantasising about a life that could be. A creature of the night, it was hard to imagine adapting to this country of dry, dazzling brightness.

An eagle soared above her head. It was far bigger than any she had seen at home and big enough to shade her like a parasol as she walked. The grass caught her attention again. She wanted to touch it, see if it was as real and as soft as it looked. She stooped to caress it and pulled her hand away with a sudden shock of pain. Looking down she saw a tattoo of tiny red pricks patterning her palm.

It was a sharp awakening.

In a nearby bush mischievous spirits disguised as small, finch-like birds twittered and laughed at her discomfort. The eagle dropped upon an animal nearby and the unseen victim cried out. No, she realised then, she hated this place as much as any other. Nothing would induce her to run off into it. It was too big, too empty, too dry, and like everything she had encountered since leaving home, that which looked kind invariably wasn't.

Mai had always lived in close proximity to others. The greatest punishment imaginable to her was to be left alone. Surely, anything was better than this. Turning her back on the phantom birds and the evil pricking grass, she hurried back to the others and the safety of the bus.

The countryside changed again. Every now and then the ground would drop away on either side of the road in gradations of orange and red. The gorges here were so steep it looked as if the ogress Pantoorat had gashed them from the primeval earth with her axe.

They'd been driving almost non-stop for nearly twenty hours and no one had had much sleep. Mai's eyes were full of grit, as were her clothes, hair and toes, and her palm still stung from the prickly grass. But however bad she felt, she knew Rick fared worse. To counter the effect of the ganja he'd smoked at the last roadhouse, he'd been devouring the small white pills as if they were sweets, rattling them down with water from a plastic bottle. Mai swapped seats with one of the other girls and sat in the single seat near the front of the bus, close behind him. He shook his head to and fro to help wash the pills down. Dandruff speckled the neck of his black T-shirt. If she had Jimmy Jack's knife, she thought coolly, she was close enough to reach out and cut his throat.

The tension crackled and jumped between the two men as if the air were filled with *goong den,* dancing shrimp. Jimmy Jack kept telling Rick to pull over and swap seats so he could drive and Rick kept on refusing. Jimmy Jack shouted something and Rick swore back. Rick turned and yelled at the girls to shut up. His eyes were netted with red veins, his pupils wide as satellite dishes. No one had said a word.

Jimmy Jack raked through the bag at his feet and produced his mobile phone. 'Pull over now fucker, or I'll call the Mamasan, tell her what an arse-wipe you are.'

He'd already called the Mamasan, several hours ago; Mai knew that, she'd heard him talking to her on his mobile phone during their last stop.

'Don't be a jerk, JJ. She just wants us there fast, doesn't give a flying fuck how,' Rick said.

'We won't be getting there at all at this rate.'

'And we'll be arriving a day late with you driving like a grey nomad—what'll the Mamasan say when she finds out she's lost a day's income?' Grey nomad was the name the men gave to the old people who towed caravans and held up traffic. Mai had heard them say the phrase a lot since the beginning of the journey and it was usually accompanied by much swearing.

To prove his point, Rick surged forward, almost nudging the caravan crawling up the road in front of them. Leaning on the horn, he swung into the middle of the road to overtake, only just missing the gravelly shoulder and deep drop on the other side.

Jimmy Jack swore, the girls behind screamed. The open road stretched before them once more across the desert, smooth, straight and empty. Rick laughed and turned to them. 'Scared youse, did I, girls? Don't worry little darlings, you're in safe hands with Uncle Rick.'

With disgust, Jimmy Jack threw his phone to the floor of the bus. 'Out of fucking range. Pull over arsehole,' he said. He put his knife to Rick's throat and buried the blade in his beard, stopping just before it reached skin. Mai's stomach lurched. Pepped up with speed, she knew Rick's reactions would be unpredictable at best.

'You're a pussy, JJ, you wouldn't dare,' Rick growled, keeping his bleary eyes fixed on the road ahead.

Mai leaned over and placed her hand upon Jimmy Jack's shoulder. It was all very well for her to dream about doing this herself, but JJ doing it now was a crazy idea. With her other hand she covered his on the knife and carefully tried to ease the blade from Rick's throat. 'Please ...'

Jimmy Jack shrugged her off, swore and kept his grip tight upon the knife.

Rick slammed a heavy foot onto the accelerator. The sudden jolt of speed made Jimmy Jack drop the knife and lunge with both hands for the dashboard.

'You want me to pull over, JJ?' Rick shouted as he gave the wheel a sharp left turn. 'You got it!' The bus careered off the road, smashed through the safety barriers and commenced a flight path across a deep ravine.

Everyone screamed. For several seconds they flew through the air.

Hung there.

And then they dropped.

They hit the ground, catapulted around the bus in a tangle of arms and legs, loose luggage and shattered glass. Mai's head hit the roof of the bus. Something slammed into her leg. The snap of bone, jarring pain, she felt as if her leg had shattered into sharp splinters. Her screams joined those of the others as the bus rolled into darkness.

i Sometimes thought
Ralph did'nt belong to Percy at all
I thought he
belonged to one of my rapists

ridiculous
but I could'nt love him

he got back at me did'nt he
in the end

SATURDAY

CHAPTER TWENTY-SIX

Stevie gritted her teeth against the pain in her shoulder as Monty pulled her into a hug. She speared her fingers up his neck and into his russet hair and massaged his scalp in the way he liked. They stayed like that for some time until she felt the cold begin to leave her bones. As he continued to hold her she marvelled how almost everything that was precious in her life came from this man: Izzy, the life they shared as a family. The house didn't matter. What mattered was that Monty had pulled through the operation and within a few months he would be as good as, if not better than before his health problems had started.

'Are we going to have to start all over again?' Monty asked.

Stevie avoided the soft brown eyes that seemed to stare straight through her. Pressing her cheek into his neck she breathed his scent, surprisingly untarnished by hospital odours. 'I don't know, Mont, I really don't know.' Who gives a stuff about bricks and mortar? she said to herself. It was only a house. She would not read anything more into it.

Nevertheless she'd still not told him about the explosion or her trip to the emergency department, only told him about the fire, what she'd told her mother and Izzy too.

'It's my fault,' he said when they finally pulled apart. 'I should have taken that first electrician's quote instead of farting around for the cheapest. If I wasn't such a tight-arse the wiring would all be done by now.'

Stevie forced a smile. 'You're a Scot. You recycle dental floss.'

'How's Izz taking it?'

'She's furious, blames me because we weren't there when it happened. If we were, she thinks we could have put the fire out and saved your fish, our computers, her toys—she doesn't give a stuff about anything else.'

'Thank God you weren't there.' He hesitated, unusual for him. 'I don't seem to have much luck with fish do I?' His last fish had been 'murdered' a couple of years ago by a couple of thugs who'd broken into his flat. 'Maybe I should find a new hobby.'

She knew he felt the same as she did about their house. The flippant comment, meant to trivialise their predicament, was contradicted by a look in his eyes she couldn't meet. Was he thinking about their relationship too?

Surely not practical, pragmatic Monty.

She slipped off the bed and kissed his cheek. 'I can't stay. I need to get to Dot's for a shower and a rest before meetings with the architect, the engineer and the insurance guy.' And the arson squad, and Inspector Veitch and Angus, and ... She wondered when this nightmare would end.

So much for the best laid plans: Stevie headed toward the MCI car yard, having only minutes ago been torn from Dot's soft spare bed by the trilling of her phone. Col hadn't said much;

only that she was to meet him, Fowler and Tony Pruitt asap. Her stiff shoulder objected with every turn of the wheel as she pulled into a parking spot. Pushing through the unlocked gate, she found the men grouped around the battered remains of a Nissan minibus.

'Sorry to get you out of bed, heard you had a hard night,' Col said as she approached. 'But I thought there'd be even more trouble if I didn't call you about this.'

Stevie nodded a greeting to Pruitt and Fowler. 'What's all this about, Col?'

'A horror bus crash south of Newman—six dead and two in the ICU, brought down here by Flying Doctor. No one was wearing seatbelts.'

Stevie regarded the concertinaed hunk of metal and wondered how anyone could have survived at all. 'You got this wreck down to Perth quickly—when did it happen?'

'Yesterday morning. We had it trucked down, it's only just arrived,' Col said. 'The first cop on the scene was suspicious about the passengers and called me almost straightaway, suspecting the female passengers to be illegal immigrants. Only a couple of the girls survived, but they're critical, too sick to be questioned. Two Australian men, probably travelling in the front of the bus, are also dead. We're running ID checks on them now.'

'How can you tell the girls were illegals?' Stevie asked, making brief eye contact with Fowler.

'Come and I'll show you.'

As they followed Pruitt toward his demountable office, Fowler said to Stevie, keeping his voice low, 'I hear there was a fire at your place last night—what happened?

Stevie's mouth fell into a grim line. 'Faulty wiring.'

He shot her a look of concern. 'Really?'

She indicated to Col with a tilt of her head. *Don't tell him, he might tell Monty.* Fowler nodded back and rubbed his nose, 'Ah.'

Almost every spare inch of space in the demountable office was covered in bulging plastic bags. Pruitt explained that the personal effects were being temporarily stored here while they were waiting for transport to the larger storage facilities at the depot in Maylands. All the bags were labelled. Detailed descriptions of the contents filled several separate files stacked on the desk.

Stevie gestured to a metal trunk on the floor near Pruitt's desk. 'What's in there?'

'Evening gowns of varying sizes, and expensive lingerie,' Col said. 'Also paste jewellery, bags of sex toys and bulk packets of condoms. The contents had spilled down the ravine during the crash and alerted the attending officer as to what he might be dealing with. The presence of all those Asian girls in the bus confirmed his suspicions.'

'And here?' Stevie pointed to a collection of luggage and smaller individually bagged items laid out on a trestle table in the middle of the office.

'We think these must be the girls' personal possessions; most of the bags contain simple outfits, underwear and toiletries. Other stuff from the bus spilled onto the ground. It's been photographed, boxed and labelled.'

'Jeez, those guys in Newman have been busy,' Fowler said.

Stevie scanned the pathetic amount of personal possessions, donned gloves and, with Col's permission, joined Fowler in searching through some of the smaller bags:

CDs, iPods, magazines, a stuffed toy in the shape of a white kitten with an embroidered love heart on its chest. Izzy had something similar. With an ache sharper than the wound in her shoulder, she wondered if it had survived the fire.

She dug into a small Thai Airways holdall and removed a green silk housedress, holding it up for Fowler to see.

He looked at it and shrugged. Amazed that he didn't recognise it, she pulled a 'duh' face at him. After all that fuss over her and Skye's initial interference, surely he knew what he was looking at. Stevie carefully laid the dress out on the table, then went to her handbag and removed the button that Fowler had refused to take from her what seemed like a lifetime ago. Taking the button from the paper bag she held it against one of the buttons on the dress.

'A match.' Fowler shook his head in amazement. He pointed at the gap left by the missing button. 'And look, there's a tear in the dress where the button was ripped off.'

'Yes. Skye thought she must have caught it on the gate.'

Col and Pruitt stared at the two of them blankly.

'This button,' Stevie explained, holding it for them to see, 'was found outside the Pavel house just after Skye and I came across the abandoned baby. At one time or another, one of these girls must have visited there.'

'Which means at the very least there's a connection between them and Jon Pavel, a suspected people trafficker. It could very well mean,' Fowler added with a glance at Stevie, 'that one of these girls was responsible for feeding the baby after the parents disappeared.'

'Wasn't the baby Asian?' Col asked.

'Sure was.' Fowler grinned at Stevie, his face transformed with a boyish look she'd not seen before.

'We need to speak to the surviving girls,' she said.

'I'll ring the hospital, but I don't think you'll be allowed to see them yet,' Col said.

Stevie said to Fowler, 'That gives us plenty of time to organise an interpreter.'

'Do you know the names of the survivors?' Fowler asked Col.

'One of the girls was conscious when the officers reached her, said her name was Mai and the other survivor, Lin. These names don't correspond to any of the documentation found in the bags, but the papers are probably fakes anyway. We think Lin and Mai are their correct names. Some of the suitcases and the gowns are named: Kitty, Babe, Vixen—take your pick,' Col said, wryly.

Stevie clapped Fowler on the arm. 'Come on, we've got work to do.'

'Wait,' Pruitt called out, 'there's a couple more things you need to see before you go.'

Stevie turned from the door, struggling to curb her impatience. With great mental effort she forced herself to stand still and not fidget as Pruitt took a couple of the labelled bags from his desk and handed one to each of them. Fowler held up the bottle of pills he'd been given and gave them a shake. 'Amphetamines?'

Pruitt nodded. 'Dexies probably, but we're still waiting on the test results. They were found on the floor on the front passenger side.'

Stevie was only listening to this exchange; her attention was focused on the bag she'd been given and the long-bladed knife inside it. She carefully felt down the length of the blade, noticing the small serrations and the sharp pointed end, smeared with what appeared to be blood. It hadn't completely dried and clung to the inside of the plastic evidence bag sticky as jam.

'Samples have been taken,' Pruitt said as Stevie continued her examination of the knife. 'Although we already have a pretty good idea which victim the blood was from.'

'Who?' Stevie and Fowler asked Col simultaneously.

'The paramedics on the scene think that one of the men's injuries was not immediately life threatening, that he might have survived the crash with prompt treatment. It was the slashed throat that killed him.'

A pause while Stevie and Fowler considered this.

Stevie held up the knife to Pruitt. 'Where was this found?'

'Lying on the ground between him and the other male. The other guy was flung through the windscreen and died instantly from a broken neck.'

We were having words

There I go again
precious words

Ralph wanted to sell the house
I said no
I questioned him

he told me what he was doing
and what I had done

SUNDAY

CHAPTER TWENTY-SEVEN

Most of the flowers in the vases had died and the green tinge
of stagnant water overrode the smell of disinfectant in the
hospital room. 'It's a sign,' Monty said, wrinkling his nose. 'I
knew it; I've outstayed my welcome.'

The surgeon, following closely on Stevie's heels that
morning, had announced that Monty could go home the next
day.

Stevie had been waiting anxiously for days for Monty to be
given the all clear. Now, after everything that had happened,
she wished he could remain in hospital just a bit longer, out
of harm's way. At least until she could drag herself from the
mire into which she felt she had sunk. It didn't seem to worry
him that they would have to stay with Dot, but it worried her.
Despite her bricks and mortar mantra, it felt as if they'd taken
a step back in their relationship.

While her mind had been shooting off at dozens of
tangents ranging from people traffickers to medications,
physios to paedophiles to pornographic magazines, house
fires to change-of-address notifications, Monty's thoughts
were focused on the minibus crash. He turned from where
he had been standing at the window watching the traffic

crawling below, hands deep in his dressing gown pockets.

'Any news about the two dead men from the bus?' he asked, lowering himself gingerly onto the hard chair alongside Stevie's.

'The fingerprint results are back,' Stevie said, rocking back with her feet resting on the bed, attempting a look of relaxed calm. 'The one with the slashed throat was Rick Notting. He'd been in and out prison for most of his life for a variety of charges ranging from GBH, possession with intent to sell and, in later years, procurement. The other guy, Jimmy Jack Robinson, is a known pimp, but clever or lucky enough to have avoided doing time, so we don't have much on him.'

'Where are they from?'

'Both of their driver's licences list false names and addresses. But through their real names and social security records, Fowler has been able to trace their last known abode as a Northbridge address with Robinson's name on the lease. When Fowler and his people arrived, the joint was being thoroughly gone over by a group of professional cleaners who told them a woman phoned the job in and paid by credit card. She said her name was Joyce Grenfell.' That name. Stevie tugged at a thought that remained hidden. How many people out there, under a certain age, would even know who the old British actress was?

'Someone was having a laugh at our expense?' Monty said.

She frowned, still puzzled by the choice of alias. 'Yeah, surprise, surprise—but the transaction did go through.'

'Stolen card.'

'Fowler's following that lead too.'

'What about the knife?'

'We think it belonged to Robinson—his prints are all over it. Wayne put word out on the street for information and one of his sources came back to him saying they vaguely knew of this Robinson guy—Wayne said his informant was very careful about distancing himself—said that Robinson always carried a distinctive fishing knife ...' Stevie paused, pulled at her ponytail. 'But another print, also isolated from the handle, belonged to one of the girls.'

Monty's eyebrows shot up. 'They think one of the girls might've done Rick Notting in?'

Stevie shrugged. 'Melissa Hurst hasn't finished the autopsy, but I guess when she examines the throat wound, she'll be able to work out the angle of entry. We might be able to figure it out from there.'

'Do you have a seating plan for the bus?'

'No one was wearing seat belts, bodies were flung all over the place, with the two men and the body of a girl ending up outside. SOCO and MCI are dealing with the problem now.'

'Wouldn't the steering wheel have stopped the driver from going through the window?'

'The bus door slid open, they think the driver fell out.'

Monty got up from his chair and began scooping up the get well cards that filled every available surface in the room. After glancing through them all, he put a handmade creation from Izzy into his pocket and tossed the others into the bin. 'You and Fowler getting on a bit better these days?'

Stevie made a balancing motion with her hands.

'Sounds like he's doing a good job on all this following up. Angus was in to see me yesterday; he's still pissed with you, even if Fowler isn't.'

'He'll get over it.' Stevie moved over to the bin, pulled

out the discarded cards and shuffled through them before tucking them into her bag. Monty made no comment except to turn his eyes upwards.

'Back to the Northbridge house,' she said, thinking it was a good thing they still had so much to talk about; the last thing she wanted to discuss now was office politics. 'It was obviously being used as a brothel, fitted out with several cubicles as well as a dormitory-like bedroom and a bar downstairs. Fowler managed to get hold of some prints before the cleaners wiped the place clean. Some of them matched those of Notting and Robinson; the others are still being compared to the dead and surviving girls. Which reminds me.' She looked at her watch. 'Fowler and I have a meeting with the interpreter in about five minutes. The doctors says one of the girls is well enough now to be questioned.'

Monty moved to follow Stevie from the room, but she stopped him with a hand upon his shoulder. 'The girl's been traumatised enough, Mont. She's already going to have to face me, Col, Fowler and the interpreter—one more person will be one too many.'

Monty gave her one of his dog-in-the-pound looks. 'Of course I wasn't going to participate in the questioning. I was merely going to accompany you upstairs. I do need to exercise, you know.'

Stevie knew he would try get away with it if he could. No matter how much Monty had been talking about retirement, being a cop was as natural to him as breathing, and he couldn't help himself.

He walked with her to the lifts where they met Fowler and Col and the pathologist, Melissa Hurst. Fowler explained that the interpreter was running late, but as they'd run into

Hurst in the foyer just after she'd finished the autopsy on Rick Notting, they'd decided to hold an impromtu case conference. Wayne and Angus were to meet them shortly in the doctors' common room downstairs.

'I suppose I'd better get back to bed,' Monty said, making no move other than to look expectantly from one face to another.

'If I were your surgeon,' Hurst regarded him sharply over her half-moon glasses,' I wouldn't want you wandering around the hospital, discharge tomorrow or not—there's no resuss trolley in the common room, y'know.'

Monty looked down at the diminutive older woman, opened his mouth and closed it again. Turning on his slippered heel he muttered, 'I know when I'm not wanted.'

Hurst shot Stevie a wink. They both watched as he made his way back to his room, growing taller and straighter with every step he took.

Hurst took them downstairs to the semi-deserted common room where they met with Angus and Wayne. Wayne acknowledged Stevie with a bear-like clap to her sore shoulder, which almost made her cry out. Angus gave her a smile, not quite as frosty as it could have been. 'Sorry to hear about your house,' he said, pulling up a chair beside her. 'The arson squad seems to have it under control, but I still want to look into it.'

'Me too, just as soon I come up for air. But please, Angus,' she put her hand on his arm, 'don't tell Monty what caused it. He's doing so well, a shock like this could set him back.'

'He'll need to know it was a deliberate attack.'

'I'll tell him when he's fully recovered or when this case is wrapped, but not 'til then. Have you had any luck with tracing the man who gave the mag to Izzy?'

Angus frowned. 'No one outside the school seems to remember seeing the man at all, can't tell us anything ...'

'Thanks for meeting me here,' Hurst broke in, addressing the team gathered around the table. 'The Notting autopsy is the only one I've had the chance to complete so far, and I've still got a queue of trolleys in the basement waiting for me.'

'Wish I was that popular,' Wayne said.

Unsmiling, Hurst reached into her briefcase and handed out colour photos of the deceased, some taken at the scene and some from Notting's autopsy itself.

Stevie examined the pictures, interior shots of the bus showing portions of dark-haired girls squeezed between crumpled seats and twisted metal, another girl thrown free and clearly dead. She focused mainly on a shot of Notting lying on his back outside the bus. In his case, the sadness she usually felt at viewing such scenes was absent. He reminded her of a wolf, his lupine grin eerily mimicked by the deep red slash in his throat, exposing slashed blood vessels and a gaping trachea. Flies spotted the pool of congealing blood in which he lay; the vivid stains of his shirt looked alive and creeping under her gaze. A limp male hand, presumably belonging to Jimmy Jack Robinson, was visible at the very edge of the frame, the knife on the ground between them.

Col put down the pile of photos he'd been leafing through. 'The cause of death looks pretty obvious to me; what else have you got for us, Melissa?'

'His blood contained a cocktail of chemicals—high doses of amphetamines, sedatives and marijuana, which could explain the randomness of the accident. The guy was as high as a kite and would have been totally out of control. And if he was the driver, well ... he was an accident waiting to happen.'

'That makes sense,' Angus said. 'Pruitt's report states

there were no signs of brake marks on the bitumen. It was as if he deliberately drove straight over the ravine.'

'But how do we know he was the driver?' Stevie asked.

'MCI are still busy working out body projectiles, but they think from the position he was lying in, he most probably fell out of the driver's side door,' Angus told her.

'But they can't be certain, surely,' Wayne queried the pathologist. 'If he was alive, might he not have moved or crawled away from where he landed when he first hit the dirt?'

'Unlikely, Sergeant, given that his spinal cord was severed in the T3 and T4 region,' Hurst said.

'So he was paralysed?'

'If he'd lived he'd have been a paraplegic from the lesion down. At the time of the accident, due to shock and swelling, he probably wouldn't have been able to move a muscle.'

Everyone around the table paused to consider this.

'Is it possible that someone cut his throat while he was still driving the bus?' Stevie queried.

'Only if someone had a death wish,' Wayne scoffed.

'These girls might not feel they had much to live for,' Stevie said, exchanging a glance with Hurst, who agreed with a barely perceptible nod of her head.

'Okay then, could Jimmy Jack have threatened him by putting the knife against his throat? It's a sharp knife—his hand might have slipped if the bus hit a bump,' Angus suggested.

Hurst allowed a slight smile; she enjoyed listening to the detectives trying to work it out for themselves. Stevie knew that she probably had the correct card up her sleeve, but wouldn't produce it until she was sure every possibility had been covered, and then her word would be final. As well as

Chief of Forensics, she lectured in pathology at UWA. She loved to teach, and could never let an opportunity pass her by. They had all learned a lot from Professor Melissa Hurst.

'What about the angle of the wound?' Angus asked.

'Left to right slash,' Hurst replied.

'Left to right,' he mused. 'Meaning our offender was right handed.'

Stevie pushed away from the table and stood behind Wayne. 'I need to get something clear here.' Reaching for a butter knife from the table, she told him to hold still. With her left hand pulling back upon his forehead, she held the knife above his throat and made a left to right slashing motion.

Angus smacked his hands together. 'I've been wanting to do that for years.'

Stevie pulled a disconcerted Wayne to his feet. 'Okay, now, lie on the ground,' she commanded. Wayne looked around the empty common room to reassure himself no one else was watching and positioned himself on the hard carpet squares as if rigor mortis had already set in.

Stevie positioned herself behind his head and went through the same motions as when he was sitting. When she'd finished Wayne heaved himself from the floor returned to his seat and flexed his shoulders. 'Well, I hope that was worth my pain and humiliation.'

'It was, Wayne,' Hurst said, 'well done. Stevie was demonstrating how similar the throat cutting technique is, irrespective if the victim is lying or sitting when the attack is made from behind. The knife wounds would be almost identical too, which means we can't rely on them.'

'If Notting was driving, let us assume Robinson was in the passenger seat—he did go through the front window—so if he did the throat slashing surely the cut would have been more like a jab to the left side of the neck,' Angus said.

'But still possible for the passenger to angle himself and slash from behind with negligible difference to the slash mark provided it was performed in one swift motion, left to right.' Hurst switched her gaze from Angus to a woman bearing down on them with a tray of coffee. The hospital worker's gaze slipped to photos strewn across the table. Hurst hastily bundled them underneath the file. The woman's complexion took on the green hue of her hospital uniform. Stevie wondered how long she had been eavesdropping and waited for her to leave before she continued.

'So the angle of the blade in these two scenarios can't tell us whether he was killed in or out of the bus. What about blood spatter?'

'We're getting there,' the pathologist said. 'There was some of Notting's blood on the bus, but also some of Robinson's. The lab concluded it was from the impact of their heads on the windscreen. The spatter patterns are just trickles and drops and not indicative of a powerful spray.' She removed the photo of Notting once more, this time tapping it with a neatly trimmed fingernail. 'The neck was pulled back, making the muscle and the trachea more prominent, protecting the carotid artery but exposing the jugular. He would have died of suffocation from the severed trachea before he bled out; still, there would have been a massive gush of blood. It flowed away from the wound when he was lying down, as dictated by gravity. If you look at this photo you can see the pattern flow down either side of the neck and across the ground. The clothing along the victim's back was also saturated, but as you can see, there is only a little on his shirt front. If he was sitting on the bus when he was killed most of the blood would be on the front of his shirt and in his lap.'

'Would it have got on the murderer?' Fowler asked.

'If the carotid artery had been damaged, yes, most probably; but since only the jugular was affected here, the spray wouldn't have been as powerful. The murderer might have been able to avoid it if he or she was careful.'

'She,' Angus mused. 'The girl, Mai, was the only one conscious when the paramedics arrived. She was lying alongside her friend Lin on what was left of the floor of the bus with a badly broken leg.'

'Could either of the girls have done the deed after the accident and crawled back into the bus?' Stevie asked Hurst.

Hurst tapped her pen thoughtfully on the table. 'Well, there was a considerable amount of red dust found on Mai's clothes—much more than on the other survivor ...' She shook her head as if to silence the improbable thought. 'But I don't see how she could have done it. The pain from her broken femur would have been excruciating. Even if she was thrown clear of the bus during the accident, I don't see how she could have crawled back into it after having slit Notting's throat. And the Lin girl is out of the equation totally. She has serious head injuries. She would have lost consciousness on impact.'

Stevie drew circles through the coffee rings of the table. 'But if Mai was determined enough ...'

Fowler's phone rang and he climbed to his feet: the interpreter was ready for her appointment. Speaking to Col and Stevie, he said, 'Let's go and meet this young lady. Find out how determined she might have been.'

And my head exploded
and all the words
were lost

CHAPTER TWENTY-EIGHT

The interpreter from the Thai Consulate, a straight-backed young woman in a raspberry-coloured skirt suit, met them at the nurses' station. They were told they could stay with the patient for fifteen minutes maximum. Stevie saw the head nurse look at her watch. She envisioned a stopwatch and a starter's gun and had to hold back from sprinting to Mai's room.

It was decided that Stevie would conduct the interview. Their footsteps clattered down the corridor. They must sound like approaching storm-troopers to the frightened girl in the room, Stevie thought. While it was unavoidable that Fowler and Col accompany her, she would have given a month's pay to see Mai alone.

A uniformed AFP guard jumped to his feet as they approached. Col showed his ID even though it was obvious the young man knew exactly who he was. Mai could be an important witness against the people-trafficking mob and they weren't taking any chances over her safety.

Fowler and Col sat as far away from the bed as the small room would allow; Stevie and the interpreter, Pimjai Sarangrit, on chairs pulled up close to the bed. A plastic bag containing the green housedress sat on the floor between them.

Mai's face was as pale as the pillow on which she lay propped and highlighted the darkness of her deep-set eyes. A cascade of eggplant-black hair framed her face. Her bandaged leg rested in a splint that looked like a medieval torture contraption, exposing bare toes, swollen and blue. It seemed the overworked nurses had not yet had time to give her a thorough wash. Streaks of red dirt were still visible between her toes. To Stevie, the sight of the dirt made Mai's presence in the clean white bed less surreal. It served as a vivid reminder of what might have happened out there in the desert.

Stevie introduced herself through Pimjai, pulled her notebook from her bag and with Pimjai's help carefully wrote down the girl's complete name, Mai Prawanrum. She explained that the interview was to be recorded. Out of the corner of her eye she saw Col tap the record button of the camcorder.

When Stevie asked the girl how she was feeling, Mai's shrug said it all: how do you think I'm feeling?

'Can you tell me where you were going on the bus?' Stevie asked, careful to keep her eyes on Mai and not Pimjai.

The delay between question and answer was like an overseas telephone conversation on a faulty line. 'She says she was going to Broome,' Pimjai said at last.

'Why were you going to Broome, Mai?'

A quick reply.

'To work,' Pimjai said.

Stevie glanced at the two men in the corner of the room. 'And what is your work?'

'She works at ...' Pimjai hesitated while she listened to Mai, then lowered her eyes, 'at pleasing men.'

Mai seemed to share none of Pimjai's embarrassment. Her sloe eyes remained fixed and unwavering upon Stevie, clear proud eyes that seemed to be challenging her to react as Pimjai had done.

Stevie had no trouble keeping her expression neutral; in her job, this was just par for the course. 'You were brought into this country illegally. Did you want to come here or were you forced?'

Mai looked at Pimjai as she answered Stevie's question. The interpreter from the consulate sat straight in her chair, stockinged legs clamped at the knees. 'They said they would kill her baby if she did not come to Australia with them.'

'And where is your baby now?'

Mai turned her head away, her voice cracking with her first sign of emotion.

'Somewhere in Australia,' Pimjai said. 'She doesn't know where, but she thinks he is safe now. She saw him on the television news after he was found in the house.'

Mai pointed to Fowler as Pimjai spoke.

'She saw that man on the news too,' Pimjai said.

Stevie reached for Mai's hand and noticed streaks of red dirt embedded in the creases of the girl's fingers. She wondered what those hands had been up to, if this young girl really was capable of cold-blooded murder. Could that delicate hand have pulled a knife across a man's throat? As she looked at Mai she attempted to smile away the thoughts. She must diffuse the suspicion in her eyes and keep the girl on side. For the time being she would stick to those least likely to cause distress: get details; clarify what they already suspected. And meanwhile, any minute now, the nurse might appear and ask them to leave.

'Your baby is safe, and soon you will have him back.' Stevie leaned toward the housedress in the bag on the floor. Stopped. That was another thing that would have to wait. Timing, strategy and interpretation was what it was all about, with everything to gain and everything to lose.

The temperature had risen in the overcrowded room; the antiseptic air tinted with the metallic smell of dried blood and Pilbara dirt. Unbuttoning her shirt cuffs, Stevie slid her sleeves up her arm.

Pimjai clapped her tiny hands as she translated Stevie's words, telling the girl her baby was safe. This interpreter was showing more emotion than she should, Stevie thought; then again, so was she.

Bugger it.

When Mai's face transformed with a joyful smile; Stevie grinned back.

'But there are still some things we need to ask you,' she said, wishing she didn't have to dispel the euphoria by getting to the heart of the case. 'I know you're tired, but I need to know everything that happened, starting with how you came here to Australia.'

She waited patiently for the echo of her question. Mai's reply seemed to take forever. Crossing her legs, Stevie relaxed back into her chair as if she had all the time in the world. Inside, her pulse ticked like a clock. She tried to focus on the soothing rhythms of the girl's voice, the swooping movements of Mai's delicate hands, small and pale except for the creases of Pilbara dirt.

Earlier she'd googled the Thai language, discovering that

it contained forty consonants and twenty-four vowels—not an easy language to learn, surely. When spoken, it relied on five tones: middle, high, low, rising and falling, meaning that up to four different words might have the same spelling. Being an experienced interrogator was not enough, a different set of skills was needed to analyse this translated version of events. Tone and innuendo did not exist in the same manner as they did with an English speaker. As she continued to sit on the hard hospital chair, hearing but not understanding, she could have been listening to someone speaking from under the sea.

'She was sold to a brothel in Bangkok when she was a small girl,' Pimjai eventually translated. 'She stayed there for a few years and sent money home to her parents. Then a few years later she had her baby and was sold to a different group. They said if she didn't go overseas to work for them they would kill the baby. They said she could take him with her. But then, when she came to Australia, they took him away from her. They said it was the only way they could be guaranteed that she would work for them and not run away.'

'What happened to her baby?' Stevie asked as Mai flopped back against her pillows and closed her eyes. Stevie still hadn't reached the questions at the forefront of their minds. She glanced over to Col who made hurry-up motions with his hands.

'The man who arranged for her to be brought over,' Pimjai said, 'decided to keep Mai's baby for himself because his wife could not give him a child.'

Fowler and Col straightened in their chairs; Stevie sensed them all asking the same question—Jon Pavel? But she couldn't feed the girl the answer; for legal reasons she still had to ask the name of the man.

When Mai answered, there was no need for translation. A collective sigh of relief reached Stevie from the corner of the room.

'Do you know what happened to Jon Pavel?' Stevie asked.

She heard the word 'Australian' in Mai's reply.

'They killed him. They also killed his wife and the Australian man, Ralph,' Pimjai said.

Stevie moistened her dry lips with her tongue. 'Who killed them?'

'Mamasan and The Crow.' No hesitation. Mai did not seem to be frightened of recrimination.

Fowler hissed out a breath.

'Why did they kill them?' Stevie inched to the edge of her chair.

'Pavel brought the girls over for the Mamasan,' Pimjai said, 'but he also brought others of his own, using the Mamasan's network of contacts, even the Mamasan's money—he lied to her about what he paid for them. He kept them at his house while he waited to sell them on. Mai was one of the ones he organised to keep for himself. Then the Mamasan found out. His excuse was that he didn't think she'd mind because she had never been interested in girls who'd given birth ...' The pale skin of Pimjai's neck flushed. 'She says the clients don't like them as much ...'

These girls were investment commodities, Stevie reflected, items to be bought, sold, stolen and devalued.

'Mamasan warned him to stop and set his house on fire to make him listen. He gave Mai back to the Mamasan, thinking that would be enough to please her. But he and the Australian, Ralph Hardegan, continued to bring the girls in. They were making so much money it was like a drug to them, they couldn't stop. When the Mamasan found out, she killed Pavel, his wife and the man Ralph as an example to anyone else who tried to cross her.'

Just as they had suspected, Pavel and Hardegan had paid the price for undercutting the Mamasan. You take my girls and I take you: skin for skin.

'We haven't been able to locate Jon Pavel's body yet,' Stevie said.

Pimjai listened to Mai. 'Mai saw them kill him,' she said with a shudder. 'They tortured him, burned off his skin, and then took his body out to sea in a boat, weighted it down and dumped it over the side.'

No wonder they hadn't found the body. Stevie decided not to press for details of the torture, not yet, even though they would have to be documented later. Looking from one pale face to the other, she wondered how much more either girl could take.

Col beckoned her over and handed her a computer image of an aged Jennifer Granger, a picture Stevie had not yet seen. Pulling a photo of the young Granger from her jeans pocket she compared the peachy round face, wide innocent eyes and gap-toothed smile to the woman in the age-enhanced picture. Could the cherub really have turned into this dugong-faced creature? Stevie's inability to spot a single shared feature made her sceptical of the picture's value. She knew the age-enhancing process involved a mixture of science, art, facial growth data and heredity, and had often been invaluable in the hunt for long-term missing persons. But she had trouble coming to terms with the idea that an artist or scientist could predict the influence of lifestyle and experience on a face, when he had no idea what those influences might be. In this instance, he certainly seemed to have expected the worst.

She made eye contact with Col. 'Surely this doesn't take plastic surgery into account? You said she'd had various makeovers.'

He shrugged—God only knows—and urged her back to Mai with a firm nod of his head.

'Do you know who this woman is, Mai?' she asked, forsaking her chair to perch on the edge of the bed.

Mai's head dipped as she examined the picture of the older Granger, a veil of hair falling over her face, hiding it. Pimjai took a peep at the picture too and said something to Mai who returned a single word answer. Pimjai responded with an uneasy laugh.

'Well, Pimjai?' Stevie asked.

'She said the woman is very ugly.'

Stevie blew out a breath of impatience. 'Yes, but does she recognise her?'

'Wait, give her longer.'

Shit, how long does she need? Stevie fidgeted with her shirtsleeves while she waited, trying to roll them into neat folds of military precision, ending up making uncomfortable knots at her elbows instead. Her gaze dropped once more to the picture Mai held in her hand.

And then her breath caught.

She bent over the picture and examined it again, her cheek almost touching Mai's. She knew that face, she was certain, there was something about the mouth. Must be a known Madam, she reasoned, familiar from one of the reams of mugshots imprinted on her mind. She would send this composite to her colleagues in Sex Crimes and see if it rang any bells.

Mai took a bolstering breath. 'Mamasan.' The single word needed no translation. Col pointed a told-you-so finger at Stevie before indicating for her to continue with the questions. 'But now she looks different,' Pimjai added after listening again to Mai.

'Different, how?' Stevie asked.

'Mai, do you know an old woman called Mrs Hardegan?' Fowler asked simultaneously. Stevie could have murdered him.

'No!' Mai gasped in English, having obviously recognised the name. Her dark eyes flitted in panic away from Stevie's. She pulled the sheet over her head and lay as inert as a body under a shroud.

'She's an old woman who lives next door to the Pavels.' May as well finish what Fowler had started, Stevie decided. 'Mai, you must know who she is.'

Mai shook her head vigorously under the sheet, making a low, keening sound. Stevie glanced toward Fowler, who looked on with exasperation.

Pimjai turned on Stevie. 'This must end now—you, your questions, you are upsetting her.' Before Stevie could react, Pimjai gave the nurses' call button three sharp jabs—emergency—then let rip with a rapid stream of Thai.

'Hey, wait on a minute ...' Stevie began.

'No more talk,' Pimjai said, 'If she has to speak to you again it must be with a lawyer.'

Stevie plucked at the sleeve of Pimjai's Audrey Hepburn suit and shook her head in desperation. 'Pimjai, Mai's not in trouble, she's a witness only—you're hardly being professional about this ...'

A nurse dashed into the room and pulled up short when

she realised it wasn't an emergency. Despite Fowler jabbing his thumb accusingly at Pimjai, they were told they had to leave.

'Shit,' Fowler said as they stepped into the passageway, his lower lip jutting with disappointment. 'What an obstructive little cow, she doesn't miss much does she? Talk about the sisterhood. We're going to have to lodge a complaint against that one.'

Stevie bit her tongue; the situation was hard enough without Fowler making it worse. Some of her hair had come loose; it must've been from all that frantic head shaking at Pimjai. She smoothed it back and tightened her ponytail. What she really wanted to do was get out of here, return to her mother's house and sleep for a week.

'Pimjai was only doing her job, Fowler,' she said. She glanced back into the room and saw Pimjai reach for the sobbing girl and felt the last of her energy drain away. After everything that girl had been through and despite her best intentions, all she'd succeeded in doing was make Mai cry.

Fowler folded his arms and glared at her. 'You should have been tougher, Hooper, cut to the chase sooner, shown her the dress and asked her about the bus crash.'

'Look what happened when you cut to the chase,' Stevie said.

Fowler appeared not to hear her. 'What a waste of bloody time that was.'

'Bull it was,' Col said to Fowler with uncharacteristic sharpness, the strain was getting to him too. 'We now have proof of everything we suspected and more. The hunt for Mamasan and The Crow can begin for real now we have that positive ID.'

'If you believe in that kind of composite garbage—the girl said Mamasan looked different now.'

'Jesus, Fowler, stop and listen to yourself,' Stevie said, his negativity was getting to her even though she had a feeling that he might be right. In small doses she found she coped quite well with Fowler—there were even moments of camaraderie—but after a while his minor irritations built up like lead poisoning in her system. He was more of an old woman, she decided, than Mrs Hardegan could ever be.

'And what's more,' Col continued, flexing his fingers, doing his best to ignore the growing tension between the detectives, 'we now know that Jon Pavel is seriously dead and not still driving around terrorising people in that green Jag of his. Any luck with the trace so far, Fowler?'

'Not yet, sir, Wong's people are still on it,' Fowler said moodily.

'Stevie,' Col went on, 'I'll organise a lawyer from Legal Aid and then maybe you can sweet-talk Pimjai into letting you have another word with Mai. If not we'll have to find a different interpreter. I want to talk to the other girl's doctors too, get a progress report. Last time we spoke they seemed to think she'd be waking up soon.'

'What will happen to Mai and Lin?' Stevie asked.

'They'll be offered amnesty—and a happy ending, hopefully.'

Stevie raised an eyebrow at him. 'Provided Mai had nothing to do with Notting's death.'

Col paused. 'Well, yeah.'

'She was a whore, anyway,' Fowler said, 'It's not like she was being forced to do anything she hadn't done before.

Get her off the hook and she'll end up right back where she started.'

Stevie's pent up frustrations exploded. 'Haven't you learnt anything over the last few weeks? The fact that Mai was a sex worker makes no difference; she was coerced into coming to this country to work, a sex slave no less—she did not ask for this. It's time you got over this madonna–whore complex of yours. The nature of her work before she came to this country is totally irrelevant.'

Fowler lowered his head. If he had any sense at all, he'd have to know what she was alluding to. 'I'd better go and report all this to Wong,' he mumbled, thwacking his hand through the air. Things hadn't gone the way he'd wanted, how any of them had wanted, but jeez, Fowler, get over it.

'He's an odd one,' Col said as they watched the detective stride down the ward, swatting imaginary flies.

'You get used to him.' She gave an indifferent shrug, too tired even to keep her anger simmering. 'Kind of.'

When you asked for my help I could
do nothing
full of thoughts and unable to
speak

is this how you felt when
you came here
Sitting Silent next to
beside me on the plane

I think of that often
and all those poor lost girls

CHAPTER TWENTY-NINE

Monty was dozing when Stevie crept into his hospital room. Without disturbing him, she slipped onto his bed, fitted herself to his body, and was asleep within seconds. Fowler woke her with a tap on the shoulder an hour and a half later. She washed the sleep from her eyes and combed her hair in the small bathroom, avoiding the mirror lest she see the hard face and ruffled collar of an interrogator of the Spanish Inquisition staring back at her.

The lawyer from Legal Aid, a young man called Russell Simpson, was waiting for them outside Mai's door.

The gentle aroma of baby powder had replaced the earlier unpleasant smells in the room. A stainless steel bowl of scummy water sat upon the tray table. Mai's hands had lost all traces of red dirt and her hair gleamed with every sweeping stroke of the hairbrush gripped tight in Pimjai's hand. Stevie spent a moment watching the Thai women as companionable as sisters despite their being at opposite ends of the social spectrum. She glanced at Fowler and guessed what he was thinking. Jesus, Fowler, she thought, sometimes I wish I could just blank you from my mind.

Mai's eyes were closed as if she was revelling in the

sensation of this small act of kindness. Stevie found herself yearning to do something positive too for the girl who appeared to have so little.

Pimjai put the brush on the tray table and Mai joined her hands with a word of thanks. Stevie introduced the lawyer, who sat down in the chair Col had occupied earlier, and exchanged pleasantries with the women: 'Feeling better, Mai? How's the leg? Pimjai has made you look beautiful.' She knew she risked being condescending, but was rewarded with a small smile from each of them.

Fowler pressed the record button on the camcorder as soon as the questioning began. Stevie removed the housedress from the plastic bag and held it up for Mai to see. 'Is this yours?'

The girl slowly reached for the dress, rolled the silk through her fingers; she felt the hole left by the missing button and nodded her head.

'Mai, did you go to the Pavel house and feed your baby after Delia and Jon were killed?'

Pimjai listened and then interpreted Mai's reply. 'Yes, she overheard the men talking about what had happened—Jon Pavel was still alive then. The Crow shot Delia from the kitchen window, then took Jon with him and left Mai's baby in the house. Mai travelled by bus several times to the house and fed her baby. But then Rick found out, told The Crow and he burned her feet.' Pimjai pulled back the bedclothes to expose Mai's unbroken leg. The burn was healing, although the skin on the sole of her foot was still red and flaking in places. Stevie winced. Fowler and Russell Simpson leaned forward in their chairs to inspect the injury. The young lawyer wiped his mouth with the back of his hand.

'Before this she tried to call the police and tell them what was happening,' Pimjai said, 'but they did not understand what she was saying.'

Fowler shifted in his seat with embarrassment—as well he might, thought Stevie.

'And you used Mrs Hardegan's phone?' Stevie queried.

Mai paused as she listened to Pimjai and shook her head violently, her eyes once more eyes brimming with tears at the mention of the old lady's name.

'She phoned from call box,' Pimjai said with a decisive snap to her jaw.

'No.' Fowler could remain silent no longer. 'There was no call box listed in the phone log. Each phone call was made from the same private number listed as belonging to Mrs Lilly Hardegan.'

Pimjai told Mai what he'd said. Mai shook her head, but Stevie knew Fowler was right. All the unintelligible calls were made from Mrs Hardegan's phone, including the final, successful call from Skye.

Why would Mai apparently tell the truth about everything else, but lie about this one insignificant matter? Was she trying to protect the old lady from something—were they in collusion? Stevie expelled a breath; it didn't make sense. She would have to visit Mrs Hardegan again. Perhaps she'd get some sense out of the old lady once she knew Mai was safe.

'The bus crash, Hooper, ask about the bus crash,' Fowler hissed in a stage whisper.

She shot him a look; all in good time. But Pimjai took it upon herself to ask Mai before Stevie could stop her. Stevie sighed and made a mental note to enquire if the Academy offered courses in 'Techniques of interrogation through translation'—both of these sessions had been bloody nightmares.

It wasn't dark but it was getting there; the sky filled with the soft purple of evening. Mrs Hardegan's light was on but she had not yet drawn the curtains. As Stevie made her way down the back garden path, she found herself smiling at the scene before her, an absurd shadow puppet show—Long John Silver, bird on shoulder, watching the evening news.

After tapping on the window she entered the room, her tread light and springy on the lino floor. The interview with Mai hadn't gone as well as she'd hoped, but it buoyed her that for once she was not the bearer of bad news.

'She's safe, Mrs Hardegan, Mai is safe.' Stevie beamed at the old lady and put her arm out to the bird. It hopped from Mrs Hardegan's cashmere shoulder onto Stevie's naked forearm, digging in with its nail-like claws, much lighter than it looked. She put it in its cage, closed the door and turned back. The old lady said nothing, sat there, a lopsided grin from ear to ear, the first Stevie had seen from her. There was no denying it, she knew exactly whom Stevie was talking about.

Stevie made them tea, told by Mrs Hardegan to use the best cups—this was a celebration, wasn't it, boy? The old lady herself poured out small measures of brandy into balloon glasses and they alternatively sipped tea and spirits. Stevie sat on the footstool at her feet and told her what they had learned about Mai's life in the Perth brothel, and then the bus crash.

'But you knew Mai, didn't you, Lilly?' Stevie didn't think the old woman would mind the use of her first name. 'That was why she came to you when she discovered that her baby had been left alone in the house.'

'We tried to call the smudgin' fulletts but they wouldn't listen to us.'

'But why does Mai deny ringing the police from your phone? In fact, she denies knowing you at all.'

Mrs Hardegan ran a finger over a bushy grey eyebrow. 'He is a good boy; he is trying to look after us. We'll tell you, but it won't be easy. Wait there for a few days, we need to gather up bits and bobs.'

Stevie's phone rang. It was Col, wanting to tell her about his interview with Lin. She rose from the footstool, turned her back on the bustling Mrs Hardegan and gazed absently at the darkening view from the window. The girl was highly traumatised, Col told her, and the doctor had suggested a psych consult. My, my, Fowler would have approved of Lin, Stevie thought. Lin the innocent would fit perfectly into his checkerboard view of life where everything was black or white, innocent or guilty. She was still brooding on this when two startling silver-blue eyes cleaved the blackness of the street. Through the closed window she heard the predatory growl of a powerful car's engine. Her mind flashed back to the Freo alley.

'Stevie, are you still there?' Col's voice prickled at her sudden silence.

She blinked, looked into the street again. The headlights had gone, but their imprint continued to glow on the inside of her lids.

'How's the search for the Jag going, Col?' she asked, apropos of nothing he'd been talking about.

'Nada.' He blew air down the phone. 'But have you been listening to anything I've said?' Of course she had, she said.

He continued filling her in on Lin's background: she was an orphan who'd been hoodwinked into believing she was being sent to Australia to manage a reflexology centre for Jon Pavel.

Stevie stepped into the back garden with the phone clamped to her ear, listening to Col. She explored the space behind the wood shed and the back fence, climbed on a plant pot to peer into the neighbour's yard. The freshness of an early spring evening filled the air, mingling with the sweet aroma of night-scenting shrubs. Not a breath of wind stirred the leaves of the flame tree in the corner of the garden, but despite this, she felt a chill. Absently, she undid the folds of her sleeves, pushing them over the goose bumps on her arms.

Scanning the street on all three sides of the garden fence, she saw nothing resembling Pavel's green Jag. At a large house down the road, automatic doors opened for a silver BMW. Another smaller car pulled up opposite — commuters coming home from work.

Back in the house she forced herself to give Col her full attention.

When Lin regained consciousness, he said, she'd backed up everything Mai had told them about the death of the Pavels, as well as confirming that Mai was the mother of the baby. She'd been unable to remember much about the bus crash other than that she'd seen the men arguing just before it happened and Mai trying to pull the knife away from Rick Notting's throat.

'That's what Mai said, too,' Stevie said. 'It could easily account for her print on the handle. Mai flatly denied getting off the bus and killing Notting. Even if she'd wanted to, she said she couldn't because her leg was too painful. I believe her.'

'But she was covered in red dust, how can that be explained?'

Stevie reached for the brandy balloon and took a sip. 'That dust could have come from anywhere within a wide radius of the crash site. She told me she'd got dirty when going for a walk during their last rest stop.'

Col sighed down the phone. 'You're beginning to sound like a defence lawyer, Stevie.' And you're beginning to sound like Luke Fowler, Stevie thought. How much easier it is to blame the whore.

Stevie forced herself to loosen her grip on the brandy balloon. Even if a lawyer could argue provocation or self-defence, the thought that Mai might have to stand trial for murder after everything she'd been through was almost too much to contemplate. She took a calming breath and said to Col, 'After the crash, when Mai came to, she was disorientated and wanted to find out where they were. She managed to pull herself up on a seat and look out the bus window. She saw the two men, Jimmy Jack Robinson and Rick Notting, lying outside the bus, and a third man stooping over Notting.'

'Who the hell was that supposed to be? SOCO found no prints other than those belonging to police and paramedics.'

'Tracks could easily be wiped away from that thin dust.' Stevie paused. 'She thinks the man was The Crow.'

'Bullshit, how come he was there? Why didn't he go and finish off the girls too?'

'Maybe he was following the bus; maybe he knew he couldn't trust Notting? Robinson might easily have called him. Mai said that after she saw The Crow bend over Rick, he walked over to the bus. She ducked when she saw him coming and played dead.'

'She must have been very convincing. Christ, Stevie, and you believe her?'

Stevie nibbled on her lip and said nothing. Of course she believed her, but why? Because she wanted this version of events to be true, that was why.

'Where are you now?'

'Mrs Hardegan's—telling her about Mai.'

'Hopefully you can get some sense out of the old lady this time, find out what she has to do with all this.'

Stevie turned from the window, watched Mrs Hardegan purposefully shuffle around the room, banging doors, opening the drawers of her oak sideboard; filling up their brandy glasses. Stevie lifted hers in a silent toast and Mrs Hardegan raised her glass back.

'You know, Col, this time I think I might.'

Stevie disconnected and dropped her phone on the sewing table next to a stack of recently placed objects: picture cards, magazines, the tapestry, which in the days since she'd last seen it, had taken on Bayeux-like proportions.

'We said it was all our fault and now we can show you why.' Mrs Hardegan unfurled the tapestry and placed it across the things on the sewing table. Stevie hastily moved the stool and positioned herself alongside the tall armchair and stared at the tangle of coloured wool before her.

Then, like an optical illusion, the pattern of colours and small exes began to take shape and a crude tableau appeared. A row of blue exes depicted the sky, green, the earth, peopled by stick figures sewn from wool. Mrs Hardegan pointed to one of the figures that stood out from the others because of the messy nest on its head—a hat or thatch of hair—Stevie couldn't tell.

'There we are,' Lilly said, solving the mystery. Next to herself she had sewn three identical figures. 'The boys,' she added.

'Jon, Delia and Ralph?'

'That is correct.'

The old lady made walking motions with her knobbly fingers across the tapestry from one depiction of herself to another, ending up at a fluffy yellow orb sewn onto the sky.

'The sun?' Stevie queried.

'Yes, the sun—they sent us there to play. It was wintertime here. Cold.'

Stevie stared blankly at the old lady. 'I'm afraid I don't understand.'

Mrs Hardegan's pursed her lips. Flexing her fingers she took on an impatient tone. 'They sent us to that place that has the animals with long noses, very sunny, and we went on a car with wings.'

Leaving the tapestry for a moment, she riffled through her picture cards, withdrawing a child-like picture of an aeroplane. 'A car with wings,' she explained as she pointed to several cross shapes hanging upon her tapestry sky.

'You went on a plane?'

Mrs Hardegan briefly turned her eyes to the ceiling. 'Yes, clever boy,' she said as if talking to her parrot. 'They put us on the car. Paid for us to go here ...' The picture card she reached for now depicted a holiday scene: sea, sand, buckets and spades.

Ah, of course, the sun. 'They paid for you to go on holiday—where did you go?'

She pointed to a circular tangle of grey wool situated on the brown exes of earth. The grey blob had something long and thin sticking out from its top. 'We went to the land of the long noses where the snoodle pinkerds live.' *Christ*, sounded like something Dr Seuss might have dreamed up. Stevie massaged her brow and tried to think.

Long noses, elephants, Thailand—they sent her to Thailand! Oh God, now she understood. Jon and Ralph had used Lilly as an unknowing escort for their girls, generously paying for her holidays to Thailand. What immigration official would question the papers of a young girl who couldn't speak English, escorted by an innocent old lady? They'd used her as their mule, in the same way dealers planted their drugs in the luggage of innocent passengers to move them from A to B.

'We were told they were coming here to work in those zoos belonging to the boy,' Mrs Hardegan said.

Stevie stared at her hands as she puzzled this out: a zoo, a place where a variety of creatures live. 'You were told they were going to work at Jon Pavel's nightclub?' That was an easy one.

The old lady nodded. Maybe Stevie was getting the hang of this after all. Much of Mrs Hardegan's language, she realised, did contain a strange kind of logic.

'And food places,' Mrs Hardegan said. 'He makes long-nose food too.'

'A Thai restaurant?'

'Indeed. And the boy with the small boy was bringing him over for them to adopt.'

'So, you escorted several girls over here. But when it came to the girl, Mai, you thought she was bringing the baby over on behalf of the adoption agency?'

'That is correct.' Lilly sniffed and pulled a tissue from her sleeve. 'And then I thought he stayed on to help as a maid person. We did not know he was a prisoner. And then he left and the small boy stayed. We are a stupid, ignorant old boy—all those poor snoodle pinkerds. The boy told us what we'd done and then we had the brain thing. We had to help that snoodle pinkerd and his small one—so very small. He came to see us and asked for our help and when we tried, no one would believe us.' Mrs Hardegan closed her eyes for a moment. They flew open again as an electrical sound clattered through a speaker in the wall near the chair. The doorbell.

'Food,' Mrs Hardegan said in response to Stevie's raised eyebrow. 'We have an order—every week we like to have long-nose food.'

She lifted her tapestry and opened the sewing basket underneath, peeled some notes from a rolled up wad of cash and attempted to press them into Stevie's hand.

Stevie patted the wallet in her jeans pocket and said, 'No, Lilly, this is on me.' Paying for the old lady's takeaway was the least she could do. 'I'll get it.'

The old lady accepted the offer, settled back in her chair and closed her eyes again.

Long-nose food. Stevie shook her head, smiling, and made her way down the passageway towards the silhouette on the other side of the frosted glass door.

And still I think of
the sign above the brothel door.
to all those Soldiers

to the enemy

the sign that Said
We obediently dedicate our minds
and our bodies

our bodies to you

CHAPTER THIRTY

Stevie opened the deadbolt and smiled at the face under the porch light. The woman from the deli smiled back and held up a plastic bag of takeaway.

'Great service—Eva, isn't it?' Stevie asked.

'That's right, love. And this is pad thai, the old dear's favourite. I'll bring it in, like to say hello if you don't mind. Haven't seen her for a while.'

Stevie reached out to relieve Eva of the food. Stopped. Her hand hung in the air and she looked at the woman through the sepulchral light.

Shit. She knew that face.

When she'd first met the woman, the gapped front teeth made her think Madonna. Now she saw it as the sign of Venus, the goddess of love. Of all the surgical changes, this would be the one original feature someone in her profession would choose to retain.

Stevie took a quick step forward to bar the woman's entrance. Hooking her foot around the door she attempted to close it, hoping the deadbolt would buy Lilly some time.

A blow like a bag of wet cement to her shoulder cut off her warning cry. She fell back into the hallway and cracked her head on the corner of the bookcase. Barely clinging to consciousness, she heard a loud crash. The door was kicked fully open, books toppled to the ground. A tall man stepped through the doorway and turned on the light. Stevie moaned and attempted to move. A kick to the stomach drove the wind from her. Curled into a ball on the musty hall carpet she closed her eyes and fought for breath. *Oh God, we're going to die.*

When she opened her eyes again she was looking at a pair of grey-booted feet and grey dress pants. Looked like expensive material—Zegna? Monty had always fancied a Zegna suit. She never understood why, he'd have wrecked it within a few days, spilled sauce or red wine down the front—Jesus, the things that go through the mind when you're about to die.

Rough hands pulled her to her feet. She felt the stitches in her shoulder stretch then snap. A tide of warm blood rushed down her back. The hallway spun. She found herself half pushed, half carried down the passageway to Mrs Hardegan's backroom.

The old woman looked up and let out a startled cry. The man hurled Stevie to the ground at her feet.

'Bloody Japs! Bloody Japs!' the parrot screamed.

The blast of a shotgun tore the cage apart, shattering the air around them. Stevie held her breath and waited for the second blast that never came. With her ears still ringing, she attempted to pull herself up from the floor and failed.

A cloud of smoke filled the room, sucking at the air. Stevie struggled for breath thinking she must have been hit. The pain in her shoulder was excruciating and felt far worse than the original injury. Bolts of light streaked across her eyes.

She sagged against the side of Mrs Hardegan's armchair.

Everything had happened so quickly, she was having trouble grasping quite what was going on. She became aware of a bony hand pressing at her undamaged shoulder—Lilly throwing her a lifeline, warning her to stay put.

The smoke cleared, Stevie finally found her focus. The man was tall and very good looking, which was a ridiculous thing to think under the circumstances. He wore a finely striped business shirt with no tie, sleeves rolled to the elbows revealing muscles thick as twisted rope. The shotgun held casually at his hip was pointed towards the middle of Stevie's chest.

The Crow.

Jennifer Granger, aka the Mamasan, stood by his side. Stevie leaned against the chair, only a metre away from the woman's shapely legs, small feet pressed into stilettos.

Stevie avoided looking at Granger's face for as long as she could. Her gaze flitted to the shattered remains of the parrot's cage. Somehow she found her voice through the dryness of her throat. 'Good for us, bad for you; everyone in the street will have heard that racket. Better leave while you still can.'

'It never worried them before, love,' Granger said, picking a pale feather from her hair. She examined it between her manicured fingers, let it go and watched it flutter to the floor.

Stevie searched the woman's plastic perfect face. 'You mean when you shot Delia Pavel?'

Granger turned to The Crow. 'See, what did I tell you, son, she knows far too much.'

The Crow looked at Stevie and licked his beautifully shaped lips.

'What's wrong with you, don't you talk?' Stevie demanded,

relieved to hear no sign in her voice of the tremble that shook her from the inside out.

The Crow reached for the open bottle of brandy, took a long pull then wiped his bare arm across his mouth. He inspected the bottle, turning it over in his hand. When his eyes met those of his mother, Stevie was reminded of an animal looking to its trainer for instructions. Granger gave him a go-ahead nod.

He was going to smash the end off the bottle, cut her with it. Stevie tensed, looked at the sewing table and wondered if there was anything she could use as a shield or weapon. The objects on the table were still covered by the tapestry. She had trouble remembering what was there, let alone imagine how her dulled reflexes could dodge the jagged end of the bottle.

He took another swig of brandy; eyes never leaving hers. He wiped his mouth again, then trickled the rest of the brandy in a circle around the armchair. When he'd finished, he put the empty bottle carefully back on the table and picked up Stevie's phone.

He wasn't going to cut her after all, she thought as he crunched her phone under his boot. And then a thought drove the reality home. She remembered what Col had told her about The Crow. No, he wasn't going to cut her.

It was worse than that.

She turned her head and risked a glimpse at Lilly who still sat rigid in her chair, one hand resting on Stevie's undamaged shoulder. Stevie felt an energising jolt of anger. Some of the fogginess lifted. Lilly hadn't come so far to die like this.

Hell, neither had she.

The Crow took a silver cigarette case from his shirt pocket, removed a cigarette and lit it. After a puff he squatted at the ring of brandy and put the glowing tip to the alcohol. Within seconds a blue ring of fire surrounded them.

Mrs Hardegan gasped. Stevie patted her hand. 'It's okay, he only wants to frighten us.'

The Crow smiled at her, cigarette hanging from his mouth like James Dean. He handed the shotgun to Granger and left the room.

'Christmas pudding,' Mrs Hardegan said as the last of the impotent blue flames petered out.

'Why doesn't he talk?' Stevie asked, tipping her chin to the back door through which The Crow had disappeared.

'Just a temporary problem according to the doc. Smoke inhalation from the last burning,' Granger said. 'He can't resist the sizzle and smell of burning meat. Put his face too close to Pavel's body and damaged his voice box.'

'Poor baby,' Stevie said.

Lilly chuckled.

'I wouldn't be thinking that was so funny if I was you, Senior Sergeant Stephanie Hooper.'

Stevie stared unwavering at the woman before her. 'How long have you known who I was?'

'From the moment you reserved that DVD: name, address the works. After a quick word with that tall, blabbermouth cop, I figured out what was behind all them questions of yours; you weren't the painter you were pretending to be, you were some bitch of a cop.'

'And you killed Skye?'

'He did.' With the shotgun, Granger pointed in the direction her son had gone. 'Nice girl; often picked up takeaway from us. He heard her phoning you outside the deli, knew she must have found something out from the old dear. Well whaddaya know—we thought she only spoke gobbledegook.'

Mrs Hardegan stiffened in her chair.

'And he had a go at me in Freo, too.' Stevie deliberately omitted Fowler's name, even though she had a feeling he would be next on their list. 'Was it The Crow who gave my daughter the magazine?'

'Just one of his little jokes, always had a great sense of humour.'

Using the side of the chair Stevie hauled herself to her feet. Granger didn't try to stop her, although she did keep the shotgun barrel pointing steadily at her chest. Stevie staggered as another wave of dizziness swept through her, forcing her to reach for the arm of the chair. When she looked down, she noticed the front of her shirt saturated with blood.

The Crow entered the room through the back door with a sloshing can of fuel.

Something cold rolled down Stevie's spine. 'You've been using Pavel's car—where've you kept it hidden?' she said, desperately bidding for time.

'Just at the deli garage, love; changed the plates, only use it at night.' Granger paused and looked to her son as he circled Mrs Hardegan's chair with the fuel, the same way he'd done with the brandy. 'You'd have liked to have used that car more often—wouldn't you, son? We can have it painted when this business is over with, then you can use it whenever you like.' To Stevie she explained, 'The Crow loves the finer things in life. Lucky our delis pay so well.'

A horrible rasping sound escaped through the sneer of her son's mouth. Eva seemed to understand what he was saying, though Stevie hadn't a clue.

'You bought that deli so you could keep an eye on the Pavels?' Stevie asked.

'One of many small businesses.'

'A handy way of laundering money. And I guess you staff them with ignorant teenagers like Leila who wouldn't think to ask too many questions.'

'But more than anything, The Crow likes the sound of cooking meat.' Granger was clearly keener to terrorise them with tales about her son than to explain her business practices. 'Nothing like the sizzle and pop of the eyeballs as they explode like overcooked eggs—isn't that right, son?'

The Crow smiled, revealing a row of perfect, bone-white teeth. He finished pouring the circle of petrol, grabbed Mrs Hardegan's telephone and yanked out the cord. He looked toward his mother. This time it was he giving the silent instructions. These two didn't seem to need words. With an eerie sense of wonder Stevie marvelled at the bond between them.

'Grab the cop's stuff first,' Granger said. 'We may as well take it with us and get rid of it—it'll make identifying her body that bit harder.'

The Crow pulled Stevie's wallet from her jeans pocket and put it in her bag from the coffee table along with the pieces of her crushed phone. He placed the bag by the door to collect on their way out.

Mamasan gave Stevie two sharp prods to the stomach. Stevie doubled up, making the pain appear worse than it was and collapsed across the sewing table. As she lay there, her heart thumping wildly against her ribs, she thought, I only have one chance. Reach under the tapestry into the open sewing basket and grab the sewing scissors. Leap at the skanky bitch before she gives the shotgun back to her son. No mercy, rip right into her.

The scissors felt cold in her hot, blood-sticky fingers. Still bent over the table she made a play at gathering her breath, poking the small pair of scissors up the open cuff of her shirt, blades pointing towards her wrist. She pushed her palms against the table and readied herself for the spring.

And slipped on a pool of her own blood. Chin-first she hit the table hard.

She groaned, more from frustration than pain. Another vicious prod of the gun barrel made her pull back and she found herself crammed next to Lilly on the armchair.

The Crow wrapped the telephone cord around them. The old-style cord, a knotted rope of wires, only just reached and he had to use all his strength to pull it tight. Stevie felt the old lady next to her straining against the cord, wheezing as she struggled for breath.

The Crow reached into his pocket. It wasn't a lighter he pulled out this time; it was a small metal tube.

'This is one cremation we won't stick around for, son,' Granger said. To Stevie she added, 'We need to reach the other cop before he hears about your death and goes to ground. If we play this right, he'll cark it at about the same time as you.'

Stevie stared hard at the small tube The Crow held up in his hand. It looked like the homemade timer bomb Aubin said had been used to destroy her house.

'An incendiary device,' Granger read her mind. 'By the time this acid mixture eats through the cork and reaches the fuel, we'll be long gone.'

Stevie craned her neck around the side of the chair. She remembered Paul Aubin saying 'cocky to the point of stupidity'. But these people weren't stupid. They were confident. They thought they were in control.

The Crow placed the tube upside down at the circle of fuel behind them, where they hadn't a chance of knocking it away with their feet.

With a rush of panic, Stevie twisted at her bonds. The scissors dug into the flesh of her good arm. There was slight room for movement but pain from her damaged shoulder prevented her from twisting far enough to reach them. Lilly seemed to be aware of what she was trying to do and attempted to reach them herself. Like Stevie she managed to move a few centimetres but had to give up, her arms pinned too tight.

Stevie wondered at what rate the acid was eating through the cork. They might have five minutes; they might have half an hour. The Crow and Granger didn't seem to be in too much of a hurry despite their plan to visit Fowler next.

'It'll be all too easy for the cops to tell this wasn't an accident,' Stevie said, craning her head back towards Granger, now rooting through the drawers of Lilly's oak dresser.

'Couldn't care less, love, it won't be traced back to us. And besides, if things do start to get a little er, hot, we'll just move on like we always do.' To her son, rifling the drawers next to her, she said, 'Turn the drawers out, make it look like robbery.'

Stevie discovered she could see what was going on behind them in the reflection of the TV without having to strain her neck. Granger pulled open the cutlery drawer and dumped the contents on the floor. She picked up a knife. 'Silver plate,' she said to her son. 'Shame to waste it but I can't risk it being traced.'

'Cheap picnic set,' Lilly said under her breath.

Stevie turned to look over the top of the armchair. A thin spiral of smoke rose from the metal tube behind them.

Granger saw it too. 'C'mon son, we'd best get going.'

About to sweep the contents of the sideboard to the floor, The Crow came across the picture of Lilly's husband in the silver photo frame. He held it up for his mother to see. Granger brought the frame to her mouth and tested it with her teeth. 'Solid, but leave it, son, we can't bother with this kinda junk.'

Stevie felt Lilly stiffen beside her and made hushing sounds at the old lady. She'd just managed to shake the scissors free from her sleeve and didn't want Lilly drawing their attention. She prayed the mother and son couldn't see what was going on behind the chair, hear her sawing through the tough cord with the scissor's blades.

'Hold on, Lilly,' she whispered as the cord snapped. Instant relief. 'Stay still, they'll be gone soon and then we can get away.'

In the reflection of the TV they saw The Crow punch the photo from the frame and grind it under his heel. Lilly flinched as if she too had been punched. Muttering to herself, she reached for something down the side of her chair. Stevie plucked at Lilly's dress and tried to pull her back, but the old lady shook herself free and climbed unsteadily to her feet.

The Crow and Granger were still busy at the sideboard when Lilly crept up behind them. Stevie attempted to move, but found herself riveted to the spot with shock.

Lilly rushed at The Crow.

'Bloody Japs!' Lilly screamed, wielding the Samurai sword like a hockey stick. The Crow turned, but too late to save himself. Lilly slashed at his middle and a silent scream uncurled from his mouth. He dropped the shotgun, clutched at his ripped stomach, and crumpled to the floor.

Stevie and Granger lunged for the gun at the same time. Granger was closer and reached it first, but Stevie landed on top of the smaller woman, knocking the air from her. The gun went off with a deafening crash and the fuel around the armchair flared. Heat seared Stevie's face as she struggled with the woman on the floor, at last pinning Granger's hands behind her with the telephone cord. Any minute now the fire would ignite the bomb and the chemicals would erupt into an inferno. She risked an upward glance and saw Lilly prodding the metal tube with the sword, trying to push it away from the flames.

'Lilly, leave it! Get out!' she cried.

The armchair caught fire. The heat was intense. Toxic fumes scratched at Stevie's lungs. The hem of Lilly's dress began to smoulder. Lilly paid it no heed, her face tight with concentration as she tried to knock the tube from the spreading flames. The heavy sword began to dip in her hands as if it might drag her into the fire too. Stevie hauled herself from Granger's back and stumbled toward Lilly.

With her last reserves of strength, Lilly gave the tube a mighty whack and sent it skittering from the fire and along the floor. The bomb might still explode, but she had bought them time.

Stevie grabbed the vase of wilted daffodils from the sideboard and threw the water over Lilly, dousing the twitching flames on the hem of her dress. Appearing unhurt, the old lady stood over a wailing Granger. With one hand on the oak sideboard to steady herself, she placed a slippered foot on the back of Granger's neck like a hunter with a trophy.

Stevie pulled her away and pushed her out the back door. 'Stay there, Lilly,' she commanded, turning back into the room. The Crow lay in the deep stillness of death, one hand licked by the flames of the burning chair.

Granger moaned as Stevie hefted her toward the door. The act of shoving the woman into the fresh air sapped her remaining strength. She dropped Granger to the ground and felt herself begin to fall.

Someone in a white shirt caught her before she hit the ground.

'Fowler—what the hell are you doing here?'

'I came to get those books off Mrs Hardegan. Looks like I arrived just in time.'

Stevie struggled against his hold. 'Just in time? Jesus ...'

'Where's the old lady?' Fowler asked.

She managed to pull away from him, her panic infusing her with the strength she thought she'd lost. She spun around. 'Shit, she was here a minute ago.' People from the street were beginning to spill into the back garden. She heard someone yelling out for the fire brigade.

She made a move toward the back door just as Lilly re-emerged, coughing and soot-streaked, cradling something in the folds of her cardigan.

'We couldn't leave our feathered friend,' Lilly said through her coughs. She held the cardigan up for Stevie to see the contents; Captain Flint, bloodied, charred and almost devoid of feathers, lay inert in his cashmere nest. Stevie felt the tears begin to well.

Mrs Hardegan chuckled at Stevie's distress. 'Not dead.'

She gave the parrot a poke.

The black-skinned creature opened a beady eye. Its grey blob of a tongue levered up and down for a moment, and then it croaked, very softly, *'Bloody Japs.'*

My dear
I very much regret the part
I have played by
in your misery

If words had not left me
I could have stopped
Some of this but not the
worst of what

my Son did and his friends

but really the fault
is with me

A FEW MONTHS LATER

CHAPTER THIRTY-ONE

Stevie and Monty sat in silence on the park bench. The light was beginning to fade. Gleaming whitecaps replaced orange sequins as dusk closed in. Seagulls swooped through the balmy air and flurried around packed picnic tables, competing for tasty morsels. 'Time for tea!' parents called to kids still playing in the sucking tide.

'Shark o'clock,' Monty said.

Stevie smiled, sniffed the salty air and brushed the sand from her bare legs. It had been a good day. Reconstruction had commenced on their house and the doctor had given Monty the all-clear to return to work. They'd celebrated with a bottle of champagne and a dozen oysters, then a sunset walk along the beach with Izzy running on ahead, playing catch-me-if-you-can with the lacy fringe of the sea. Now their daughter swung on the swings, whooshing high, screaming with delight as she leapt from the seat into the air, trying each time to jump further than her last line in the sand.

Monty got up from the bench and stretched, the red worm of his scar peeping above the V-line of his Hawaiian shirt. 'How's Granger?' he asked, out of the blue. It had been days since either of them had mentioned the Mamasan, and it seemed almost sacrilegious to bring up the subject on an evening like this. But ever since she'd told him the truth behind the house fire, they'd made a pledge of no more secrets. Say what you think, don't hold back; sometimes protection causes more damage than it prevents.

'No further suicide attempts, though she's still being treated for depression.'

'My heart bleeds for her.'

'She was a victim first, you have to remember that. And she loved him.'

Monty shuddered. 'If that's what you call it.'

'I got a call about Lin yesterday,' said Stevie.

'The young girl?'

'She's been offered permanent residency and she took it. Unlike Mai. She's decided to return to Thailand now the murder charge has been dropped.'

'Hardly surprising Mai's enthusiasm for Australia has waned after what she's been through,' said Monty.

'She visited Lilly a few times before she left.'

'Where is she?' said Monty.

'With Captain Flint, at Lavender House, while the house is being fixed up.'

'The one near the golf course?'

Stevie grinned. 'Lilly calls it 'Withering-on-the-Vines.'

Monty laughed.

'She was thrilled when I took Mai to see her, clucked all over baby Niran. God knows how they were able to communicate, but they seemed to manage okay. Lilly said she was going to learn Thai once she'd re-mastered English so they can stay in touch.' Stevie paused and gazed thoughtfully at the grey line of the horizon. 'Those two have an interesting chemistry—I can't figure it out.'

'Wasn't Lilly's husband a prisoner of the Japanese during the war?'

'Yes, the Samurai sword was a souvenir he brought back with him. Wish I knew more of her history. Skye once told me she served during the war in the navy too, but that's all I know.'

Monty shook his head. 'Feisty old bird.'

A wail cut into their conversation, Izzy made a crash landing and both parents rushed to her aid. She reached out to Monty as if Stevie wasn't there. The grazed knee wasn't life threatening; he kissed it better and carried her to the tap at the top of the steps and cleaned the wound. Minutes later she was back on the swing as if nothing had happened.

Monty returned to the bench. Sensing Stevie's despondency he took her hand. 'She only came to me because I've been home so much lately.'

'I'm not much of a mother, am I? I might have spent weeks reuniting Mai and her child, but I've totally neglected my own.'

'You're a wonderful mother. Don't over-analyse things.'

Stevie swallowed down her emotion. 'I think it's time for a change.'

There was an awkward silence. Monty's gaze dropped to their clasped hands. 'What kind of a change?'

'I'm going to put in for a transfer, something less demanding, more regular hours. I've had enough of sleaze and exploitation.'

He expelled a breath of relief, 'Christ,' and pressed his hands to his eyes. 'I believe they're after a lollipop lady in Maylands.'

Pulling his hands away she kissed him on the lips. 'Sounds perfect.'

He got up from the bench and headed toward the ice-cream van in the carpark.

'Hey,' Stevie called out to him. 'Where are you going? You know you can't have ice-cream.'

He ignored her, walked past the van and stopped pointedly at the top of the beach steps near the shower. Then he turned back and grinned at her through the fading light.

I hope that things Will
turn out for you
and your boy now my dear

I hope you will find it
in your heart to forgive me
your loving friend
hilly

EPILOGUE

Niran's mother holds his chubby hand as they make their way through the busy market. All around people yell, selling food from their stalls. Niran whines, says he's thirsty. The earlier train journey was fun, but he doesn't think much of all this walking. Eventually his mother gives in, buying him a coconut with a straw in the top of it. He sucks the sweet juice and listens to his mother talk to a walnut–faced old woman behind the stand. A boy with a machete works behind her, skilfully hacking the husks away from the nuts. Niran thinks it looks like a fun job. He'd like to ask for a turn, but he knows he is still too small; he is barely strong enough to hold the coconut with two hands and he knows his mother would never let him try. He puts his drink back on the stand and hides among the folds of his mother's silk dress, inhaling her perfume.

He hears her asking for directions to the house his mother wants to visit. The old woman says it is not far away, just a short walk. Niran turns his mouth down; his legs are burning, he hates that word 'walk.' He wishes they could hire a tuktuk but he hasn't seen any of sign of the cheap Bangkok taxis in this dusty old village. When the old woman finishes telling them how to get to the house, his mother rewards her with a folded note from her diamond purse.

A little further on from the market stalls they stop at the village tap. Niran's mother pulls a handkerchief from her sleeve, wets it and wipes Niran's face and sticky hands. She reminds him to bow when he meets these strangers, keep his eyes lowered and say nothing unless he is spoken to first.

She increases her pace and Niran has to jog to keep up with her. Her hand grips his so tightly he almost cries out. They eventually arrive. Still gripping his hand, Niran's mother speaks to a girl smaller than he is, playing with some empty bottles under a bamboo house. She has filled them up with water and they make *ding dong* sounds when she hits them with a stick. Niran would like to play too, but remembering his mother's warning, he stays silent. The girl runs up the wobbly steps, calling out to her father. Another older girl dressed in shorts and a T-shirt looks at them from the house for a moment and then disappears. She comes back, minutes later, wearing a blue dress. Her father brings her down the steps and then hands her a plastic bag. Niran thinks it must contain clothes, it looks squashy. The girl in the blue dress looks back up at the house, sees her mother looking down at her and begins to cry.

'Don't cry, Pi,' her father says with his hand upon her shoulder. 'This woman is here to help you if you will help her.'

Niran's mother looks the girl up and down. 'She's not very big.' For some reason, Niran's mother looks sad when she says this. 'I thought she was older. I don't like to start them off too small.'

Pi's father makes circles over his chest with both hands.

'She'll grow. Meanwhile, she can look after your son while you work—she's good with children.'

Niran's mother runs her hand across her chin as she thinks. Pi's mother looks down at her from the house, holding hard onto the veranda rail.

'Say hello to Pi, Niran,' Niran's mother finally says. 'This girl is to be your big sister.'

Pi's mother lets out her breath and claps her hands with joy.

Pi is still crying.

Niran bows to Pi as he has been taught. He has to tell his feet to stand still and not jump all over the place. He has always wanted a big sister. He hopes the girl will stop crying soon and play with him.

ACKNOWLEDGEMENTS

There are several people I'd like to thank for helping me to get this novel to print. Firstly, three of my harshest but most valuable critics: Carole Sutton, Trish O'Neill and Christine Nagel. Also my daughter, Pippa Young (RN), for updating me on nursing practice in the noughties; my agent Sheila Drummond; Wendy Jenkins for her advice and assistance; and Georgia Richter, my talented editor from Fremantle Press. Last but not least I'd like to thank my mother, Angela Wilmot—Mum, you know why.

OTHER STEVIE HOOPER TITLES

AN EASEFUL DEATH

She was naked, her body was hairless and she'd been sprayed with bronze paint. She was posed in a provocative manner with her legs open, her chin resting in her hand and her elbow on the stone table in front of her. I think the intention was to make her look like she was some kind of nude supermodel or a mannequin even.

The woman's face was an expressionless mask ... Easeful Death was printed down the length of her right thigh in black marker pen.

Someone is killing beautiful young women and taking extra-ordinary risks to carefully pose their painted bodies in public places. The first is bronze, then silver—who will be gold?

Detective Sergeant Stevie Hooper, young, hard-edged and newly seconded to the Serious Crime Squad, finds herself haunted by disturbing flashbacks as the bizarre case unfolds. As she closes in on the killer, the carefully drawn line between her professional and personal life becomes increasingly blurred until Hooper no longer knows who she can trust.

Available from www.fremantlepress.com.au

OTHER STEVIE HOOPER TITLES

HARUM SCARUM

Bianca thought of Katy Enigma … would Katy go with this man? He had soft brown eyes and, despite his strange nose, his face looked kind. He smiled. Bianca placed her hand in his and felt him shiver. She didn't know why, it wasn't cold at all.

When the body of eleven-year-old Bianca Webster is found dumped, it is soon clear to DS Stevie Hooper that the murder is connected to paedophile Internet site, the Dream Team. Another murder leads her to suspect that she might have a vigilante on her hands.

Cyber technology spins at the heart of this thriller: Katy Enigma, Lolita, Harum Scarum—just who or what lies beneath these Internet nicknames? Stevie Hooper finds herself racing against time to discover the identities before another child is taken.

Available from www.fremantlepress.com.au

First published 2010 by
FREMANTLE PRESS
25 Quarry Street, Fremantle
(PO Box 158, North Fremantle 6159)
Western Australia
www.fremantlepress.com.au

Consultant editor Georgia Richter
Cover design Nada Backovic
Cover photograph Woman in city at night, Alamy Australia

 A catalogue record for this
book is available from the
National Library of Australia

ISBN 9781921361838 (paperback)

Fremantle Press is supported by the Western Australian State
Government through the Department of Cultural Industries, Tourism and
Sport.